MW01535038

GARRY MICHAEL

All the White Lies We Tell

Copyright © 2022 by Garry Michael

All rights reserved. No part of this publication may be reproduced, stored or transmitted in any form or by any means, electronic, mechanical, photocopying, recording, scanning, or otherwise without written permission from the publisher. It is illegal to copy this book, post it to a website, or distribute it by any other means without permission.

This novel is entirely a work of fiction. The names, characters and incidents portrayed in it are the work of the author's imagination. Any resemblance to actual persons, living or dead, events or localities is entirely coincidental.

Designations used by companies to distinguish their products are often claimed as trademarks. All brand names and product names used in this book and on its cover are trade names, service marks, trademarks and registered trademarks of their respective owners. The publishers and the book are not associated with any product or vendor mentioned in this book. None of the companies referenced within the book have endorsed the book.

First edition

Cover art by Roopali Creations
Editing by Carlie Slattery
Editing by Ebony Stokes

This book was professionally typeset on Reedsy.
Find out more at reedsy.com

This is for my fantastic four.

To Dawn Barrell for never letting me slack.

To Tina Alicea who created dozens of book aesthetics/story edits before reading Foster and Isaac's story.

To April Lynn for being the best PA ever!

And to Brittany Bailey this story was developed last winter after brainstorming with you.

Contents

Acknowledgement

This Journey has been the most exciting and nerve-wracking experience of my life. I've met great people along the way and I will be forever thankful for the wisdom, love and support.

To Mr. Z- I love you to the moon and back.

To my Mom and Dad who have encouraged me to ALWAYS be true to myself. I never had to come out because you knew all along and never made me feel less than amazing.

To my brothers and sisters. This is for you.

To my partner in crime, Jeris Jean- Thanks for being an amazing friend and cheerleader.

To Michaela Cole- Thank you for sharing your knowledge and for always being an extra set of eyes with everything I do.

E.B. Slayer- You, for being a great advisor. THANK YOU!

To my Peen Posse- This group is a well of valuable information and laughter. I am so thankful you adopted this gay man to your group.

To my Steam Queen Group- Your support is always appreciated. Thank you for always helping me promote my books.

To all the amazing Independent Authors. I apologize in advance if I miss you. Please know that I appreciate all of you.- Tempest Phan, C.M. Danks, Swati M.H, Sue Watts, Matthew Dante, Devin Sloane, S.M Lanyon, Janice Jarrell, Jenni Barra, Lizzie Stanley, Selena Moore, Zee Shine Storm, Barbara Kellyn, N. Dune, Nola Marie, P.K Morrison. Sionna Trenz, Monica Arya, Aurora Page, Ish, Ruby Ana, Charm White, Anna Fury, Elle Bor, and Robert Karl.

To all the book bloggers and fanatics who help me spread the word about my books. Dawn, Tina, April, Brittany, Lyndsay, Stefka, Anna, Marla, Michelle, Anita, Jenny, Melissa, Nedra, Jerrica, Taima, Tammy and all the bookstagrammers.

To Roopali, thank you for the great cover designs and for always accommodating my last minute requests.

To Sam and Dar who think I can do no wrong. I love you both.

Elly and Reenie, two of my fave people. Thanks for adding joy to our lives.

Last but not the least, the readers. We are nothing without you. THANK YOU FROM THE BOTTOM OF MY HEART.

All the White Lies We Tell

by
Garry Michael

One: Isaac

Sixteen Years Ago

"Andrew Sorensen from the United States has never won an Olympic gold, and he's currently eighteen points behind France's Hugh Olivier, the leader in the overall standings since the day started," the man on the television said, the moment the American skier got off the platform. "Andrew is a powerful and consistent skier, but has struggled this Olympics."

I didn't know what I was watching, but my attention was glued to the screen, mesmerized by Andrew gliding across the powder-white snow, framed by a background of blue sky. He looked like a superhero from one of my favorite comic books. His clothes were tight, just like Captain America, with red, white, and blue colors that looked like an American flag. His tinted goggles reflected the sun's rays, while the snow plume that trailed behind him made him look like he was flying on clouds. I turned up the volume to hear the swooshing and crunching of his skis. The surprisingly pleasant sounds sent tingles down my spine.

"Pop, what do ya call this?" I asked, pointing to the television as my dad entered the room from outdoors, arms full of logs.

After placing them next to our fireplace, he took off his black winter coat. The snow that had gathered on the hood fell to the floor and melted into a small puddle. He rubbed his hands and slowly brought them closer to his lips, blowing air onto his cold fingers. He joined me on the floor, where I was sitting with my legs crossed, then wrapped an arm around my shoulder, a gesture that always gave me a sense of safety. He took the remote control and turned down the volume. "It's called alpine downhill skiing," he answered.

"That looks like a lot of fun. That's Andrew, he's an American like us." I pointed to the screen while looking at my dad. "He's so fast. I think he's gonna win, Pop."

"I hope he does, bud, but he's gonna have to ski a perfect run to win gold. See those little flags at the bottom of the screen?"

I looked at the images and numbers displayed in a grid, and the only flag I recognized was the American flag, sitting below six other flags. I was only nine years old; I hadn't learned the rest of the flags yet.

"He's gonna have to do better than everyone above him to win gold," Pop explained.

The man on the television hadn't stopped speaking since Andrew took off. "I like what I'm seeing, especially his top-flight speed," he said. "Right here is where he can make up ground." Andrew took a right turn and touched an orange flag outside the blue line marking the slope's path. "Uh-oh, I don't like the way he exited that turn."

I didn't have a clue what the announcer was saying—'making up ground', 'top-flight speed', blah, blah, blah—but one thing I knew for a fact: Andrew was fast. Lightning-fast.

"Oh no! He lost his balance. I think that wobble may have cost him the podium this Olympics. He's bleeding more time," the announcer declared, a mix of excitement and disappointment in his voice.

My dad flinched, watching the scene unfold.

"What happened? Was that bad?" I looked up at him. My heart was pounding and my palms were sweating. My nervousness and exhilaration were uncontained.

"Did ya see him drift outside that blue line almost to the orange net lining that slope?"

"Yeah," I said, nodding.

"He lost a second when that happened."

Confused, I asked, "But that was just a second. That's just one Mississippi, right?"

"Sure is, Isaac, but in a race like this, a second can be the difference between winning and losing."

The announcer's voice drew my attention to the screen. "Here's the final turn. You can see his disappointment. Andrew was a favorite to win a medal this year, but he's going to finish in seventh place. The 2006 Winter Games won't be his best Olympics. That's gotta hurt."

"Is that it?" I asked, as Andrew fist-bumped and high-fived the other skiers and a row of fans lined behind a barricade. He took his goggles off and rested them on his head. He was smiling, but his eyes were sad. He stared at the screen where the results were displayed and shook his head before letting it hang low.

"That's it. That was the final."

"So, who won?"

My pop stood up and walked toward the television to show me the standing. "See these three flags right here?"

I nodded. My eyes concentrated where his finger was pointing at the screen.

"This is France, they won gold. This is Austria, they won silver, and this is Switzerland, they won bronze."

"I wish we won," I said, leaning back on the foot of the couch.

3

"That's OK, Isaac, there are more games and races that we can win. We can't win them all. But Andrew should be very proud for making it to the Olympics."

I placed my index finger on my chin. "I'm gonna go to the Olympics and win gold when I'm older," I declared, my eyes still trained on the video replaying Andrew's turns in slow motion. "Do you think I could be an Olympicker?"

My pop chuckled and tousled my hair. "They're called Olympians, bud," he said.

"Oh. Could I be an Olympian?"

He was quiet for a while, his light-brown eyes looking directly at me. His brown hair was similar to mine, and I remembered all the times I wished to be as tall and handsome as he was. It took him a while before answering and I was afraid he would say no. "I'll tell ya what—if ya keep good grades in school, and stay outta trouble, we'll get ya a pair of skis."

I got up from the floor and hugged him. "Thanks, Pop! I'll practice every day so I can be an Olympian, I promise!" I jumped up and down, barely able to contain my excitement. My own skis!

The door opened and in came Ma carrying bags of groceries.

Pop greeted her with a kiss and took the bags from her, using his other hand to pull off her coat.

"What's got you excited, baby?" she asked after giving Pop a quick hug and taking a seat near the fireplace in the rocking chair my dad made.

"I'm going to be an Olympian," I yelled. My heart was full of joy about my new dream. I wrapped my arms around her, and she leaned over to kiss the top of my sweaty head. She smelled like lilacs, and the scent was becoming my favorite.

"Ya are?" she asked. She sighed as she took her shoes off, then rubbed her feet. Her neck cracked when she stretched it left and

4

right.

"Yes, ma'am. Pop'll buy me skis if I stay outta trouble and keep my grades up."

Ma's smile faltered for a split second before glancing at my pop, who was watching us from the kitchen doorway. He shrugged and mouthed, "It's OK," before joining us in the living room.

My attention was back on the television. The medal ceremony had started, and a lady put a medal around each of the three skiers' necks, the skier from France last because he won gold. "Please stand for France's national anthem," a voice said, and everyone stood when the song started playing. Tears streamed down the French skier's face, his hand on his chest, singing along with the anthem.

"I'm gonna be just like him someday, Ma," I said, reaching for her hand.

She placed her other hand over mine and gently squeezed.

"I'm gonna win gold for us and the USA."

She didn't say anything. Instead, she leaned toward me, and when we were eye to eye, she squeezed my chin and nodded.

* * *

Later that evening, when my parents were asleep, I snuck back to the living room and turned on the television with the volume muted so I could keep watching the Olympics. They were showing a replay of the race we watched earlier, and although I knew the results, I was just as excited as the first time I witnessed Andrew skiing. I stood up, mimicking his every move, my hands sliding up and down, front and back, copying his turns as he slithered down the snow-covered hill.

"I'm gonna win gold," I whispered to myself. I laid back on the carpeted floor and stared at the ceiling until my eyelids grew heavy, falling into the most amazing dream.

Two: Foster

College Days All Over Again

I was born to continue a legacy; raised to be great. My life was the result of a series of calculated decisions, many made for me as a child, some on my own. All those decisions led to where I was: *greatness.* Just like my father. The man not only shared the same name as me, but left a legacy I'd been trying to surpass.

With thirty minutes left before I boarded the seaplane that would take me to the San Juan Islands, I checked my phone to see if my mom had returned my texts and calls. I'd just arrived in Vancouver yesterday after winning the European Cup in Austria. Once I took a breather, I was headed to the World Cup in Aspen before this year's World Championships in Canada, then ending the season in Beijing for the Winter Olympics. The phone screen showed nothing except the notification of my impending flight. I expected my dad to ignore my messages, but not my mom. Anxious to hear from her, I scrolled through my contacts and pressed their land line instead.

First ring. I said a silent prayer for her to pick up.

Second ring. "Come on, pick up, please?"

Third ring. I was about to end the call when it suddenly connected.

My heart somersaulted, relieved to finally be speaking with my mom, until I heard my dad's voice.

"Allo?" he said, his Quebec French accent unmistakable. He was born and raised in Montreal, and only moved to Vancouver, British Columbia, when he and my mom got married twenty-seven years ago. Back then my dad was an up-and-coming alpine skier and hadn't yet become Foster Donovan, Olympic gold medalist and World Champion.

"It's me, Dad," I replied with fake cheer.

"Foster? Why are you calling this early?" he asked, with all the enthusiasm of a funeral director.

"It's ten in the morning," I said, trying to hide the hurt in my voice. "Did you get my messages? I've been trying to get a hold of Mom."

"What messages?"

My nostrils flared but I kept my emotions in check. I took a deep breath and gritted my teeth. "The ones I left two days ago, and the ones from yesterday."

"Je suis désolé, fils," he apologized. "Your mother's phone broke and we ordered a new one."

"Is your phone broken too?" I quipped, and wondered if he was ignoring my calls or simply didn't give a shit about me.

"Quel sont les messages?" he asked me what the messages were about, and I knew I'd lost his attention. His disinterest was infallible. He only spoke French to us to cut a conversation short, knowing full well that my French was limited since we moved to northern California when I was ten.

"I won the fucking cup, if you must know," I yelled. I felt guilty about raising my voice at him, but what the actual fuck?

I won a freaking gold medal and I didn't even get a *hello* or *congratulations?* Especially from my dad, who once enjoyed the same career trajectory I was currently on.

"Foster! Language," he scolded. "You need to stop hanging out with your American friends. You're starting to sound uncouth."

That was when I completely lost it. My friends were the most honorable people I knew, and I wasn't about to let anyone disrespect them. "You don't even know them, not that you've tried—"

"Are you just calling to throw a tantrum?"

"Oh my god! I called to let you know I won a gold medal."

"What? The European Cup?" He laughed humorlessly. "That tournament is so small, people hardly know about it."

"You're kidding, right?"

I was about to give him a piece of my mind when he asked, "What was your time?"

"What?" I asked, taken aback by the sudden interest.

"What. Was. Your. Final. Time?" he said, enunciating every word as if I was a child.

"Um, one-minute and fifty-three-point-twenty-one-seconds," I answered. I felt suddenly exhausted by this conversation, the twenty-six-year-old me reverting to the teenaged me when my sole aspiration was to please my father.

"That's almost a couple of seconds slower than your *slowest* time from last year. You really need to stop taking a full six months off between seasons."

What? That was all I was going to get? "So, you're saying that I should move to freaking Patagonia during spring and summer to find a slope to ski?" I combed my hair with my free hand, trying to stop myself from having a complete outburst.

9

"Not full-time, just a couple of months should do the trick."

"Jesus, Dad! I've been undefeated since last year." My voice was low, surrendering this battle with him.

"Are you going to wait until you win silver?"

Un-fucking-believable. My day was officially ruined thanks to my ever-supportive father. "You know what—" I was about to tell him to buzz off in French before I heard my sister's voice in the background.

"Is that Oz?" Sophia asked, using the nickname she gave me as a child. Because of her Down syndrome, it took a while before Sophia was able to speak and she had struggled to say my name, calling me Oz instead of Foster. I still loved it.

"Oui," my dad said.

"Can you please give her the phone," I asked, but before I even finished uttering my request, Sophia's voice came through—he had passed the phone to her, an obvious manifestation of my dad's eagerness to end our conversation.

"I miss you, Oz," Sophia said, the enthusiasm in her voice contagious. I smiled.

The negativity my dad had just dumped on me evaporated. "I miss you too, baby sis," I cooed. It was true what they said about Down syndrome children—they were the most loving, caring, easy-going people on the planet. If it wasn't for her, I would have moved out of Vancouver a long time ago, but I'd miss her too much. I hardly had time to see her with my hectic schedule. Moving out of Vancouver, or even Canada, would only make it harder to spend time with her.

"I'm not a baby anymore, Oz," she chuckled. "I'm almost eighteen now." She might be *almost* eighteen years old, but she'd forever have that innocence.

I couldn't help but laugh. "Are you sure?"

"Yes!"

"Guess what?" I asked.

"You won the gold!" she screamed.

"What? How did you know that?" I knew how, since she was the first person I texted after winning. Also, it wasn't a hard guess, really; even if she said that every time I raced, she would only have been wrong a couple of times.

"I just knew you would. I'm so proud of you." Her last statement made my eyes sting. Sophia's excitement was the validation I didn't know I needed.

I swallowed the lump forming in my throat to prevent making a scene in public. A few of the seaplane passengers had recognized me even with my baseball cap and shades on, and they'd started aiming their phones in my direction.

"When are you gonna come visit?" she asked.

"I'm visiting my friends, but I'll come to see you right after."

"Promise?"

Our pilot gave me a thumbs-up, letting me know we were ready to board. "Anything for you, Red. Listen, the pilot is ready and I need to go. I love you."

"I love you too, Oz."

I hung up and stared at my phone for a couple of seconds, before grabbing my bags and walking the ten yards to the Kenmore Air dock on Vancouver Harbor.

* * *

The plane ride from Vancouver to San Juan Islands was just over two hours. After traveling from Austria to Switzerland, I wasn't looking forward to more time on a plane, but I hadn't seen my best friends since last year.

The San Juan Islands came into view the closer our two-passenger seaplane got to the harbor. A small section of the bay was lined with lit buoys that guided float planes like ours to a water landing.

Avery, Wyatt, and I went to UCLA together with our buddies Travis and his husband, Ashton. The five of us just clicked and spent almost every day hanging out, until life pulled us down different paths. Avery and Wyatt joined the Marines, Ashton went to medical school, Travis went pro and became a tennis superstar, while I followed my father's footsteps in becoming a professional skier. I was dying to meet Wyatt's boyfriend, Kai. I spoke with Wyatt on the phone yesterday to give him my schedule, and I couldn't believe how relaxed he sounded.

Speak of the devil, Wyatt was on the dock waving when the pilot maneuvered the plane into one of the slots.

"That's everything," the pilot said after unloading my two overnight bags that were stored in the undercarriage.

"Thank you." I pulled a bill out of my pocket and handed it to him.

"Oh, thank you!" he exclaimed, pocketing the hundred-dollar tip. He hopped back in the plane and slowly sailed it away from the dock for his takeoff.

Wyatt and a very good-looking man with sun-kissed skin greeted me at the halfway point of the wooden dock, which was a little too wobbly for my taste. Wyatt strode toward me, his long legs closing the gap between us quickly. Then he did something out of character—he hugged me, shocking the shit out of me.

"Whaaaat? A welcome hug?" I teased, even though I couldn't help but be happy for my friend. He'd been through a lot these past few years. I didn't know the extent of his experience from his deployment, but the Wyatt who came back was barely a shadow of the warm, exuberant man currently with his arms around me.

"Shut up and let me help you with that." Wyatt grabbed one of the bags after the embrace. "This is my boyfriend, Kai. Kai, this is my good friend, Foster. You've heard Avery and me talk about him."

I reached out my free hand to shake Kai's. "Hello, Kai. Nice to finally meet the person who tamed this guy," I teased, giving Wyatt a little elbow.

"Nice to meet you too, Foster." Kai beamed, his perfectly positioned dimples on both cheeks deepening, making him look even more handsome.

"How's everyone?" I asked when we were inside Wyatt's red vintage Chevy.

Wyatt and Kai gave each other a knowing look before Wyatt looked at me from the rearview mirror, a shit-eating grin on his face. "We have something special for you," he said.

"You know I hate surprises," I said. "What is it?"

"You'll love this one," Kai interjected.

I shook my head but couldn't find it in me to feel anything but delighted to be around my friends again. I looked out the window and marveled at the beauty of San Juan Islands. It was green everywhere you looked, even in the middle of winter.

Wyatt parked the truck in front of a two-story home I didn't recognize. It had gray shingle siding, similar to the houses you'd find in Cape Cod.

"Whose house is this?" I asked.

13

"This is Avery and Elizabeth's new place. We'll get your bags later. Let's get you inside." Wyatt grinned, his gray eyes sparkling.

Kai took my hand and led me to the walkway. "Close your eyes and no peeking," he instructed when we reached the door.

"What are you guys up to?" I asked, even though I did what I was told anyway.

I heard a door open and I was led inside, holding my breath. I could hear soft chatter, but I couldn't make out the conversation.

"You can open your eyes now," Wyatt whispered.

Slowly, I opened my eyes to the chorus of "SURPRISE!" I put my right hand over my chest as I took in the scene in front of me. Below a big white banner with *Congratulations, champ!* written in red, my favorite color, were my close friends, who were like my family. Avery and Elizabeth had their boy, Elijah, in front of them. Travis was standing behind his husband, Ashton. I held back the tears and swallowed hard. If only my dad was this excited. I shook off all the negative thoughts and rushed toward my friends. This was college all over again.

Travis and Ashton sandwiched me in a hug. "We've been replaying your race from the European Cup," Travis said.

"You were incredible," Ashton added.

"Thank you. Congratulations yourself, I'm sorry I missed your wedding." Travis and Ashton had some last-minute hiccups with their wedding planner and ended up moving their wedding date sooner than expected to when I was in Austria training for the European Cup.

"No worries, bro," Travis assured me. "Trust me, I get it."

"Let's continue this at the dining table." Avery put his arm around my shoulder and guided me to the dining room, with

14

everyone close behind us.

The table setting was a tropical motif with green napkins and fresh, bright-red hibiscus flowers. Several glass serving dishes full of delicious-smelling food were placed down the middle. "A Hawaiian luau? I can't remember the last time I had Hawaiian food," I said and, on cue, my stomach grumbled.

"Kai and I made everything from scratch while video-chatting with Kai's ma," Elizabeth explained.

"I hope you like it," Kai said.

My heart swelled with joy over the effort my best friends had gone to for this special evening. "Thank you, everyone. So much."

Wyatt clinked his glass with his fork once we were seated. "I'd like to make a toast," he began, and raised his glass. "To our amazing friend, Foster. We are so proud of you. We wish you luck this coming Olympic year."

"He doesn't need luck. He's got this," Ashton added.

"You might not need luck, but we hope all your dreams come true," Wyatt said. "To Foster!"

"To Foster," the others said in unison as they raised their glasses.

The dinner was filled with stories about Kai and Wyatt remodeling the San Juan Winds, the business Avery, Wyatt, and Elizabeth had built from the ground up. Ashton and Travis updated me about their honeymoon plans and Travis' tennis schedule that would start up in spring. I was genuinely delighted that my friends had found their *someone*. But a slight feeling of jealousy came over me out of the blue, reminding me of what I didn't have. Was there something fundamentally wrong with me? Why couldn't I land a decent guy?

After dinner, Travis and Ashton cleared the table of dirty

dishes, and Avery went upstairs with Elijah to get him ready for bed.

While everyone was busy, I stepped outside onto the patio for some fresh air. Even though it was frigid, I always loved the way winter air felt in my lungs, reminding me of the mountains and slopes that were my second home. Where it was just me, the speed, and the next turn.

* * *

Four Months Ago

"You're breaking up with me over brunch?" my soon-to-be-ex-boyfriend asked after he set down his espresso cup with a clink and angrily wiped the sides of his lips. His raised voice earned us several glances from other patrons inside the coffee shop.

"Can you lower your voice, please?" I asked, leaning forward with my index finger on my lips. "Let's not make a scene here." Delaney's was one of my favorite places and I didn't want to be too embarrassed to come here anymore.

"You should've thought of that before you brought me to this dump. Seriously, Foster, what's so special about this place?" David asked, motioning to the inside of the café.

I looked around and raised my hand in apology when I caught the barista's glance. I pulled a hundred-dollar bill out of my wallet for our coffee and apologized for David's arrogance even before we finished our chat.

"Is there someone else?" David asked, ignoring the fact he was causing a scene.

"What? There's no one else, Jesus!" And that was the truth. I

16

wasn't a cheater.

I met David at a gala hosted by one of my sponsors during Christmas last year. He was a social media influencer and well-known for posting workout videos for his seven million followers. If people only knew the truth about him. He hated working out, and used steroids to bulk up. He even had implants put in his calves. He'd made a great living being famous for just being famous. I understood his appeal—blond hair, blue eyes, a chiseled face, and the body of a Roman god. Who wouldn't fall for that? Our attraction was instant, but with no real connection and zero things in common, I was surprised it lasted for six months, and even more shocked that he didn't see this day coming. It also bothered me that he wasn't being truthful with his followers. I thought I could look past it, but I hated the trickery he used to get what he wanted.

"It's not you, it's me," I said, almost vomiting on the cliché. But that was the best I could do. I didn't know what I wanted, but I knew it wasn't this.

"I can't believe you're doing this to me," he fumed. "I'm a fucking catch." He grabbed his phone from the table—another reason he and I didn't work. I couldn't be with someone who, after not seeing each other for weeks, spent our entire time together staring at his phone. "You'll be back." He stood up and headed toward the door, looking around the place with disgust.

"Take care, David," I called out.

He turned around, his face red and his lips pursed. "Fuck you, Foster," he yelled, giving me the middle finger for good measure.

* * *

"Are you not having fun?" Wyatt asked as he handed me a bottle of beer.

"Are you kidding? This is the best dinner I've had in years." The truth behind that statement amplified just how linear my life had been lately. Training, racing, with no time for real connection. It wasn't like I didn't try, but it seemed like I attracted the same kinds of men: drop-dead gorgeous with the personality of cardboard, or career-driven guys with no substance. It was fun for a while, but it was getting old.

"Yeah, we really need to do this more often."

If I wasn't looking at Wyatt when he said those words, I would've thought they were from someone else. "You really have changed, bro. And I am so happy for you and Kai. I've known you since freshman year and I've never seen you this happy."

"I am happy. It wasn't easy, and I had to keep fighting the urge to self-destruct, but being with Kai made me want to keep trying. To be better, you know?" Wyatt took a swig of his beer then looked at me. "I hope you find that too."

"What if I don't?"

"You will. Look at me. I would be the last person you'd expect to find true love...and don't you dare roll your eyes at me," he teased, pointing a finger at me. "If I can find it, I have no doubt you will. You need to keep your heart open. You might meet him in the most unexpected place and time. And when you do, never let him slip away."

"OK," I said, even though I doubted it, and we clinked our bottles together. "Let's head back in and join the gang." I hoped that by being around the others, Wyatt would drop the subject for now. I couldn't afford to dwell on this, not when I had slopes and competitions on my mind.

Three: Isaac

You Earned It

The uncertainty was in waiting for the moment of truth; the decision that would dictate the direction of my season this year rested on the twenty-one-member board of directors. I looked at the rearview one last time, making sure I was presentable for the meeting that I'd been planning for since last fall. Not wanting any distractions, I sent a quick group text to my parents before putting away my phone. *I'm about to head in. I'll call you when I'm done.* After pressing send, I put my cell in the glove box of my rental.

I entered the state-of-the-art headquarters of the US Association of Ski and Snowboard, located in Park City, Utah. The floor-to-ceiling glass windows framed the breathtaking view of the snow-covered mountains, making me wish I was on the slopes. After I checked in, I sat in one of the cold leather chairs in the lobby, where nine-paneled flat-screen monitors replayed a montage of old ski and snowboarding competitions. Magazines lay on the glass surface covering a large reclaimed tree trunk, and my attention landed on one with Foster Donovan Jr. on the cover. I grabbed three magazines and pretended to peruse them all, with the intention of keeping the one where a smoldering Foster was looking right at me. I didn't want the group of skiers and snowboarders to know I was ogling him. I didn't know why I cared either; I'd been out since high school, and I didn't have a problem being who I truly was.

After placing the other two magazines back on the coffee table, I leaned back and began flipping to his interview. A black-and-white image of Foster wearing nothing but a pair of dark jeans greeted me when I found the correct page. He was leaning on gray polished concrete, arms spread at his sides, exposing his impressive chest above eight-pack abs and the top half of his pronounced oblique muscles. His blond hair was purposely disheveled, and his lips were curved into a smirk that was finished with an intense gaze. The revealing images momentarily caused me to forget why I was here.

I cursed myself for getting distracted minutes before one of the most pivotal meetings of my life. I tossed the magazine on the table, causing a flop that echoed in the tense room of athletes. *I'm sorry*, I mouthed when a couple peered in my direction.

I need to refocus.

"I'm just going to use the bathroom. Give them a heads-up in case they call for me," I said to one of the three receptionists sitting behind the counter.

"I'll be sure to let them know," she said, flashing me her pearly whites.

I made my way to the men's restroom, passing by a group of men and women who were here for the same thing—the association's support. "Stay calm," I murmured in front of the bathroom mirror after splashing cold water on my face. I stared at my right hand and slowly made a fist. A sharp pain pierced my wrist, but I ignored it. I didn't need to be reminded of the injury that cost me my chance to qualify for the United States Olympic team almost four years ago. "You've got this, and you deserve to be here." I pumped myself up with one more pep talk before heading out to join my peers, who were also waiting for their chance to plead their cases. I was in a great position. I'd spent the past few years recovering and working back to the level I was at before my fall. I'd accumulated enough points by racing in small club events sanctioned by the association.

It was out of my control now, and the thought made me feel helpless.

The frosted-glass sliding door opened and out came a man with salt-and-pepper hair wearing a black suit with a blue shirt. "Isaac McAllister," he called out, combing the lobby filled with snowboarders and skiers around the same age as me. At twenty-five, I wasn't a rookie, but I'd been a late bloomer, only making small progress the past couple of years.

"Here, sir," I said, raising my hand before standing up from the chair I'd occupied since I arrived an hour ago. I drove my rental straight from the airport, since I didn't plan on staying in this stylish town. Besides, I had to fly to Aspen, Colorado, after this meeting—assuming I'd get the resources I needed to compete in the qualifying race that would earn me a spot in the World Cup. I was here for one reason, and I was about to find out.

"I'm Jonathan," he said, shaking my clammy hand.

"I'm sorry about that," I apologized, wiping my hands on my suit pants.

"Don't worry about it. Come in." He opened the door wider so I could enter.

21

I was greeted by all twenty-one board members sitting at a long shiny table made from mahogany wood with thick glass that ran through the middle. Jonathan, one of the board members, joined the five men and four women seated on my left. Eight men and two women sat on my right, and an older man, who I assumed was the chairperson, was sitting in the middle at the far end, with a vacant seat opposite.

"Have a seat, Mr. McAllister," the chairman said.

My sweating continued, and my breathing became irregular. I looked around the table; twenty-one pairs of eyes were on me.

"Thank—" I started, but I had to clear my throat, which had become dry all of a sudden. Perhaps all the fluid in my body had been excreted by my last trip to the bathroom. "Thank you for seeing me, and please call me Isaac," I continued, relieved I was able to form a coherent sentence with my mind going one hundred miles per hour.

"I think the board is with me when I say that we're pleased by your accomplishments these past four years. You've had some decent wins and you just keep getting better," the chairman said. I smiled thinly, hoping his kind words weren't a prelude to a *thanks-but-no-thanks* speech. "Building your points high enough to make it on the team is very commendable."

I knew that. I was well aware I had enough points to make it on the team, but that wasn't why I was here. I was here to find out if my performance was good enough to earn their support.

"Thank you. It was tough, I ain't gonna lie," I said nervously, looking around. "But this is what I wanna do and that's why I'm here."

One of the women sitting three chairs to my left flipped

open a folder and asked, "How's your right wrist, Isaac?"

They'd done their homework. "It's better, ma'am. It hasn't given me any issues since I finished rehab." I couldn't tell her that it still bothered me once in a while, and that it had aggravated me enough two weeks ago to force me to pull out of a race. I should tell them that, but it would make them run faster than a skier on ice.

"That's very good, Isaac," Jonathan replied, nodding.

"Well," the chairman said, "I guess we'd better get to the point."

I held my breath and looked down at my joined hands resting on my bouncing legs. The moment of truth was finally here.

"We'd like to offer you the association's support. We'll provide you with a coach, take care of all travel logistics, and provide your gear this season."

My head jolted up. I didn't hallucinate that, did I?

"You're a good skier and, with the right team, I think you could be a champion," the chairman continued. The board members nodded in agreement. "But we're going to need you to be one hundred percent committed. That includes off-season training."

"I will do anything." There was no stopping the tears cascading down my cheeks; this was the best outcome I could've asked for. "Thank y'all so much. Ya have no idea how much this means to me. Thank y'all." Jonathan stood and offered me his hand, and I followed suit, shaking it with a bit too much enthusiasm.

"Congratulations, Isaac. You earned it," he said.

I thanked the board one more time and said goodbye as Jonathan and I made our way out of the conference room.

"Which part of the South are you from?" Jonathan asked

after the door closed behind us.

"I beg your pardon?" My heart started to pound, but for a completely different reason.

"I swore I could've heard a Southern twang when you thanked us. It's crazy because you don't have it now." He shook his head. "Don't mind me, we've been meeting skiers and snowboarders since yesterday, and I'm starting to hear things." He chuckled.

"No worries, sir," I said, grateful he answered his own question.

"We'll send you an email with how things work, as I'm sure you have tons of questions, but for now relax." He clapped my shoulders, before turning back toward the room. "Oh, Isaac," he called out before I even made the first step. "When are you flying to Aspen for the qualifying?"

I glanced at my watch. "In four hours."

"Cool. Stop by the front desk and give them the name of your hotel so we can send your new coach, Alex, your way."

I nodded once and grinned like a lunatic the entire walk back to the front desk. "They told me to give you the name of the hotel where I'll be staying in Aspen? Actually, I'll be in one of the towns outside Aspen, do you think that'll be a problem for my coach, Alex?"

"Oh, Alex is the best!" the same receptionist as earlier exclaimed. She typed in my hotel info and assured me Alex would contact me soon. "Congratulations!"

"Did you get it, bro?" one of the guys still waiting asked me on my way out of the reception area.

"Yes," I responded, still floating on cloud nine.

"Right on, dude! See you out there." He gave me a fist-bump.

As soon as I got to the rental car, I pulled out my phone.

"Did ya get it?" Pop asked after one ring. "Honey, Isaac is on the phone! Let me put ya on speaker."

"I did, Ma and Pop." I choked on my words, a maelstrom of emotions flooding my every sense.

They were silent for a while, and all I could hear was heavy breathing and sniffles. Pop cleared his throat and asked. "Did ya get a coach?"

"Coach. Equipment. Everything." My pop had been my first coach and had trained me until I was eighteen years old, but when my dream of becoming a professional skier required me to travel out of state, he decided to stay with my mom, a decision he didn't take lightly, but it was for the best. They'd sacrificed enough.

"I'm so proud of ya, Isaac, ya deserve this," Ma said.

"This is yer moment, kid. Do ya hear me?" Pop said, the conviction in his voice barely able to conceal his obvious tears.

"Thank you, Ma and Pop. I never would've made it without your support and all the sacrifices you made."

"We just want ya to be happy," Ma said.

"Don't forget to have fun too," Pop added.

"I'm happy, but the fun will just have to wait."

"Isaac—"

"I have to catch a flight to Aspen. I just wanted to let you know." I did not need his familiar old lecture about taking skiing too seriously bursting my bubble. "I might not be able to come home this spring and summer, they want me to commit to off-season training."

"Don't worry about all that. We'll be fine," Pop said. "Call us when you get to Aspen."

"Travel safe, love," Ma said.

I disconnected the call and looked at my reflection in the

rearview mirror. How is it that I looked no different and yet everything had changed? I took a deep breath. "You're almost there," I whispered.

Aspen, my next conquest.

Four: Foster

The Best at Everything

Hearing my sister's laughter followed by the first five notes of her favorite song filling my condo made me smile. After being away for months, it was nice to be welcomed home. Before Taylor Swift belted the chorus of 'We Are Never Ever Getting Back Together', there was a soft knock on my door. "Come in," I called out, and just like all the other times she and Mom spent weekends here, Sophia came rushing in and plonked on my bed.

"Time to get up! Mom and I made breakfast."

The scent of cinnamon and brown sugar wafted through my open door, followed by Mom carrying a tray of hot cinnamon rolls. "I hope you're hungry," she said. The smell of brewing coffee started to tickle my olfactory nerves, waking every cell in my body.

"I don't think my coach or trainer would appreciate it if I ate cinnamon rolls for breakfast before two big races. In an Olympic year no less," I said with empty protest.

"We made bacon too," Sophia said.

I groaned while holding my stomach. "Crispy?" I asked.

"Of course!" As if she would ever forget my preference.

"Oz?" Sophia asked.

"Yeah?"

"Can we stay one more day before you go to Aspen?"

There was nothing more I wanted than to have her stay an extra day, but my schedule was packed with training, prior engagements, and I still needed to pack for the World Cup.

"Sweetie, remember what I told you? Your brother is going to be busy? We'll come back after the ski season," my mom said.

Sophia's smile faltered and she looked like she was about to cry. *Oh no.* She so rarely got upset that it always kicked my protectiveness into gear, even when it was against myself. I'd cancel everything before I broke her precious heart.

"You know what? Do you want to come to help me with my photoshoot?" I asked. "You can be my assistant today."

Her demeanor changed. She clapped her hands before jumping off the bed and leaping across my room. "Yes!" she exclaimed. "Thank you, Oz. Can we listen to music when they're taking pictures of you?"

"I'd love that," I said, and winked at my mom.

Mom smiled. She loved it when we spent time together. I stood up and grabbed Sophia's hand, and led both of them to the living room. I relieved Mom of the breakfast tray and set it aside, and she wrapped her arm around my waist and leaned her head on my chest

"Let's start the song over." Sophia unlocked her phone and restarted the song. It was the first song on her Spotify playlist she created when I gifted her my old cell phone three years ago. Mom and Dad had since asked if she wanted a new phone, but she refused because it was a gift from me.

Mom left the room and came back with a steaming cup of

coffee. She handed it to me and said, "Don't read too much into your dad's behavior lately. He's just stressed, but he is really proud of you."

I shook my head. He was a middle-aged retired skier with more money than he could spend in this lifetime. What could he be stressed about? *Whatever*. I wouldn't let him ruin my day. "I'd rather not talk about it now. Let's try to have some fun."

* * *

Sophia hijacked the sound system in my black Tahoe SUV. The temperature had been around zero to three degrees Celsius consistently, and the city was covered with a blanket of snow that had accumulated over the past month. The evergreen pines were the only signs of life.

"I love winter," she said, after selecting a song from Ariana Grande this time.

"Oh yeah? What do you love about it?" I asked.

"The snow. It's so nice and it's pretty everywhere."

"Me too." And I did. Winter was my favorite season, not just because of sports, but I always felt at peace. The season when everything was planned and each day this time of the year had a purpose. Times when I didn't have to worry about failed relationships and the loneliness that had consumed me these past few years.

"Do you want to pick the next song?" Sophia asked.

"You're in control," I answered. I reached out and ran my hand down her silky light-brown hair. "What do you want for your birthday this year?"

She looked out the window as we crossed the Lions Gate Bridge over the Salish Sea separating West Vancouver from Stanley Park, where the studio was located. "I wish for two things," she said. "A Polaroid camera. Like the one on TV. It's so cool to have a camera that prints pictures right away."

"That's very cool. What's the other one?"

She looked at me and giggled.

"What?" I asked, giving her a quick glance.

"I can't tell you the other one. It's a secret."

"How about a clue?"

"Oz! I can't tell you. Otherwise, it won't come true."

Respecting her wishes, I stopped pressing and focused on finding a place to park as we had reached town.

"I think you're gonna win gold at the Olympics again," she said, holding my hand on our way to the studio.

"Oh yeah? What makes you think that?"

"Because you're the best at everything."

I smiled and squeezed her hand as my phone began to vibrate in my back pocket. I took it out and groaned. Dad. *I don't need this today.* "What's up, Dad?" I answered.

"Hi, Dad!" Sophia called out.

I put my phone to my chest. "Dad says hi," I said, even though he didn't, and she radiated.

"What's up, Dad?"

"I've been thinking about what I said regarding training in Argentina during their winter…" He trailed off, and for a second I thought he felt bad for insinuating that I was slowing down and not good enough to win my next competition. But then he continued talking. "I spoke with my friend who has a place near Catedral Alta Patagonia and mentioned your interest."

What interest? My jaw tightened, my blood boiled, and I had to look down at Sophia's beaming face to cool the inferno that was about to envelop me, enough to thaw every ounce of snow covering the entire city. "I can't talk about this right now. I have to go." I ended the call before he had a chance to protest.

"Are you OK?" Sophia asked after tugging my hand holding hers, perhaps noticing my agitation.

I gave her my most genuine smile and said, "Absolutely. I'm hanging out with my favorite person."

"You're the best, Oz."

I was the best at everything, alright. Except for being a son or being in a relationship. Other than that, I was fucking phenomenal.

Five: Isaac

Yes is the Only Acceptable Answer

Pacing back and forth at the foot of my bed, I rehearsed my potential interaction with my new coach, Alex. Even though this partnership was final, according to my conversation with the association's director, I was convinced that something I'd do or say would make them take their support back.

I pushed a stray strand of hair into place and glanced at my reflection in the full-length mirror next to the door of the hotel room before heading out. "I'd like you to help me harness my speed and teach me the discipline I need to get my game to the next level," I whispered on the way to the lobby. I needed to convince Alex that I wasn't here to waste his time, to let him know I was legit.

"Hi, Charlie. My name is Isaac McAllister," I greeted the hotel receptionist after reading his name tag. "I was expecting someone and I was wondering if he's checked in yet?"

"Hi, Mr. McAllister. No one has asked about you yet," he said, checking his computer.

"This is the only lobby, right?" I asked, scanning the waiting area again, worried that Alex might be looking for me elsewhere. The thought of being even a minute late made me uneasy.

"It is, Mr. McAllister, and—"

"Isaac?" I looked to my right to find the source of the voice. A tiny woman crossed the lobby determinedly in my direction. A stocking cap was pulled over her shoulder-length brown hair, and her makeup-free face shone bright red from the cold. She was wearing a black winter waistcoat with brown fur around its hood.

"Yes?" I asked, my tone acknowledging and questioning at the same time. I didn't have a problem engaging fans, but not when I was almost late meeting my new coach.

"Let's sit over here so we can get started," she suggested, waving toward two overstuffed leather chairs next to a handcrafted coffee table.

"What?" I asked.

"Oh, have you had dinner yet?" she asked. "I could use a coffee." She pulled a manila folder from her black tote that matched her outfit before pulling the zipper of her coat down.

Still confused, I asked, "I'm sorry, get started with what?"

"Hey, Mac," a group of skiers coming out of the elevator called out.

I acknowledged them with a nod before returning my attention to the woman in front of me.

"Our game plan," she answered, like I had a clue what she was talking about.

Assuming she was one of the sports journalists who were in town to cover the World Cup, I said, "I'm sorry, but I have to go. I was supposed to meet someone—" I glanced at my digital watch "—five minutes ago." I moved away from the reception desk to let Charlie help the next person waiting in line.

"I know. You're meeting with me," she said, irritation evident in her tone. "I'm Alex, your new coach."

It was as if someone dumped a bucket of ice water on my head. My face burned from embarrassment. "Oh, I'm sorry. I just—"

"You're expecting a dude, right?"

"Well, yes. I'm sorry." I hoped she could detect sincerity through my nervous voice. I went back over my conversation with the association staff and never once did they say Alex was a woman. Not that it mattered, of course, I didn't have a problem with that. A heads-up would've been nice so I didn't look like a complete ass in front of my new coach. *Way to make an impression, Isaac.* I hated not being in control of situations.

"Do you have concerns with your coach being a woman?" She put the folder back in her bag and crossed her arms, waiting for my response.

"I don't care if you're a woman. My only concerns are," I raised my right thumb, "can you help me win?" I lifted my index finger next. "Are you any good?" Then I lifted my middle finger. "And do you want to coach a gay skier? If you answer no to any of these questions, then we aren't a great fit, because yes is the only acceptable answer," I said.

She grabbed the folder out of her bag and smirked. "OK, I get you."

"I'm serious."

"The answer is yes to every single one of your questions. Chill, man. Why did those guys call you Mac?" She motioned her head in the direction of the gym, where the skiers had been going.

"It's short for McAllister."

"Cool. Grab your stuff, Mac. We've already wasted precious

minutes standing here. I only coach winners."

I like her.

* * *

My hamstrings burned as I pushed the last rep from the NordicTrack weight machine in the hotel gym. I'd spent the last sixty minutes training my quads, calves, and hamstrings to stay in shape for the tour. Fearing injuries before the big race, I purposely reduced the weights from my usual one-twenty pounds down to eighty, but that didn't mean easier training. No, sweat still dripped down my thighs as I lay back, legs elevated, taking a well-deserved break before a fifteen-minute cool-down run. "I hate leg day," I murmured.

My legs felt like rubber when I stepped off the weight machine and headed toward the treadmills below the row of televisions playing events from last year's Winter X-Games.

"What's up, Mac," a voice called out from behind me.

I turned. "Hey, Yoshi! Ready for the weekend?"

Yoshi and I were two of the few skiers staying at this hotel outside posh downtown Aspen. At eighteen, Yoshi was one of the tour's youngest skiers, and because he was the fourth-ranked Japanese skier, he didn't have the endorsements his compatriots had. As for me, being twenty-five didn't exactly scream *protégé*, and this place was decent enough without breaking the bank. I booked this lodge before I met with the association, and after that, all the hotels in town were sold out for the World Cup. "I am. I'll probably do a couple more runs tomorrow just to see if I can shave a couple of seconds off my time. You?"

"I was hoping to head up there with the guys, but they went earlier today, so I'll probably just wait until this weekend. It'll probably do me good to rest up. I've been working out since I arrived." He sounded disappointed but smiled anyway.

"I was going to do two runs tomorrow, but you can have one of my spots." I was surprised that I offered. I'd never trained with anyone and preferred to be on my own, the result of being an only child. I sometimes wondered what it would feel like to have a sibling. Yoshi being left behind by his team reminded me of when I was the outsider looking in.

Yoshi grinned, his plan of resting evaporating into the air. "Are you sure?"

"Absolutely. It'd be fun. Plus, it'd be nice to scout the competition," I joked.

"What do you mean by *scout the competition*?" he asked, his brow furrowed.

"It's an expression we silly Americans use. It means checking out others to see if they're any good."

"Ah, I see. They have the same expression in Japan."

"Oh yeah? What is it?"

"It translates to *let them see you*."

I shook my head, clueless about what he meant. "I don't get it."

"I was just teasing you; I know what you meant. I was born in Tokyo but raised in San Francisco, and I am as American as it gets." He laughed. "Are you done with your workout?"

"Almost. I just have to do a quick run before I meet with my coach."

"Cool. See you tomorrow?"

"Meet you up there at nine o'clock."

Yoshi waved to my reflection, and I replaced my headphones and built to a comfortable jog. Foster appeared on the screen in front of me. He was striding out of a hotel in a charcoal pea coat. He raised a black leather glove to shield his eyes from the onslaught of flashing camera lights. He smiled at the reporters peppering him with questions. Below his gray scarf were the words *The King of Slopes Arrives in Aspen.*

I increased the speed of the treadmill and turned up the volume of my headset. "One race at a time," I muttered.

Six: Foster

Big Mac

I was a rock star, but I didn't have a band. Instead, the snow and the mountains were my orchestra. I enchanted fans with jumps and turns on the slopes. Sports analysts had run out of superlatives to describe my talent. I wasn't boasting, just stating the facts. Facts that were backed by stats and the medals sitting on my shelves. Yes, there are many shelves in different rooms at my place. I'd been skiing since I could stand up, and I didn't plan to stop. One would think I'd get sick of it, but it was the opposite. The more I won, the more I wanted to keep winning, especially after my last conversation with my father a couple of days ago.

Are you going to wait until you win silver? His question played over and over in my head even after I'd arrived in Aspen.

No chance I'd ever let that happen.

Cameras flashes greeted me when the doorman opened the glass door for me to exit The Villa. It was a nice place. My team always booked five-star hotels to ensure added security and privacy so I could be laser-focused on my upcoming race.

This competition was my chance to add another first to my name: the first ever to win three consecutive World Cup titles.

I was no betting man, but if I was, I wouldn't bet against me. I ruled the slopes, because on a mountain I felt completely true to myself, and no one could beat me when I was at ease. No one had come close.

"Foster, what do you think about your chances this weekend?" a reporter waving his hand asked.

"Do you think you'll break your own record?" another yelled from the back. The record in question was the fastest time ever clocked on this slope.

"How do you feel about the possibility of surpassing your dad's back-to-back wins from fifteen years ago?" I couldn't even tell where that voice came from. With the increase of curious onlookers, it was hard to keep track of which questions belonged to which reporter.

"I feel pretty good coming into this event. The competition is tougher this year, so we'll just have to wait until the race. Thank you all." I delivered one of my well-rehearsed, non-committal, to-the-point print-and-television-approved answers loud enough for everyone in the back to hear.

More clicking and flashing followed by more questions, but instead of answering, I waved to the crowd and hurried to the driver side of my rented black SUV. The hotel offered a chauffeur service, but I preferred to drive whenever I could.

* * *

I parked the SUV facing the mountain range on the other side of the glassy lake. I scrolled through my playlist until I found my favorite classic 70s rock, before reclining my seat low enough to unwind and still be able to enjoy the scenery. My shoulders relaxed when I exhaled and forced the rest of my body to follow. The view was as breathtaking as I remembered. Cotton-shaped clouds dotted the darkening blue sky giving way to dusk. The setting sun's final rays skimmed the top of the Maroon Bells mountains, which caused the peaks and clouds beyond to glow a brilliant yellow-orange. The reflection on the lake below made the moment even more magical. I'd never told anyone about this hidden gem, and how the mountains looked like they were on fire at this time of day. This was my spot, where nature put on a show just for me. I may be selfish, but that was how I felt.

That was how I used to feel.

The urge to share this moment caused me to snap a photo that didn't do the view justice and send it to Sophia with a text that read, *Wish you were here.* After pressing send, the nagging feeling I was sure would diminish after I sent the picture to my sister didn't go away. Instead, a dull ache spread through me. I rubbed my chest where my heart was, the small void growing and tightening its grip on my soul.

I have everything. Why am I so lonely?

I ignored that thought, not willing to entertain the meaning. I closed my eyes and tried to envision the people I wanted to share this place with, but aside from my sister and my mom, I couldn't think of anyone. Pathetic, really, considering the number of people on my contact list: from A-list celebrities to politicians. I didn't know what was up with me lately. It had been gnawing at me these past couple of days, maybe weeks, months even. As amazing as my life looked from the outside, it was missing something.

I opened my eyes and shook. I didn't need this distraction.

I needed to remain focused. I had a big event this weekend and I couldn't afford to take my eyes off the prize. I returned my seat to the upright position and turned the car ignition to life, its eight-cylinder grumble disturbing the snowbirds that had gathered close to the shore of the lake. Time to go back to town.

It was only five-thirty in the evening, but it was already dark out when I decided to take a quick detour from the hotel to the ski resort where the event would be taking place. I wanted to see it. No, I *needed* to see it to get me out of this gloom. I needed to recalibrate, and this place would ground me.

As I neared the hills of the slope, I noticed a tall man wearing a tan Sherpa jacket, jeans and brown boots standing behind the barricade at the bottom of the hill. He was taking photographs of the slope, and examining every picture. I got out of the car, keeping my eyes on him. Curious, I stood next to the SUV and watched him snap pictures.

After a couple of minutes, he turned around and our eyes met. Shock flashed across his face, before he schooled his reaction to neutral. His jawline was outlined with dark-brown stubble that matched his hair.

He had what my sister called *serious eyes*; not mean, but not friendly either. They were the kind of eyes that models tried to replicate on fashion shoots or in editorial pictures. I'd used those eyes in the past. He patted his pants and fished a set of keys from his pocket before glancing at me one last time.

Definitely serious eyes.

I followed every move he made. This guy couldn't be a skier. There was no way a skier would see me without talking to me or, at the very least, sneaking a photo. This man seemed unaffected and I wasn't sure how I felt about that.

41

* * *

"You feeling OK?" my coach, Stan, asked after I hopped off the ski lift. We headed for the small square structure that was erected for this weekend's event. It was covered with this year's logo and housed the platform where skiers would take off.

"I'm fine, don't worry," I assured him as we made our way inside. The place was humming with skiers and coaches waiting for their training runs.

"Congrats, bro. That final turn you took from the European Cup last week was epic," a skier I didn't know said.

I didn't even bother to look at his event pass to learn his name. I was often bombarded at competitions by hopefuls who wanted to rub shoulders with the greats.

"Yeah, that was pretty sick, man. I watched the replay on YouTube and it was impressive," another skier enthused. Lyle, I knew—he had finished second in that event.

A small crowd gathered around me within seconds. I glanced at Stan and blew out a breath. My hope for a quiet training run was shot.

Over Lyle's shoulder, I spotted the man from last night walking toward me. The scene around me reduced to slow motion. Behind him, a brunette with *Coach* written on her credentials whispered something to him before he glanced up and our eyes connected. Just like last night, all I got was a quick glance before he looked away and took his coat off.

The sight that followed made my mouth water, and I swallowed hard, trying to ignore how my body reacted. He was unusually muscular for a skier. His tight gear accentuated his broad shoulders and muscular back that narrowed to a trim waist. And that ass…because my blood had suddenly gathered around my now-semi-chub, it took a second for my brain to catch up to the fact that he was a skier and competing in the same event.

"Who's that guy?" I asked one of the skiers.

"That's the American, Isaac McAllister; we call him Mac," someone said.

"Haven't you heard about him?" Stan asked. "Surely you've seen him race? He's been killin' it on the USA circuit."

I shook my head, my eyes never leaving him. I would have remembered someone like Isaac.

Isaac turned and eyed me once again. He started stretching his arms and then his legs, while my perusal traveled down to his impressive bulge.

Sweat started to form on my back, but I couldn't take my coat off because it was the only thing hiding my fully erect cock. *Jesus! What's wrong with me?* It wasn't like this was the first time I'd seen a striking man wearing a speed suit.

"Hey, ready?" My coach's voice snapped me out of my delirium as one of the skiers from Japan joined Isaac, blocking my view of him.

"Give me a few minutes," I answered. I had to meet him.

Isaac's frown lines deepened as the gap between us narrowed. He was even more handsome up close. His naturally rugged looks were doing all sorts of things to me. My heart started to race, and I felt hot and bothered with my cock straining against my tight speed suit.

Then we were face-to-face. I offered him my hand and wet my lips. "Foster Donovan," I said.

He took my hand and shook it. His callused palms and

43

strong grip almost made me bust my nut, reminding me it had been months since I last got laid. "Isaac McAllister," he replied with a deep growl that was smooth like honey.

I cleared my throat. "Um, do you want to train together?"

"I'm sorry?" he asked, glancing at his coach.

I momentarily questioned my wits and wondered if I had mumbled something incoherent. It wouldn't surprise me considering my current state. "Wanna train together?"

"Oh. Um, I'm actually training with Yoshi." He jerked his thumb at the skier next to him.

The skier waved. "Hi, I'm Yoshi."

Was that a no? I shook my head, surprised by the turn of events. There were very few guys on the circuit who didn't want to be in my presence. Scratch that, there was *no one* on tour who didn't want to be in my presence, and Isaac—*Mac*—McAllister turning down my offer to train stung.

So this was how it felt to be rejected.

Who the fuck does he think he is? I didn't need to train with him. I didn't need to train with anyone. Asking him to train with me was my lame excuse to get to know him. "No worries," I said as casually as possible before heading back to my team.

We'll see how good you are, Isaac. I'm not a huge fan of burgers, but I'd like to take a bite of that Big Mac.

Seven: Isaac

Replaceable, Expendable, Dispensable

What the hell was that about? I exhaled loudly the moment Foster left. It took every bit of my energy to stay in the present and not think about the tingling sensation his obvious perusal did to my body. How had I managed to never come across him, only to run into him two days in a row? After seeing him last night, his intense gaze had been the last thing on my mind before I succumbed to sleep, but not before jerking off twice while imagining Foster's lips wrapped around my cock, glassy eyes begging for my pleasure. "Goddamn it," I whispered and turned to face the wall, readjusting my growing erection in the tight fabric. It was a wonder I was able to wake up in time this morning.

"Did you just blow him off?" Alex whispered.

"No," I countered.

"Um, yeah you did. I can't believe you said no to training with him!" Alex shook her head. "Do you know how many of these guys would die to get a chance to train with him?" She motioned her index finger to the group of skiers camped in the small building housing the platform.

"Then why not ask them?" I said.

"Mac, that isn't the point. He is Foster Donovan. If he asks you to train with him, you say yes!"

I shrugged. I knew that, but I promised Yoshi that I'd train with him. And if I was being completely honest, I didn't need the distraction. And a man like Foster Donovan wouldn't go unnoticed.

My heart skipped a beat when Foster retreated to the other side of the room and glanced at me. His blue eyes were intense, replacing the playful look he had when he came over. His lips were pressed into a line and his jawline was pronounced. I forced myself to look back at Alex. "I don't need his help, and besides, I'm training with Yoshi." I looked around for Yoshi and found him holding two sets of skis in the air, examining each one intently.

Alex leaned in. "Look, I don't know Yoshi, but would you rather train with him or the best skier in the world?" she whispered. "You know who Foster is, right?"

"Of course I know who he is." Did she think I knew nothing about my own sport? I shook my head. A few minutes with him and I was already out of sorts and arguing with my coach, an affirmation that I had made the right decision. "I gave my word to Yoshi. You can't just drop someone because something better comes along." My chest tightened at the thought of being the cause of someone's disappointment. I knew how it felt to be replaced.

* * *

Thirteen Years Earlier

46

"Have a great time and make some friends," my mom said, readjusting my favorite red, white and blue beanie and kissing my forehead.

"I will, Ma," I replied, before climbing onto the bus that would take us to the cabin near Washington, D.C. for a four-day ski clinic. Ma and Pop had surprised me with this trip after I finished at the top of my sixth-grade class last year, and I'd been looking forward to this day since. At twelve, it would be my first time away from my parents. I drowned out my fear of being on my own with the excitement of making new friends and skiing all weekend long. Once seated, I looked out the window and waved at my ma one last time before the bus made its way to the snow-covered road.

After almost two hours on the road with intermittent stops to pick up more kids, our bus pulled in under a covered driveway that led to a log cabin twenty times larger than the one my pop built himself. One by one, we filed off, the stuffy bus air giving way to a cold winter breeze and swooshing sounds coming from the slopes to the right of the log cabin. A thrill ran through me. Ski lifts carried skiers and snowboarders, whose chatter and laughter reverberated through the air.

The camp staff checked us in and assigned us a roommate for the weekend. "Isaac McAllister?"

"Right here, sir," I raised my hand and made my way to the front of the line.

"You'll be with Aiden Gregory in room 108." The staff member pointed to the other kid and checked off something on his clipboard.

When he moved on to someone else, I walked over to Aiden. "Hey. My name is Isaac McAllister."

"I'm Aiden Gregory. You wanna go check out our room?"
"Yes!"

I helped Aiden carry one of his three bags as we searched for our room. *"Why do ya have three bags? Are ya stayin' longer than Sunday?"*

"My mom packed four different winter coats and boots for each day that I'm here," he said. "Is that all you have?" he asked, pointing at my backpack.

"Yes, this is all I need. My ma packed my clothes for the next four days, but I only have one winter coat. This one." I pointed to the coat I was wearing; blue, my favorite. I didn't understand why anyone needed a different coat and boots for each day, but I kept that thought to myself. I didn't want Aiden to be mad at me.

"Cool," he said as we found room 108. Once inside, Aiden rushed toward the beds. "Dibs on the top bunk!" He unzipped his bag and pulled out a brand-new Nintendo DS.

"OK." I didn't mind having the bottom bunk. I didn't care where I slept, as long as I was there. Plus, Aiden might let me be his friend if I let him have the top bunk. I dropped my backpack on the bed and looked out the window. The bus driver was busy unloading boxes of ski equipment. "When do ya think we can start skiin'?"

Aiden looked up from his video game and peeked through the window. "Maybe tomorrow. It's almost dark and I don't think they'll let us ski at night."

I pulled an old ski magazine I brought from home out of my bag and laid on the bed, propping my head up with my elbows, and started reading an article titled 'How to Take Your Skills to the Next Level.' I needed to prepare for tomorrow.

* * *

The following morning, our instructor asked us to pair with someone to practice on one of the bunny hills so he could see our form before graduating to a big slope. "Wanna be partners?" I asked Aiden immediately. I was afraid someone would ask him before I did.

"Sure," he shrugged and sat down. I was a little dismayed that he didn't sound as excited as I was. "What happened to your skis?" he asked while putting on his ski boots.

"I broke it last month, but my pop fixed it up," I answered. I'd been gutted when I wiped out last month after turning a curve too fast. I was worried I'd have to stop skiing when I saw the snap. They were my only pair of skis. My pop was worried I had hurt myself because I was sobbing when he reached me, but when he realized I was alright, he promised me he'd fix the broken ski like it was brand-new. And aside from the obvious fracture a few inches from the tip of my ski, it was as if nothing had happened. It hadn't affected my speed, and sometimes I thought it made me faster.

"That looks goofy. Why not just buy a new pair?" Aiden asked. "It works just fine."

"I hope it won't slow us down in the race later," he said before turning his back on me.

We spent hours practicing on the bunny hill, and I was starting to feel bored. I'd skied on bigger slopes than this and I didn't need this much practice. But some kids weren't as advanced as me, evident from their struggles on this small hill.

"Fuck," Aiden yelled after face-planting in the snow for the third time.

I looked around to see if our instructor heard him cuss, but he was busy helping a group of kids who were holding onto a rope to keep their balance. "Are ya alright?" I asked him.

"This is so stupid," he mumbled before pushing up and stalking away.

"Alright, kids, let's take a break," our instructor yelled, and we all sat in a circle off to the side of the trail.

Aiden was talking to one of the taller kids in our group. They both looked in my direction, whispered something, then came over. "I'm switching partners," Aiden said.

My heart sank. "But we're already a team," I said, then looked up to the instructor for confirmation.

"Why are you switching, Aiden?" the instructor asked.

"One of Isaac's skis is broken, and Thomas' partner is too slow," Aiden said.

"My skis aren't broken. They're fixed now." I unlocked my boots from my skis and showed them to the instructor, silently begging him to not let Aiden dump me. Tears burned my eyes and I prayed that the cold would freeze them so no one would see them fall. My breathing became heavy, fogging up the small space between the group. "It's not fair," I whispered.

"Who's your partner?" the instructor asked Thomas.

"I was," a kid said before Thomas had a chance to answer.

"What's your name?" the instructor asked.

"Sawyer."

"Do you want to pair up with Isaac?"

"Yes, he's way better than that punk anyway," Sawyer said.

I admired the way Sawyer stood up for himself.

"Thanks, Sawyer," I said. As disappointed as I was, I wouldn't let Thomas and Aiden ruin this weekend.

* * *

The sound of a three-second countdown signaling a skier's

launch brought me back to the present. I glanced at the platform just as Foster jumped off for his training run. "Is there something wrong with your skis?" I asked Yoshi.

"Oh yeah, just trying to decide which one would be better for these conditions."

"Your coach didn't tell you?" I asked.

"Nope, he gave me these to choose from." He lifted both pairs for me and Alex to see.

"Use the 78 Carbon. It's better since it's been cold and the slope is almost ice," Alex said.

"Right on. Thanks, Alex," Yoshi said with a grin.

"Thank you," I whispered.

She winked. "Are you ready? You're up next."

After climbing onto the launch pad, I assumed the ready position waiting for my countdown to begin. I gripped my ski poles, put my goggles on, and leaned forward.

Beep. I took a deep breath, harnessing my adrenaline and excitement.

Beep. After working through the ranks and busting my ass off, I was here.

Beep. I jumped in the air, skiing down the slope and into my dreams.

Eight: Foster

King of the Slopes

I slid forward the moment the countdown turned to one, signaling my launch. I planted my ski poles and thrusted in sync with my skis, propelling me forward with godlike speed. Gliding through ten meters of ground before the first turn of the terrain where the steepness of the slope dropped, I tucked my poles to my side while leaning forward for aerodynamics and preparing for the free fall that would generate the pace I needed for the first jump. My skis landed on the slippery slope with a loud thud.

Nailed it!

I maneuvered my skis to turn left while keeping my whole body leaning to the right for a series of turns leading to the finish line at the bottom of the hill.

"Fuck," I cursed when I botched the first turn of the slope. If it hadn't been for my quick reflexes keeping me in balance, I would've bled more time.

1:56.11. I could work with that. I'd blame the Big Mac distraction for the extra tenth of a second added to my final time after the training run. It was still enough to be on top of the standing for tomorrow's final race.

Isaac slid across the finish line, fist punching the air, before taking his goggles off and looking up to the screen where everyone's ski time was logged. 1:56.32 was posted next to his name, just under my recorded time. "Yes!" he screamed and looked up to the sky.

His enthusiastic reaction bothered me. I was still faster than him by two-tenths of a second, but that had been a close call.

Are you going to wait until you win silver? My dad's voice echoed in my head.

That would be the last time I'd let myself get distracted.

Isaac skied toward me. "That's a great time," he said. He was breathing hard and I could smell his minty fresh breath.

"Could be better," I said, hoping that my nonchalant tone was obvious enough to express my disinterest.

"About what happened up there." He motioned his head up at the platform before continuing, "I hope I wasn't—"

"Doesn't matter. I'll see you around." I unhooked my skis from my boots and walked away. I needed to get the hell out of there.

"Foster, wait," he called, and fuck, if my name didn't sound so fucking good coming from him. But it didn't matter. It couldn't. I kept walking.

"What happened up there?" my coach, Stan, greeted me when I entered the club inside the ski resort.

"Just miscalculated a little," I said as I stalked past him. I wasn't in the mood to discuss it. In fact, I wasn't in the mood to do anything other than get out of this tight suit, take a shower, and be left alone.

"Wait up." Stan grabbed my arm. "Are you gonna be fine for tomorrow?"

"What kind of question is that? Of course I'll be fine." I knew

I would be; it wasn't the first time my training time wasn't on par with what we'd planned, but I always won the race.

"I'm just saying," he leaned closer and lowered his voice as Isaac entered the clubhouse, "we can do another run if you're not feeling it yet."

"All I need is to get out of this suit and take a hot shower," I said, handing him my skis. I didn't mean to be an arrogant prima donna, but peace and quiet were all I needed right now. I marched to the men's locker room before Stan had a chance to say anything else. I would apologize later.

An almost-naked Isaac wearing black briefs greeted me when I entered the locker room. He was standing in front of an open locker with a towel hanging off his chiseled shoulder as he bent to tuck his speed suit into his duffel bag.

Great. Just fucking great.

I tried to focus my attention on the gray lockers past him when he looked up and our eyes met. When he straightened to a stand, his muscles glistened, and his briefs strained to contain his round ass and impressive bulge. I steeled myself when I felt his intense gaze watching me walk to the locker across from his. I released my frustration by opening my locker and slamming it into the adjacent one.

"What's your problem, man?" he asked. He banged his own locker shut, a little less brutal than I, but it forced the tension up a notch just the same.

I threw my goggles inside the compartment with a satisfying thump. "What's *my* fucking problem?" I answered, adding my favorite word for good measure when I turned to face him.

"Yeah." He stepped over the bench between us and crossed his arms. "Do you have a problem?" He put his outstretched hand on my locker trying to cage me in. He darted his tongue across his lips.

I straightened up, matching his bravado, and swatted his arm away. "Yeah, I have a problem. You!" I gritted my teeth and nodded once. "There's only one king in this realm, and I'm still breathing the last time I checked."

Isaac narrowed his eyes and smirked. "King, huh?"

Alright, I too can play your game, Big Mac. "You wanna fucking kiss me, don't you?" I asked with a breathy voice, trying to rattle him.

Isaac must have been surprised by the shift in my tone. He swallowed hard, his Adam's apple bobbing. He was staring at my lips, his chest heaving.

"Cat got your tongue, Big Mac?" I slowly licked my lips and Isaac's eyes followed the entire drag of my tongue.

His smirk returned. "Big Mac, huh? I like that. So what if I do wanna kiss you?" Isaac watched for my response, his brown eyes curious.

"You can't handle all this."

"Yeah? You might be the king on the slopes, but I'm sure I'd manage just fine down here where the commoners dwell." Isaac moved his right hand and was about to touch my face when I grabbed his arm and yanked him toward me to throw him off balance. I pushed him toward the locker, switching places with him. I placed my right hand on his chest, my palm cupping his muscular pec. His eyes widened and his smirk turned to a seductive grin.

"Not so fast, Big Mac," I said.

"You know you want to kiss me too," he whispered.

"Don't write checks you can't cash, Big Mac." I stepped back slowly and let him go, missing his touch already. I wanted to feel his lips on mine, but my self-control won. I took a deep breath to maintain my composure. *Focus.* "See you around, Isaac." With that, I left the locker room and all this shit behind. *Focus.*

Nine: Isaac

The Race is On

I blew out a shaky breath I didn't know I was holding when Foster exited the locker room. *Damn it.* What had got into me to act so boldly? That wasn't me, I rarely did anything off-script. I chalked it up to the high of my training run time. It still wasn't enough to beat Foster Donovan, but that had been one of my fastest times. The best preparation I could've asked for heading into the final race tomorrow.

I looked down at my painfully erect cock trying to free itself from my briefs, and pulled the towel off my shoulder to cover myself. I was thankful I was the only one in here. I placed my fingers where Foster had caressed my chest and denied myself the excitement I felt even after he'd left. This wasn't the place or time for shenanigans.

Foster was a distraction.

* * *

"Why can't they just lower the elevation of the starting gate out of the fog?" I asked Alex, flopping on the bed of my hotel room where we'd been since this morning. It was Sunday, and the final race had been postponed for another three hours on top of the twenty-four hours they issued yesterday. The fog had decided to camp at the launch point, making it impossible to see and dangerous for skiers. I groaned and dragged my palms across my face. It was a rhetorical question, but these sorts of things drove me crazy. "We don't even know if it's clearing up." I was kicking myself for booking this hotel twenty miles from the club.

"Oh, relax. They'd let us know if it was safe to start," Alex said, checking her cell for the umpteenth time.

"I'm so bored," Yoshi said. He had invited himself to join Alex and I in my room after our morning warm-up. He was banging his head on his skis that were propped between his legs.

"Should we head up there?" I sat up and asked Alex, who gave me a dramatic eye roll.

"And do what exactly? Wait outside in the cold?" She shook her head and grabbed the remote, powering the television on. After scrolling the channel guide, she turned to the network that was broadcasting the World Cup. A close-up image of Foster Donovan appeared on the screen as he was speaking to one of the reporters, *NBC Sports* plastered on the mic.

The man doesn't have a bad angle. I fixated on his lips and imagined how soft they were. I replayed our interaction from two days ago, only this time with an alternate ending; him pinned against the wall as I devoured his mouth, probing his velvet with mine.

"You planning on staring at him all day? Or are you ready?" Alex startled me from my sweet daydream.

"Huh?"

"The tournament director's office just called Alex to let us know the race starts in an hour. Gawking much?" Yoshi teased and pointed at the TV.

"At least close your mouth," Alex joked. "You had enough eye candy? Can I turn this off?"

I snatched the remote from her hand and switched off the television. "Buzz off. I was reading the weather conditions below." I stood up and grabbed my gear, ignoring Yoshi and Alex's cackling laughs. "Are we going or are we just gonna stand around here?" I didn't give them a chance to reply as I marched out of the room to hide the redness creeping across my face. "Can you please call and reserve one of the stationary bikes?" The club had a decent-size gym and I wanted to warm up before the finals, afraid the delay and thoughts of Foster had halted my momentum.

"I'll call them right now. Do you need one too?" Alex asked Yoshi.

"Um, yeah, if you don't mind," he said, and scratched the back of his head, giving Alex and me a sheepish grin.

"Of course not. Where's your coach?" she asked. Yoshi just shrugged and walked ahead of us out the door. She looked at me for an answer and I shook my head.

* * *

The heavy fog that enveloped the slope and caused the twenty-eight-hour delay of the championship run had dissipated when we arrived at the club; all we could see was blue sky.

Spectators lined the course a quarter of a mile past the launch platform; they waved flags from assorted countries, their colors matching their coats and snow hats while chanting the names of their favorite compatriots. The calls of "Foster! Foster! Foster!" and "Isaac! Isaac! Isaac!" cut through the bells and whistles from the crowd. There was no surprise about the love and adoration for Foster, but hearing my name warmed my heart. *Welcomed...finally.*

The overwhelming number of American and Canadian flags washed the sidelines in a sea of red, white, and blue. I could see Foster's name written on some of the handmade signs from the throngs of red-hooded fans. One of the guys held a sign that read *Marry Me, Foster* written with white glitter inside a red maple leaf. The sudden pang of jealousy surprised me.

The crowd's energy was electric—the complete opposite of the tension on the skiers' launch platform. It hummed was uneasiness, heightening the stakes of the moment. I looked around. Everyone had their game face on. To my right were the rest of the Japanese skiers with their coach, all either jogging in place or pedaling on stationary bicycles to warm up. They were sans Yoshi once again.

To my left was Foster Donovan's entourage. "You got this, champ," the man I assumed was his coach said. As if someone like Foster needed a pep talk.

Foster nodded, jumping up and down and stretching his arms. He glanced in my direction before putting his goggles on; were his squinted eyes a reaction to the brightness, or disdain at my presence? Whatever. I didn't have time to dwell on it.

Behind me, a giant television showed the ski slopes and the

swarm of fans lining the tracks and waiting at the bottom of the hill near the finish line.

The announcer started introducing the event and the racers. "It's a glorious day here in Aspen, and after twenty-eight hours of delays due to weather conditions, the men's downhill is finally underway," he boomed. "My name is Jacob Myer, welcome to the 2021 World Cup! This is the starting order for today's final run. There are some big names and some newcomers vying for medals." The screen showed each skier's name next to the country they represented and the number indicating their turn to race. The race order was randomly picked, even though some of the big-name skiers could request to be earlier or later. The screen flipped to the next group of skiers and there it was: my name was listed with the number thirty-five next to it, and below it was the Canadian flag next to Foster Donovan's name.

My heart started pounding. Foster Donovan skiing after me. I couldn't stand his attitude, but I had mad respect for his accomplishments these past few years. He had an Olympic gold medal and back-to-back World Cup wins. He was phenomenal—but this was a race, and he was my competition.

"There's a starting field of thirty-six racers who qualified to this event representing twenty national ski associations," Jacob announced. "This group includes the American qualifier Isaac McAllister, who clocked some pretty good times during the qualifying and training runs."

My ears perked up at the mention of my name; ripples of nausea churned in my stomach, threatening to turn into full-on tidal waves. I turned my back to everyone and took a deep breath.

This is yer moment. I played my dad's voice in my head to

get me through what I needed to do today.

Medal...any medal.

"You got this, Mac. Just channel the same energy and confidence from the training run," Alex said, staring straight into my eyes and giving me a fist-bump.

"Will this be lucky number three for Foster Donovan?" Jacob asked the question on everyone's mind. "If Foster Donovan Jr., of Canada, wins today, he will be the first-ever skier to win three World Cups in a row, cementing the legacy his father began. Let's ask our expert analyst for this men's downhill competition, former American skier Andrew Sorensen."

I turned back to face the screen. The camera switched to reveal Andrew Sorensen sitting at a glass desk plastered with the World Cup and NBC logos. Andrew was one of my childhood heroes, the one who ignited my love for the sport.

"What do you think of the lineup?" Jacob asked Andrew, who was wearing a black suit with an American flag pinned to his collar.

"Foster Donovan is back in action and a favorite not just for the Canadian fans, but fans around the world. However, I wouldn't count out the American skier, Isaac McAllister. Most of the viewers probably haven't heard of him until today, but I've seen him on the US circuit busting his butt to get to this level of competition."

Andrew Sorensen talking about me. I would've whooped if I wasn't so damn nervous. I tuned out the conversation, turning my focus to the slope. I wished my parents were here, sharing this moment with me. I knew they were cheering me on from a bit more than a thousand miles away, a place where most of these guys wouldn't dare give a second thought.

Any medal.

Ten: Foster

Then There Were Two

There were two men left after the thirty-fourth skier from Germany crossed the finish line: Isaac and me. The two of us were probably the most anticipated skiers of the tournament. Isaac being the American who had piqued everyone's curiosity after the training run, and me being, well, me.

I stepped aside to let Isaac prepare for his run. He'd been in the zone and hadn't glanced in my direction since the first skier hit the slope.

He staked his poles in front of him while he slid his skis back and forth, back and forth. He was breathing hard, fogging up the air around him. He gripped the pole handles and stared straight down as he waited for the countdown to begin.

"You got this, Mac," his coach said, and he responded with a nod.

The clock beeped three times.

Isaac took off and the crowd erupted. The voices roared louder than for the skiers who went before us, even louder than the applause for his American teammates.

I looked up at the giant screen to watch him ski. *Show me*

what you got.

"Here's the qualifier from the United States, Isaac McAllister. The model of consistency on the local circuit, and there's no better way to prepare for the World Cup than winning the qualifying race almost a second faster than everyone else. But his skills will be tested today against the most accomplished skiers in the world. It's hard to imagine that Isaac, the twenty-five-year-old American, has never been on this stage."

I wondered the same thing. How could someone as good as Isaac sneak under my radar? Where had he been these past few years? If his finish time from the training run was an indication of his talent, he could easily beat some of the more veteran guys out there.

After my encounter with Isaac two days ago, I'd spent an exorbitant amount of time stalking his social media accounts. I discovered that, like me, he was out and proud. But aside from being gay, there was nothing about his personal life, where he lived, or his background. Nothing. It must be nice to live incognito like that. I wouldn't mind it myself.

Just like during practice, Isaac raised his game when he risked speeding up as he approached the hairpin turn. It paid off. He leaned forward, using his aerodynamics in tandem with gravity pulling him downhill. He swiftly maneuvered a couple more twists and leaps, and the raucous crowd went apeshit with every slide and glide.

I wasn't going to admit it to anyone, but for the first time in a long while, I was a little anxious. Not because I feared losing. No, champions didn't think like that. I was anxious because I finally had legitimate competition, and this race just got interesting.

"Whoa! That was a good tactical play from Isaac," the

commentator continued after Isaac tucked himself up to make the next bend. He leaned to his side, almost to the ground, when he came out of the corner. The powdered snow from the drags of his skis proved his speed.

Bells rang and whistles blew when Isaac made it to the halfway mark. The green light next to his name on the board signaled he was currently in the lead.

"Boy oh boy, did he nail that or what?!" Stan exclaimed.

The announcers on screen seemed to agree that the smooth landing after being in the air for almost two seconds shaved critical split-seconds from Isaac's time.

"That leap!" the host said.

"Who did that remind you of?" Andrew Sorensen asked.

Me, I thought, beating them to the answer.

"That was from Foster Donovan Jr.'s playbook," the host answered. "Watch out world, Isaac is making the absolute best of his moment. He's killing it, and he knows it. Look at that concentration." A close-up frame of Isaac momentarily appeared on the screen before zooming out and giving us a bird's-eye view of him speeding to the finish line. "Is he gonna do it? Can he continue this almost-perfect race to take the lead? He's almost there."

Isaac cornered the final turn and sped up, crossing the finish line with his hand in the air. The crowd roared, banners and American flags waving madly.

Way to make a splash, Big Mac. Too bad I have to beat you.

Isaac looked up to the screen flashing his final time. "Yes! Yes! Yes!" he shouted as the camera zoomed in on him. He laid back on the snow-covered slope. "I did it!" He stood up and took his goggles off. "That's for you, Ma and Pop," he said to the camera, then proceeded skiing in front of the crowd, handing out high-fives. He hadn't won yet, but with one person left to race, he was guaranteed second place.

"I got this," I assured my team, trying to ease the worry on their faces when I climbed on the platform, waiting for my turn. I tuned out everyone around me and directed my attention to the slope. Goggles, mental blinders on. *Win or bust.*

I came out of the gates with bullet-like speed, building momentum for the first jump. Because the starting point for this event was lower than at most of the other clubs, we had to be creative in finding ways to generate free-fall speed that normally would've been assisted by gravity. I took a giant leap, which suspended me in the air, a swarm of red-and-white flags waving in my periphery. I landed with precision and tucked into a ball, streamlining my body to reduce resistance.

I skied a perfect line through the track. Metal bells rang, alerting me that I was halfway through the race, when I leaned into a bend. I pushed myself harder, making sure I had enough buffer heading into the final turn.

Across the finish line, I knew I'd won before I even looked up to check. I could always tell where in the standings I landed by how I skied, and the run I just had warranted nothing other than first place.

The spectators' cheers became a living entity that lifted my spirits. I waved to the crowd and their roar of excitement intensified, building in momentum like an avalanche. I pumped my hands in the air, urging them to keep cheering.

"Foster! Foster! Foster!"

My team rushed toward me, lifting me up on their shoulders, their other fists raised in victory.

When my team set me down, I looked to my right, where

Isaac and the skier from Norway, who came in third place, were waiting. The disappointment I was sure I'd see on Isaac's face for finishing less than a twentieth of a second behind me was nowhere to be found. Instead, he radiated pure elation.

His coach and Yoshi, who finished fifth, joined him. They brought their hands up in the air before jumping and chanting, "Mac! Mac! Mac!" It was then I wondered if they knew they'd finished second.

Yoshi pointed at the scoreboard with the standings and they all looked up, fist-bumping afterward.

It was touching to see someone celebrate a runner-up finish, but the genuine smile on Isaac's face, his taking pictures of the standings, warmed my heart. The annoyance I felt for him was replaced by respect. His exhilaration seemed ten times greater than my own—and I won the damn thing. I even set another record for winning the event three years in a row. *What's up with that?*

Isaac looked in my direction and skied toward me while waving to the crowd and the cameras. "Congratulations, Foster. Great race." He extended his hand and I took it.

"Thanks. You were impressive." I'd said those three words before, but this was the first time I'd meant them. I was impressed not only by his speed and skills, but his attitude toward defeat.

"There's always next time," he said, before veering to the crowd calling his name.

Eleven: Isaac

Suit and Tie

The idea of attending a party wearing a tuxedo after a grueling competition didn't sound appealing. At that moment, all I wanted was to go back to my hotel room and fall into a well-deserved nap before flying to Lake Tahoe for the next tournament. But as tempted as I was to cancel my RSVP, a part of me wanted to be there.

I would be lying if I said I wasn't disappointed about not winning the gold medal, but coming in second behind Foster was nothing to sneeze at. I was pleased with the week's accomplishments, and it couldn't have come at a better time, fresh from receiving association assistance and having the coolest coach in Alex. I didn't want to disappoint them and have them reconsider their offer.

I got out of the club's shower and headed to my locker while drying my hair with a towel. I grabbed my cell phone and ignored all the texts and call notifications on the screen, scrolling instead through the recent call history and pressing Alex's name. "Should we fly to Lake Tahoe tomorrow so we have more time to train for the next race?" I asked. "We can get used to the conditions before the event." Now that I had the association's financial backing, I could finally focus more on training. I still couldn't believe this was my life now.

"Mac, just breathe, will you?" she said, chuckling. "The Tahoe race isn't for another week."

"So? I just don't want to lose our momentum."

"You just completed a race hours ago. You won silver and had the best finish time of your career so far. Enjoy the moment. Don't you have any hobbies?"

"What made you think I wasn't enjoying the moment? All I'm saying is we need a new plan. And what do my hobbies have to do with any of this?" Camping was my only pastime, and I couldn't do that in the middle of the season. "We can talk about it at the Winners' Circle Gala."

She paused. "About that...I'm not planning on attending tonight."

"Wait, what? Why not?"

"Well..." she trailed off

"This is a big deal. We just medaled on our first race together. Whatever happened to enjoying the moment?" I felt a particular thrill using her own words against her.

"I know, but crowds aren't really my thing." She blew out a breath and the change in her tone was different from the confident, no-bullshit attitude I'd come to know these past few days. "Long story, but I'll tell you over a beer sometime."

I was a little disappointed, as she and Yoshi would be the only people I knew there. This wasn't the first time I'd placed in a race, but this was by far the biggest event I'd medaled in since joining the circuit seven years ago. I'd been accustomed to racing in club events, but definitely not the same prestige as the World Cup. "OK, let me know if you change your mind."

"I won't, but thank you, Mac. Try to have some fun, OK?"

Why did everyone keep saying that? What made them think I wasn't having fun? "I will. I'll call you after to talk about Tahoe."

I ended the call and typed *tuxedo shops in Aspen* into Google. I was hoping for a store other than Prada, Louis Vuitton, and Armani, but I was pressed for time and I had exactly four hours before the formal dinner sponsored by the World Cup and local chamber of commerce. It was a gala that would host the top ten finishers and their coaches. I ignored the brewing excitement of seeing Foster again, since thoughts of him always led to me jacking off, and I was in a public locker room.

I drove my rental to downtown Aspen and parked on one of the streets near the shops listed on my phone. I'd been in training and competition mode and hadn't had a chance to experience the town. It was different from most of the places I'd visited. This place was posh. The snow-covered cobblestone streets were lined with bare birch trees, light layers of snow dusted on their branches. Most of the three-story buildings were red brick with ornate façades decorated with arches etched with the year the building was erected, some dating as early as 1810.

I started my hunt for a tux at Louis Vuitton. To say I was underdressed in my jeans and tan Sherpa coat was the understatement of the year. The doorman wearing white gloves should've been my first clue, but it was too late to turn around now.

Several patrons who were dressed to the nines in fur coats glanced in my direction, and the only man who wasn't helping someone greeted me. "Welcome to Louis Vuitton. Would you like a glass of wine?"

"Oh, you sell wine?" I asked, looking around for the tuxedo rack. Since when did clothing shops start selling wine?

I received a couple of quick head-to-toe glances. I felt suddenly, inexplicably hot.

"No, sir. It's complimentary for your shopping experience," the salesperson said. A warm smile crossed his face as if to tell me, *It's OK.*

"My mistake, sorry."

"No worries. My name is Brandt, and it'll be my pleasure to assist you." He offered his hand, and I accepted it before introducing myself.

"I'm Isaac, and I'm here to check out your tuxedos." I surveyed the shop once again, but all they had on display was bags and a very limited clothing assortment. "But I don't think you have any."

"We keep them in the back. Do you know your size?"

"I wear large."

"Tuxedos and suit sizes are numbered. Usually, they range from size 26, the smallest, up to the 40s," he explained, giving me a sympathetic look. I must've looked like a fool, but if I did, Brandt's expression didn't show it, he was patient. He stood back to look at me. "You know what, you look like you're about 36 to 38. Let me check what we have. Make yourself comfortable, Isaac." He motioned to the leather chair.

I didn't want to sit down. I didn't want to stay.

Brandt came back with a rolling rack containing four different garment bags. He opened them one by one, exposing a classic black tuxedo, followed by a velvet navy blue, then a velvet maroon with a black collar, and finally another black in a slightly shinier fabric.

I stood up and he handed me the classic black to try. I

peeked at the price tag. My mouth dropped open and my eyes grew wide. "Twelve thousand dollars?" I gasped, earning me another look from the other shoppers. "Is this really twelve grand?" How could a piece of clothing cost this much? That was a good chunk of my prize money, there was no way I could spend twelve thousand of the forty thousand dollars I'd won. Especially since I didn't even have the money yet.

He gave me a compassionate look before nodding.

"Are they all that much?"

Another nod. He pulled the suit jacket from the hanger and walked toward me, bringing it closer to my body.

I staggered back, not wanting it to touch me. "I don't think I can afford—"

"Shh," he whispered. "Listen, Isaac, I get it. I know I shouldn't tell you this, but all of the stores here are just as expensive. So if you need to find a more affordable tuxedo, one that won't cost you an arm and a leg, you're going to have to rent it…and not from here. Try Harry's Tux thirty miles away. They have a great selection."

"Thanks, Brandt. I appreciate your help." I peeked at my watch. If I wanted to make it to the gala on time, I needed to hurry. I clapped his shoulder before heading out of the store, ignoring the chuckles I got from the other salesperson and the snobby customers.

* * *

The scene at the Aspen Museum of Art, the venue for this year's Winners' Circle Gala, could rival any Hollywood awards show. Heat lamps lined the red carpet, greeting limousines and town cars that led to the main entrance of the all-glass building encapsulated by woven wooden panels. Spotlights beamed on large purple silk banners on both sides of the building featuring the words *Slopes and Contemporary Art, Winners' Circle.*

Everyone was dressed impeccably. Most of the men wore black tuxedos with matching bow ties, while the ladies donned evening gowns that would make any movie star envious.

Thankful that Harry's Tux had what I needed, I looked down and examined my own black tuxedo and rearranged my bow tie before crossing the street. My hands started to shake, and I wasn't sure if it was from the cold or the brewing ball of anxiety inside me. I tucked them in my pockets, out of everyone's sight, but that move had an unexpected knock-on effect.

"Nice pose, Isaac! Look over here," a photographer called.

Before I could even register which photographer had spoken, another voice rang out. "Isaac, over here."

A woman in a black cocktail dress with a pin that read *STAFF* ushered me onto the main red carpet. "We'll have you pose for five minutes, then we'll move you to the other side," she instructed.

Flash! I covered my eyes as a bright light from one of the cameras took me by surprise. I grimaced at the piercing pain. I lowered my hand as my eyes adjusted, and when they did, there was Foster, headed in my direction.

He was a vision in black. His tuxedo looked custom, a perfect fit. His blond hair was combed up. "Hi," he said when he reached me, before turning to face the swarm of cameras and giving them a charming smile. *What a natural.* "Put your arm around me. They'll *love* that," he whispered in my ear. His warm breath made my skin prickle.

"What?" I asked.

"Just for show. The media eats that shit up, trust me."

I wrapped my arm around him, trusting his guidance since he had more experience than I did. And, well, I got to touch him again.

The number of cameras pointed at us tripled, photographers screaming, "Over here!"

Foster pointed out where to look next, and after five minutes of turning and smiling, I'd had enough. "How much longer?" I asked.

"That's it. You did well. Let's wave goodbye." Foster and I waved to the press and fans, and made our way inside the museum.

The gallery was cleared of art and the tables were covered with crisp white linens. A massive chandelier was the center-piece of the room.

"The winners sit over here," a man wearing a *STAFF* pin said, leading us to the middle table. Our names were marked on placards: Foster was to be seated in the center, with me to his left, and the bronze medalist to his right.

"Thank you," Foster said.

"Shit," I murmured as we took our seats. In front of each person was a large plate, with a smaller plate and bowl stacked on top. There were nine pieces of sparkling silverware; three on each side of the plate and two above it. A small saucer placed to the upper left had a small spatula-style knife on top, while three different crystal glasses sat to the upper right. *I am so screwed.* I patted my pocket for my cell phone before I realized I'd left it in the car.

I blew out a breath and caught Foster looking at me out of

the corner of his eyes.

Twelve: Foster

Let's Compromise

Isaac's curse was barely audible, but I'd been hyper-aware of his presence since he wrapped his arm around me, so I heard it, along with his shaky breath.

I glanced in his direction, but he didn't look back. Instead, he stared at the table setting, his lips curled into a frown. *That's odd.*

The makeshift ballroom was quickly becoming a sea of black, white and glitter. When the last guest had been seated, the event's head organizer took the mic and addressed the party. "Good evening, everyone, and welcome to this year's Winners' Circle!" It was the usual boring, sterile speech about how everyone did an amazing job organizing the tournament, and other self-serving bullshit like that. I tuned it out and directed my attention again to Isaac, who was still staring wide-eyed at the table.

The Norwegian skier sitting on my right suddenly stood up, jolting my focus back to the speaker. He accepted his bronze medal and returned to his seat. The speaker continued. "Now, let's welcome this year's silver medalist, who had a very impressive World Cup debut—Isaac McAllister."

That was about the only statement I could agree with. Isaac's route to the final race had been remarkable. I joined the applause and waited for Isaac to stand up and take his moment, but he didn't move a muscle. After a couple of seconds, I elbowed him. Finally, he looked at me. I motioned for him to stand up.

The ovation increased when he stood and leaned forward to receive his medal. He placed his right hand over the silver and waved to the guests. "Thank you," he said, over and over.

Finally. I didn't know what was up with him, but I was glad he had his wits about him and could bask in his achievement. I also didn't know why I cared.

"And finally, this year's gold medalist and three-time World Champion, Foster Donovan Jr."

I straightened my suit jacket and waved as the room erupted in applause. I turned slowly, acknowledging everyone in the room, before I leaned over and accepted my gold medal. I motioned for Isaac and the Norwegian skier to stand as well. I grabbed both of their hands, holding Isaac's tighter than necessary, and raised them over our heads. Claps, whistles, howls, and camera flashes—the reaction I'd hoped to get.

We took our seats as the commotion died down and the speaker concluded. On cue, waiters and waitresses in crisp white shirts and tailored black pants started serving the first of a six-course meal.

As the first dish was placed in front of us, Isaac cleared his throat and started playing with his bow tie, loosening its hold on his throat. It was then I realized he didn't know what to do with all the plates and silverware. I brought my left hand under the table and gave his thigh a gentle squeeze.

Isaac jolted, snapping his head in my direction. Poor guy

was all out of sorts, making me feel a little protective of him; something I'd only felt with Sophia. Slowly, I lifted my right hand to the soup spoon.

Isaac's eyes followed the movement of my hand. His shoulders relaxed when it dawned on him what I was trying to do. His lips mouthed the words *thank you*.

I winked as he turned his attention to the bowl of bisque in front of him.

As the night progressed, Isaac glanced at me with every new course. He followed my every move, even copying the way I used the white table napkin to wipe my lips. He blew a sigh of relief after the last course of the evening was served.

I should've let him figure out the plate setting for himself and given him a taste of his own medicine after the embarrassment he caused me two days ago, but his obvious distress in the moments after we were seated made me want to shield him from the same feeling. Which in itself was ridiculous, considering we weren't even friends.

"Um, Foster?" Isaac said.

I heard my name all the time, but it sounded better coming from him. "Yeah?" I answered, leaning back and placing my arm on the back of his chair.

"Thanks for all that," he said with a slight drawl. Weird, I hadn't heard an accent on him before now. "I've never seen such a plethora of plates and silverware."

"Don't worry about it. It can get confusing sometimes." I waved him off, and our eyes met. Sitting this close to Isaac allowed me to appreciate his handsome face. Even with a sleek hairstyle, his features were still rugged, with his scruffy square chin and prominent nose.

He was staring at me, and I could see so many emotions

warring in his brown eyes. Uneasiness, weariness, curiosity, interest, embarrassment, all on full display.

I leaned forward on the table, resting my chin on my knuckles, never breaking eye contact. I needed to figure out what was on his mind. I swallowed hard. Should I ask him to dance? My ego was still a little bruised from his rejection, but what I wouldn't give to hold him in my arms. Fuck it, I didn't have to see him tomorrow, so what the hell, right? "Do you wanna dance?"

He glanced at the middle of the room where couples were now dancing to the rhythm of the live band.

I held my breath, waiting for his answer.

"I'd love to," he said and stood up, offering his hand. The roughness of his palm woke my every dormant desire.

Isaac led me to the dance floor, where he placed his arms around my waist, pulling me in. He wasn't wearing any cologne, but his scent was intoxicating.

I smirked and wrapped my arms around his waist, pulling us so close that our bodies brushed together.

He raised his right eyebrow, asking the silent question, *who's leading here?* I'd been dominant in all of my past relationships and I wasn't about to change now.

His lips curled into a seductive, lopsided smile. "I think we have a little problem," he said with his low growl. He darted his tongue to moisten his lips, something I noticed he did often.

"Oh yeah, what is that?" I challenged, urging him to say what I just realized.

"Oh, come on…" he trailed off, tightening his hold on me, attempting to establish dominance. His eyes pierced a hole in my self-control.

"Come on what?" I tightened my hold on him, mimicking his every move. I felt something hard and, since we were both in tuxedos, it certainly wasn't a belt buckle. "What is the problem, Mac?"

He shook his head and peeled his body away. He lifted his left hand, palm up, and I took it in my right hand; our other hands stayed on each other's waist. "Let's compromise."

Our bodies swayed to the music, and we got lost in each other's eyes, free of competition, just being in the moment. I'd compromise...for now.

Thirteen: Isaac

You Love Yourself Some You

I'd completely lost my mind, or maybe it was the two glasses of wine I'd consumed on an empty stomach during the longest dinner of my life. That had to be the reason I was in the middle of the dance floor, going toe-to-toe with Foster Donovan. Arrogance was something that usually bothered me, but with him, I found it sexy as hell. We'd finally settled on a position we could agree on. It was clear he was used to being the leading man, but so was I. We were undeniably locked in a battle for control—and here I was thinking the tussle had ended on the slopes.

A subtle shift in Foster's hand and there it was, at the top of my ass. "Smooth," I said.

He shrugged as if to say, *I don't know what you're talking about.*

I opened my mouth to speak, but my stomach decided to kill the mood with a grumble.

Foster's eyes widened and he chuckled. "Are you still hungry?"

I looked around before I whispered in his ear, "Hungrier than before we started eating."

"That was a six-course meal!"

"I know, but each course was smaller than the last. Also, why did they serve ice cream in the middle of the meal?"

"Isaac, that was sorbet, and it was supposed to cleanse your palate."

"Cleanse my what?"

"Your palate, for the main dish."

"The portion of the food was so tiny, it hardly left an impression on my tongue, let alone my palate."

"Are you for real?" he asked, his gaze inquisitive.

"Yup. That's OK, I'll wait till we're done here and I'll stop by the food truck a few blocks from the slopes."

"Wait. A food truck in Aspen?" he asked, his forehead creased.

"Yes, they serve hot dogs," I deadpanned.

"Oh, shut up. I've been coming here for years and never once have I seen any food truck that sells hot dogs." He searched my face to see if I was joking. "What's the name of this food truck?"

"Don't laugh," I warned.

Foster responded with an exaggerated nod.

"It's called Oh My God It's a Wiener."

Foster's boisterous laugh echoed through the hall and it seemed like every person looked at us. "You're fucking with me, right?"

"I'm not making that up. I'm telling you it's a real place. Me, Yoshi, and my coach, Alex, were just there last night."

"Take me there then." His voice was playful but daring.

"Um, now?" I lifted his wrist and glanced at his watch.

"Unless you're lying."

"We can't leave now, the gala isn't over yet." With our joined hands I motioned around the party.

"I'd rather see this Oh My God It's a Wiener truck than stay in this snooze-fest. Unless, of course, it doesn't exist."

"Let's go then." I pulled him off the dance floor and ignored the questioning looks from guests and staff.

"See you all," Foster yelled. "Nice party." He tipped an imaginary hat to one of the staff members on our way out.

* * *

"Holy shit, you're right. I can't believe I've never heard about this place!" Foster took his cell phone from his tux jacket. "I need to take a picture of this." He snapped pictures of the food truck from different angles. "We need a selfie."

"What? No!" I protested.

"Oh, come on. Don't act like you're too cool for a selfie." He grabbed my arm, pulling my body toward him without any resistance. Foster stood behind me and extended his right arm to frame our faces and the Oh My God It's a Wiener sign above us. "Smile, Mac," he ordered, snapping a couple of images before putting his cell back in his jacket. "What should we order?"

A group of guys walked past us and recognized Foster. "Oh shit! Hey, bros, it's Foster Donovan!" he yelled, getting his friends' attention and waving them closer.

"Where, dude?" one of them asked, and his face lit up when he saw Foster. They started taking pictures and videos of us as they approached.

"Oh shit," I murmured. This wasn't what I had in mind

when I brought Foster here. I was hoping for peace and quiet, forgetting that he was Foster Donovan Jr., king of the slopes. "I'm sorry about—"

"It's OK, I got this," Foster said. He squeezed my shoulder and walked toward the guys, meeting them halfway. "Alright, guys. I'm good for a couple of pictures then we're going to enjoy our evening. What do you say?" he asked them.

"Yeah, man," one said.

"Congratulations," the other guy said.

After taking a few pictures, Foster shook their hands. "Tag me in your posts," he said, before heading back to me. "That's how you handle that."

"Looks like you know what you're doing." I was impressed by his quick thinking.

"I've had some practice. Now, what kind of *wiener* should I get?"

I groaned inwardly by his suggestive question. "Let's get you a foot-long," I said, then cursed myself the moment it left my lips. "Not a word," I warned, pointing my finger at him.

Foster's lips pressed into a line as he tried not to laugh, his eyes dancing with delight.

I headed to the counter and placed our order to hide my grin. It couldn't have been the wine. I'd lost my mind. That was the only explanation.

"Let's walk while we eat our *wieners*," Foster proposed, waving his foot-long at me before taking a bite, putting more than a little emphasis on the *wiener*.

"You need to stop calling it that. Don't you have these in Canada?"

"I have no idea," he said around a mouthful.

"Of course you don't. A hot dog food truck isn't fancy

84

enough to get your attention."

His eyes narrowed before he swallowed. "I'm here with you, aren't I?"

"True, sorry."

"No big deal. You're not the first person to assume how I live my life and, sadly, you won't be the last." His demeanor shifted, he was now a little subdued, his swagger gone.

Way to go, Isaac. Way to ruin a perfect evening. "I didn't mean to make you upset. I'm sorry if—"

"Nah, don't worry about it." He took another bite.

A revving engine captured my attention, and I jerked Foster closer to me as a car cornered the street and sped toward us. My abrupt action caused our hot dogs to fall to the snow-covered ground.

Foster bent to grab one of the defiled dogs and threw it at the speeding car. "Asshole!" he yelled.

It was clear Foster was all worked up, and I badly wanted to defuse the tension. I looked to the ground and said, "That was my wiener."

He glanced back at me, mischief in his eyes. "Did I grab the wrong wiener?" We both laughed. *Thank goodness for that.*

"Are you OK?" I asked, and handed him a napkin to wipe his hands. "That car almost got us."

"I'm fine. That car would've been able to stop on a dime. That's an Aston Martin. I have one of those."

I nodded. Of course he did. We continued our walk and conversation. More like, Foster talked and I listened. So far, I knew he had an Aston Martin, a Tahoe SUV, a place in Vancouver, BC, and had traveled to all the continents, even Antarctica.

"You do love you some you, don't you?" I joked after he told me the story about his most recent endorsement deal with The North Face.

"I've been talking about myself non-stop, haven't I?"

"Just a little. I don't mind it." And that was the truth. Learning about Foster was surprisingly entertaining.

"OK, enough about me. My hotel is coming up and there's a nice bar. Do you have time?" he asked.

I paused. I did need to get back to my hotel and call Alex. She was probably wondering why I hadn't called. I wanted to run my schedule for the rest of the season by her to make sure she had all the dates for my upcoming races. This was an Olympic year and I needed to be in peak condition come February.

"It's OK if you need to go." Foster snapped me out of my thoughts.

"Oh, I'm sorry. I was just thinking about the season, but I have plenty of time."

Foster's face brightened, and he gestured for me to keep walking.

* * *

"What's next on your schedule?" I asked Foster once we were seated in the bar. A man was playing a baby grand piano while a woman in a sequined red gown sang. The jazz version of Phil Collins' 'Against All Odds' had the patrons enthralled. A couple noticed our arrival and raised their glasses our way, and Foster acknowledged them with a nod.

"A break before the World Championships," he answered.

"How about you?"

"A smaller race in Lake Tahoe next week."

"Oh yeah? I have a place in Tahoe."

I shook my head and chuckled.

"I'm sorry, bad habit," he said.

"That's OK." I raised my hand to get the attention of a server.

"No, it isn't. You're absolutely right. I always find a way to make the conversation about me."

"Foster, it's OK. You just said you had a place in Lake Tahoe."

"Yes, but you would have asked me where in Tahoe it's located, and how often I go there since I live in Canada."

"Well, you would have been disappointed since I hadn't planned on asking any of that. Do you know what you want to drink?" I asked when the server made his way to our table.

"I'll have a dirty martini with three olives. And put it on my room tab, please."

"Of course, Mr. Donovan," the waiter replied.

"No way, drinks on me," I protested.

Foster raised his hand in surrender.

"What do you have on tap?" I asked.

"We have an IPA from one of the microbreweries in town," the waiter answered.

"Great, I'll have that, and *Mr. Donovan* will have his martini."

The waiter left and we listened to end of the song. A few minutes passed and neither Foster nor I said a word. "So... what should we talk about?" he asked, tapping his fingers on the table.

"Not about your place in Lake Tahoe," I joked.

"Fuck that. I'm telling you about my place in Lake Tahoe."

We burst into fits of laughter, earning us glares from the docile crowd.

Our server returned with our drinks on a tray. As he leaned over to place napkins in front of each of us, my beer slid off the tray and landed directly in my lap.

I jumped when the cold liquid splashed across my tux. Beer dripped between my legs onto my seat.

"Oh no! I apologize," the waiter said, handing me napkins and picking up the empty glass.

I dabbed at the big wet circle around my crotch with a napkin. "Don't worry about it, it was an accident."

The waiter scurried away and quickly returned with a towel to wipe the spilled beer from the chair. "I'll pay for your dry-cleaning bill," he offered, his face glowing bright red.

I put the soaked napkins on the tray. "Really, that's kind of you to offer, but unnecessary." He returned to the bar.

"You handled that way differently than I would have," Foster said when our waiter was gone. "Wanna freshen up in my room? You can use the hairdryer to dry your pants."

"Oh, I don't know if that's a good idea."

"Why not? I know I'm hot, but don't you have any self-control?" he teased. "I know *I* can behave myself." He winked and smiled in the most seductive way; it should be illegal. Foster stood and glanced down, meeting my eyes. "So, what's it gonna be?"

I pulled some cash out of my pocket and placed it on the table before standing up. "Lead the way."

Fourteen: Foster

Battle for the Top

"I assure you, I can behave myself," I said. Isaac followed me into my suite and I closed the door. "I know you think you're all that, Mac, but you aren't the first cute guy I've been around." I removed my jacket and threw it across one of the sofas in the room. He remained by the door.

"So you think I'm handsome," Isaac said. His eyes scanned the room, stopping at the large window with the incredible view of a sparkling Aspen lit up for the holiday season. "Looking at this view, maybe I don't care if you behave or not. I bet the view is spectacular in the morning."

"Let me correct you on one thing. I said *cute*, not handsome. As you may have read, I like my guys muscular and tough. Seeing you in that tux checks all the boxes."

"Funny thing, Foster. I also like my guys a little cute. It helps me focus on what I like to do with them." He removed his jacket but was struggling with the cufflinks on his white dress shirt. He held his arms out. "Help a guy out?"

I crossed the ten feet or so that separated us. The front of his tux pants was damp from the beer. "Help you out, huh? I'd be happy to help you out of those wet pants." I grabbed his wrist and carefully removed the first cufflink. His eyes met mine; I felt a tingle in my crotch. There was no doubt, this guy was smoking hot. I dropped his wrist and reached for the other one. "You always let men undress you?"

"Not usually. I'm normally the one undressing them." He watched as I removed the other cufflink and held the pair in my open hand for him to take. He continued, "I love unwrapping presents and seeing what's inside." He tugged on his already loosened bow tie. "You gonna get this too?" His sexy eyes locked with mine.

"So it looks like I'm doing the unwrapping tonight," I said. I lifted my hand to his neck, my fingers grazing his chin. The moment we touched, a shock wave of lust ripped through my body and headed right for my cock. "I like when my men let me take charge like this."

Isaac grabbed my wrist near his neck and held it tight. "So do I." He pulled me a few inches closer. I was close enough to see his nostrils flare and smell wine on his breath. "And just so you know, I only let my men undress me after I've given them permission."

"Is that what's happening here, Mac? You're giving me permission?" He gripped my wrist more aggressively. "If I wasn't so turned on, I'd tell you that you were hurting me." I peered into his eyes. "You like it rough, don't you?" I moved my hip into his and pushed him back against the door.

"I told you this wasn't a good idea. I was just going to freshen up and here we are already wrestling for control." He paused for a moment, reading my expression. He pushed his hip roughly back into me. "And...that's what's happening here, *Foster*." He said my name like he didn't give a shit, but I knew where this was headed. He just needed to know it would be me in control.

We stood motionless, our faces inches apart. Our eyes darted back and forth like two hungry wolves checking to see who'd bite first. Every second felt like an eternity. Was he going to kiss me? Was he waiting for me to make the first move? "What are you waiting for, tough guy?" I whispered. "An invitation?" He had one of my wrists still in his grip, so I grabbed him and pulled him against me.

"Are you giving up control?" he asked, glancing behind me and into the room. "You might be the boss of this dream life, but with me, you'll let me lead the way?"

"Maybe just once. Sure, I could agree to that. Go ahead, *Big Mac*. Make your move," I growled.

He leaned an inch forward and pressed his lips hard against mine. His lips were soft, but he was strong, and we held each other's wrists as we fought for an edge. He forced his tongue into my mouth, so I took a nibble and pressed back harder. His crotch came forward and he rolled his hips, grinding a solid bulge against my own cock. I let go of his wrist and brought my hand to the back of his neck and pressed forward, smashing my lips harder. Our teeth gnashed as we kept the passionate kiss alive.

Isaac pulled back. "Is this what gets you off? There's more just like it if you'd care to find out," he said. I reached up and grabbed his partially opened dress shirt with both of my hands and ripped it open. Buttons flew off, revealing a muscular chest. He'd obviously shaved it. I noticed the dark stubble between his pecs that led down his ripped abs and disappeared into his slacks. The corner of his mouth rose in a slight smile. "You're an aggressive sort, aren't you? Don't stop with the shirt on my account," he said, daring me to move things along.

"You'd like that, wouldn't you? And if I do, what comes next?"

"Probably something like this," he said calmly, reaching for my necktie. He removed it and began to slowly unbutton my shirt, one at a time. I stared at him as he concentrated on every button, making a dramatic production of it all. When he got to the bottom button that was tucked into my slacks, he undid the clasp and slid his hand against my skin on his way to release the final button. His other hand caressed my jaw before he pulled me in for a deep kiss. My cock jumped as his hand brushed over my bulging head when he pulled out my tucked shirt. I was melting in his touch. I had never been this turned on by a man in my life. He was taking control of me.

I pulled back from the kiss. "Not so fast, Mac. Not that I'm complaining, but I don't usually let someone else lead the way. And, as you know so well, I'm never out of the lead."

"That's on the slopes. Now that I'm skiing with the big boys, you best get accustomed to something different." He pulled my dress shirt off and tossed it behind me. We were bare-chested and taking our sweet time examining each other. "So this is what the famous Foster Donovan looks like without his shirt in person." He smiled and winked, letting me know he was enjoying the view.

"You're only getting half of the view, rookie. If you like this, you're gonna love the bottom half." I stood motionless, waiting for him to decide his next move. "Shall I take over now? Maybe you've never swam in the deep end?"

He chuckled. "Look at you, so full of analogies. I heard that Foster Donovan didn't have a deep side. Or has no one ever pushed your buttons properly?" He moved his hand to my zipper, never taking his eyes off mine. His eyes sparkled as his mouth parted slightly, and his tongue swiped gently across his upper lip.

My eyes remained on his, daring him to take us to the next level. I placed my outstretched hand to the door behind him and leaned in. My bicep was beside his face, and he turned toward it and nibbled on my skin. "You are a tease, Mac. You better hope I don't get bored."

His grin widened and he leaned back, sliding down the door and squatting in front of me. He tilted his head up to me and licked his lips. "Let me know if this bores you." He unzipped my slacks and fished my hard cock out of my boxers. He placed his mouth on the tip and licked lightly. I instinctively grabbed his head and tried to pull him toward my cock. I needed to bury myself in his mouth. "Easy, champ. There's no rush. Unless, of course, you're a minute man," he teased.

I stepped out of my slacks but left my boxers on since I was protruding out of the fly. "Open up and I'll show you whether that's true." I held his head firmly in my hands. "Come on, pretty boy, take it all in, if you can."

He opened wide and let me feed him my cock. I stared down at his prowess and marveled as I watched my full nine inches slide down his throat. Apparently, world-class skiing wasn't his only skill set.

"Jesus! That feels amazing," I moaned, holding his head and pumping my hips slowly.

He sucked my cock eagerly; my head fell back and I groaned softly. This, him, it felt so good. I definitely wasn't a minute man, but fuck, if I didn't feel like I could blow my load any second. I pushed his head away from me before I lost my ability to stop my orgasm. "My turn." I helped him back to his feet and grabbed his hand, leading him across the suite to the bedroom.

"You sure you wanna go there, Donovan?" he asked, following me.

"Absolutely. After witnessing your talents, it's my turn. I'm competitive that way—you of all people should know that."

"Are you sure you want to unleash me once we get in there? I can't promise I'll go easy on you."

"I'll take my chances." Isaac stood at the end of the bed facing me, and I shoved him onto the soft comforter. "Shut up and take notes, Mac." I pulled his black formal shoes off without untying them. After removing his socks, I tugged on the bottom of each pant leg and yanked them off in one swift move. He wore tight-fitting black briefs that were stretched to the limit trying to contain his erection. After seeing him near-naked in the locker room the other day, I already knew he was packing. I was delighted that he legitimately did fill it out in all the right places.

He glanced at his bulging briefs and then looked back at me. "It seems we both come with big equipment." I grinned and admired his body. It was fantastic. He was ripped, like most downhill skiers are, and he had the muscular thighs to prove it. His thighs were smooth, with a scattering of brown hair growing below his knees. He had one knee bent and a leg askew, and my eyes trailed up his inner thigh to where his ball sack was stretching his briefs.

"Nice," I said, crawling up the bed to the prize. "Lift your ass up." My hands tugged on the hem of his briefs. He did as I commanded, and I pulled them down his legs and tossed them over the side of the bed. Thankfully, the beer had not gotten past the tux pants. Not that I would have cared. I was hungry for him, and a little bit of beer wasn't going to deter me. I buried my face in his crotch and licked his balls nice and slow, making my way leisurely up his shaft. His legs stiffened at my firm touch. As soon as I got to his cock, he grabbed my head and tried to maneuver me to it. "Relax. I'm in charge now." I expected a mouthy response from him, but I guess when my mouth came around his meat, he couldn't think of anything beyond the pleasure.

"Fuuuck, Foster. That feels insane." He was rigid under me as I took him fully into my throat. Isaac was hung, and he tasted delicious. From the looks of his tool, we were equally matched in the dick department. "That's it, suck that cock." He was talking some smack now, and it only motivated me to try harder. "Careful, I could fucking shoot if you don't slow it down." Apparently, we had the same effect on each other. Maybe he had been checking me out these past few days. After the locker room teasing, I was hot as hell for him. I think he felt the same. "Come up here." He tugged on my shoulders, so I slid up his stomach with my tongue and stopped at a nipple, nibbling hard.

"Here?" I asked.

"Not exactly." He flipped me over and was on top of me in a flash. He had my arms pinned to my side with his knees; he started kissing my neck and grinding his cock into mine. "Let's get these off you." He put my erection back through the fly of my boxers and pulled them off. "You *are* a big boy, Foster. I've heard the rumors, and I'm happy to see the reports are correct." I took the break in the action to reassert myself over him; I bucked him off and rolled on top of him.

"Two can play your game, Mac," I growled, holding his hands tight and placing all my weight on him. "Looks like we're having a bit of a problem giving up control."

"It's early. I'll let you tire yourself out before I make my move." He pulled my face to him and plunged his tongue into my mouth. He tasted amazing. We ground our erections into each other as we struggled over who would control something as simple as kissing. He reached down and cupped my ass cheeks, pulling me harder to him.

"There you go, baby. Now you're feeling it. You like this position, huh?" I groaned seductively in his ear.

Just as quickly, he had me flipped over on my back and was moving between my legs, encouraging me to spread them wider so he could squeeze in between. "This is more what I had in mind, *baby.*" I grabbed the back of his neck and pulled myself up to his mouth and kissed him deeply again. Our cocks sure as hell didn't care who was where based on the stiffness of each of them.

"Maybe we don't have to figure this all out tonight, Mac."

"Giving in already?" he asked, staring down at me with a shit-eating grin. Lying under him, being this close to him, had me off my game. He was so incredible-looking that I was afraid I might say something I'd regret. "Well, are you?" he asked again.

"Nope! Just kind of hoping to get off, if you don't mind."

"OK, let's call a truce. We can save the dominance for the course, how's that?"

"I still want to play though?" I protested.

"Oh no, Donovan, I wasn't ending things. I have a great idea. Lie back," he said, motioning his head to the bed beneath me. I gave him the evil eye. "Trust me, it'll be fun. You'll love it, guaranteed. We can even rotate positions if you want." He moved off me, turned around and straddled my face. He then leaned forward and put my cock in his mouth. I looked up at his huge cock as I caught his drift: we were about to sixty-nine.

"Good compromise, Mac. Now get back to sucking it." I grabbed his dick and slid it in my mouth, and we both aggressively swallowed each other's cocks. I took him deep, his every pump coming down on me. In turn, I lifted my hips up and face-fucked him. We were both moaning, loud.

I gently nudged him and had him lay on his side. Both on our sides, we pumped our cocks into the other's mouth. It was animalistic, intense; I forgot he was my main competition. We both stroked each other's cock as we swallowed them, and the action was getting hotter.

He pulled his mouth off me. "I could shoot, stud, if you're close."

"Anytime you're ready." I took him back in my mouth and pumped my cock harder into his. Our bodies were tensing, our mouths moaning, our urges building; two athletic bodies being worshipped by the other. I had never been intimate with a peer because I'd always avoided it, and the opportunities for sex with another professional gay skier were limited anyway. Was I so turned on because of that fact, or was it simply my desire for Isaac? My mind raced as he led me down an exhilarating path of release.

"Fuuuuuuuck," he managed to say with a mouthful of me.

I groaned in response as our bodies thrusted and writhed on the bed. We were two hungry guys chasing our release. I let out a guttural moan and my toes curled; my load was getting ready to explode. He grabbed my ass and pulled me hard into his face, expecting the payoff at any moment. Isaac tensed; he was almost there too. We continued grunting, grabbing, pumping harder and faster.

"Shit! Holy fuck!" I mumbled around his cock as I released my load.

Isaac was quieter but he stiffened up, and his cock twitched in my throat right before he flooded my mouth with his seed. We fell onto our backs, breathing heavily, our heads at opposite ends of the bed.

"That works," he said, grabbing my foot and squeezing it.

"Next time, I'm on top," I quipped.

"Sure, OK. It'll probably be your last time."

Fifteen: Isaac

Walk of Shame

Let the awkwardness start, in three, two, one. I waited a couple more seconds for it to begin, but it never arrived. I pinched my leg to make sure I wasn't dreaming, and after a couple more tries, I found I was still lying next to Foster, who had his eyes half-closed, a sexed-out look on his face. It had, in fact, happened, and without the uncomfortable post-orgasm moments. *Interesting.*

"That was a lot of fun," Foster said, getting off the bed and heading to the bathroom. The sound of running water filtered through the open door.

I looked around and marveled at the size of his suite. I could easily fit three of my hotel rooms in here. The glass windows were fogged up, and I wondered if it was from the steam made by our scorching bodies.

The water stopped and Foster returned with a towel around his waist and a spare for me. He handed it to me then flopped back on the bed, using one of my arms as a pillow.

I grabbed his wrist to check the time and was shocked that it was almost midnight. I played with his hair, surprised I didn't have the urge to run away and do my walk of shame.

"Mmmm," Foster hummed, clearly enjoying my caress. "Isaac?"

"Yeah?"

"You should stay at my place in Lake Tahoe," he said.

I was not expecting him to say that.

He looked up when I didn't respond. "Nobody is using it right now, and it is literally across the street from Palisade, where your next race is," he added.

"You hardly know me," I said. "Plus, someone is already making the arrangements." I'd never get used to saying that. Having someone take care of my travel needs still felt odd.

"I know you. You're the guy who just sixty-nined the shit out of me for the first time. Plus, it'll be better for you and your coach to stay in one place."

Being the first person to give Foster a new experience squeezed my heart with warmth. "That was my first time doing that too," I admitted, leaning to kiss the top of his head. It smelled like mint and spice from his shampoo, or maybe his styling gel. I inhaled and closed my eyes.

"See, what a bond, right? But seriously, it'll be better for you and your coach." Foster sounded like a salesman. He had a point. I could take this opportunity to get to know Alex more, to build trust.

"Only if you let me pay you," I said.

"Sure. Can I take payments in favors?" he asked, grabbing my spent cock.

"Not a chance. That was a one-time thing."

Foster sat up, his mouth hanging open. "Why? It was so much fun."

"Well, I hope ya enjoyed it. It ain't happenin' again." As much I hated to admit how amazing Foster's touches and kisses had felt, it couldn't go any further. This was the kind of distraction that could derail the progress I had made these past few years. *The fun will have to wait.*

He looked at me curiously. "What accent was that? That's the second time I've heard you speak like that."

"Huh? What accent?" It wasn't what I said that made him look at me that way, it was the way I said it. My heart beat faster, and I took a subtle breath to calm the growing tension in my body. "Are you talking about my boring West Coast accent?" I joked, hoping to mask the unsteadiness in my voice. This was the second time this week that I'd slipped, almost giving away my well-kept secret. It only happened when I was nervous or uncomfortable—and being with Foster made me both.

Shrugging, Foster exhaled and stretched. "I swear I'm hearing things sometimes."

I hated that I was making Foster question himself, but I couldn't go back now, not when I was this close to my dreams. This was a casual thing. Nothing more, nothing less.

"Is that where you're from?" he asked.

"Umm, yeah." It was a fib, but not by a lot, since I'd lived all over the Pacific Northwest since I was eighteen.

"Care to narrow it down?" he asked, his eyes on mine. I hoped he couldn't read my mind.

"Portland," I answered.

"Great city, close to some prime ski slopes."

"Yup." I got off the bed and looked for my clothes. I could feel Foster watching me.

"What're you doing?" he asked. He was lying on his side with his head propped up by his hand.

I looked at him as I zipped up my damp pants. "I have to get going. I have an early flight tomorrow."

"Oh, OK. Let me put some clothes on and I'll walk you out."

"No, don't get up. I can walk myself out." I raised my hand to stop him. It was fine. Walking me out would only complicate things, and this was just a casual thing.

"You cool?" Foster asked.

"Yeah, I'm great." I pulled on my dress shirt and tried to button it, forgetting that he had ripped it off me. Frowning, I pulled on the suit jacket and buttoned it closed. It was freezing outside.

"OK." He grabbed a pen and paper from his nightstand and scribbled something. "Here's my Lake Tahoe address and my cell number. Have your people call me."

"I don't think I'll be stay—"

"Isaac, I don't mind," he insisted, and held the paper in front of me.

I walked toward the bed and grabbed it. "Thank you."

"See you around?" he asked with uncertainty.

"Yeah. See you, Foster." I raised the paper in my hand and said, "Thanks again." I slipped into my shoes.

And there it was, the walk of shame. Only it was more painful this time. It was an actual *shame* because I truly enjoyed Foster's company. Being around him was fun. I closed the door behind me and leaned back on it as I blew out a few shaky breaths to gather my composure. I looked down at my jittery hands and put them inside my pockets. *That was close.*

It was snowing when I exited the hotel, and I shivered a little when the cold air greeted me, sobering me from the high of being with him and having the best orgasm of my life. Thankful the museum where I parked was only eight blocks from here, I traced the same path Foster and I traveled earlier. The sound of his laughter and the way he said my name replayed in my head.

The roads were a lot quieter this time, and I wondered if it was because it was late or the absence of cocky but sweet company. The Foster I met this evening was a completely different person from the persona he projected. He had confidence and bravado, but behind that façade was a sensitive and generous man, both with his time and belongings. His offer to let me stay in his Lake Tahoe home made sense. Even though it was close to the club, I didn't want a handout. I hoped he would accept payment for letting me and Alex stay.

I dialed Alex's cell number when I hopped in my car, planning to leave a message on her voicemail about staying at Foster's home, but I was surprised when she answered.

"Mac?"

"I didn't mean to wake you up. I was hoping to get your voicemail because it's too long to text." I felt guilty for interrupting her evening.

"Are you OK?" she asked, concern in her voice.

"Oh, yeah. I was just calling to let you know about the plan for tomorrow."

"Isaac, you and your plans. Do you ever just have fun?"

"I had fun tonight," I admitted.

"You did? Well, that's good." The sound of a yawn cut through the receiver.

I told her about Foster's offer and how it made sense to stay in one place, and she agreed. "See you tomorrow?"

"Copy that," she said.

I pulled the piece of paper with Foster's address and phone number out of my rented jacket and entered them into my cell phone. I created a text chain and typed *Thank you for the amazing evening,* then deleted it and replaced it with *Thanks for letting us stay at your place.* I decided to press send and drove off.

* * *

"Holy smokes, this place is fancy!" Alex exclaimed once we typed in the code Foster sent me this morning and stepped inside. "I could stay here forever. Does Foster need a coach?" I responded with a death glare, eye roll and head shake, exactly in that order.

I had to agree with her though. The modern house was a mixture of polished concrete floors, metal, and floor-to-ceiling windows. The exposed staircase, with wire instead of rails connected to the posts, was the focal point of the house. I pulled my cell from my back pocket and opened the text chain between Foster and me. *Your place is amazing. Alex doesn't want to leave.* Three bubbles appeared, indicating Foster was responding.

Foster: *Then don't leave.*

Me: *Me or her?*

Foster: *Both?*

"What are you smiling about?" Alex asked.

"Nothing," I said, putting my phone back in my pocket and ignoring the curiosity in her stare as I walked past her.

Sixteen: Foster

Room for Two?

A text from Mom popped up on my phone the moment I turned airplane mode off.

Call me when you land, it read.

I grabbed my bag from the overhead compartment. Since my team only flew first class, we were some of the first passengers to exit the flight from Aspen. I put on my baseball cap and shades to conceal my presence before entering the airport. Fans knew me all over the world, but in Canada I was sports royalty.

"See you, Foster," my coach said, and headed off to baggage claim.

I gave him a hand salute and pressed my mom's name on my phone. "Hey Mom," I said when she picked up.

"Hi sweetheart, are you back in Vancouver?" she asked.

"I just landed. Is everything OK?"

"Everything is fine, I'm calling to invite you over to celebrate."

"Celebrate?" My mind reeled, trying to figure out which occasion I missed during the week I was gone.

"For winning the gold medal at the World Cup!" she

exclaimed. "Your dad was very proud of you, we all are."

Her last statement stopped me in my tracks, causing the woman walking way too close behind me to bump into my back. I waved my hand in apology. "Mom, you don't have to cover for him." A small part of me wanted to believe her. I wanted to believe that despite my dad's constant criticism, he could still be proud of me. But I knew better. He was never proud of me. Not when I won my first Olympic gold medal four years ago, and definitely not now. I sometimes wondered if he despised having his son breaking all the records he set. I shook my head to rid it of toxic thoughts. My relationship with my father was complicated enough and didn't need another layer.

"Foster, darling, it was your father's idea to get us all together. Just come, OK?"

"OK, I'll be there in an hour," I said, being the great son I was, and a glutton for disappointment. I hung up as a text came in from Isaac.

Your place is amazing. Alex doesn't want to leave, the message read.

I grinned. Fucking grinned like a psycho. Without any chill, I typed, *Then don't leave.*

Isaac replied, *Me or her?*

I asked, *Both?* I waited a couple of seconds to see if he'd reply, but after a minute of no incoming text, I put the phone in my back pocket and headed to the long-term parking where I had left my SUV.

The evening I spent with Mac had been hot as fuck—and I had gone out with models and celebrities. The battle and display for dominance was the most sensual and erotic foreplay I'd ever had. Just the thought of it stirred my cock back to life, making my pants tighter and uncomfortable. "Fuck me," I murmured, putting my hand in my pocket to adjust myself without anyone noticing. It wasn't just the sex, if you could even call it that, when all we did was suck each other to oblivion. Everything about that evening was remarkable. I still couldn't believe a place called Oh My God It's a Wiener existed.

If I didn't know any better, I would've thought it was a first date. Something about that night was very first date-y. After climbing into my Tahoe, I checked my cell one more time. No text from Mac. Disappointed, I pulled out of the parking lot and headed to my parents' home.

* * *

"Oz is here!" Sophia yelled after greeting me at the door.

"How are you, Red?" I asked, hugging her.

"Great now that you're here." She took my hand and led me to the dining room, where my parents were setting the table for the evening.

"Here's our champion," my mom said, placing a bowl of salad on the table and hurrying over to kiss my cheek. "We're so proud of you, aren't we, honey?" Dad was standing at the end of the table, watching us. Mom motioned her head for him to join us as he remained stationary behind one of the chairs. She released me from her embrace and led me to Dad. We exchanged the world's most uncomfortable hug.

I tapped his back a couple of times to end his misery.

"Aren't we proud of Foster, love?" Mom asked again after

he released me.

"Ahh, yes. We are…we are very proud of you. Congratulations." He looked at my mom, as if seeking approval for his performance.

Somebody dust off the Oscar. "Thank you," I said, and headed to my seat. Getting a compliment from him was like pulling teeth. "What did you think about the race?" It was a pointless question. I knew he was 'too important' to be bothered to watch the World Cup. It was petty to ask, but I couldn't help myself.

He glanced at Mom sitting beside him, before turning his attention to me. "I thought you were impressive." It was a generic response that didn't require watching the race. But then he surprised me. "Generating speed using your body's momentum was remarkable, and your top speed was impressive considering the lower start gate." He grabbed the white napkin from his place setting and laid it on his lap.

My mom reached out and squeezed his shoulder, a warm smile on her face.

Well, that was unexpected. Not only had he watched my race, but he also had something good to say about my performance.

"That guy from the USA was pretty good too. I'd keep an eye on him if I were you. He almost beat you."

And there it was, the dad I knew. Would it kill him to just give me kudos without any criticism? Geez. Isaac had a great race, but he couldn't have beaten me. He gave me competition, but my reign was secure.

"And he is so handsome." Sophia placed her hand on my arm and I directed my attention to her instead.

"You think so?" I asked, glad she shared my opinion.

She nodded, her ponytail bouncing. "Do you know him?"

"Kinda," I said.

"Kinda?" my dad huffed. "That's not a word, Sophia."

"Yes, I *kinda* know him." I shot my dad a quick glance then returned my focus to Sophia.

Dad mumbled something in French, but I didn't care. Not every word had to be sophisticated every time we spoke. Why did he want me to visit when all he did was pick fights with me?

* * *

After dinner, I could finally relax. I collapsed onto the brown leather sofa in the living room, my sister sidling up next to me and resting her head on my shoulder. I grabbed the green blanket from the back of the couch and draped it over our legs, and gazed into the basalt fireplace. My mind wandered thousands of miles away to my Lake Tahoe home, trying to imagine what Isaac was doing. Why hadn't he responded to my text? So this was how it felt to be left hanging. I didn't like it. *Note to self: never do that again.*

A ridiculous idea came to me while listening to Sophia chatter over the crackling of the fire. What was the worst thing that could happen if I showed up unannounced? The house was spacious enough for three people, so my presence wouldn't interfere with Isaac and his coach's routines. I could refund half of what I charged him, although the amount I asked him to pay wasn't even enough to cover the maid service, but he didn't need to know that.

"Why're you so quiet?" Sophia asked.

"I was just daydreaming," I answered, and tickled her feet.

"Oz, stop!" she yelped, giggling. "Is it about your next race?"

"Umm, not really." I looked around to make sure my parents were nowhere around before I continued. "I'm thinking about someone."

"Oh yeah?" Her eyes widened and she leaned over to whisper in my ear. "Who is he?"

Sophia knew about some of the men I'd dated, and she'd always found the good qualities in them, even after hearing about the breakups.

"I can't tell you yet, but I kinda like him." I didn't want to tell her about Isaac as I wasn't entirely sure myself. He intrigued me, and it didn't hurt that he was hot as fuck.

"OK," she said, respecting my wishes. "Dad doesn't like the word *kinda*." She chuckled. "Can you tell this guy you like him?"

I wished it was that easy. "I don't know," I admitted.

"Why not?"

"I don't know him very well."

"Yet," she corrected me. "Maybe be friends with him first."

"You know, that's a great idea." Look at that, my sister giving me relationship advice. I pulled my cell phone from my pocket and looked for the next flight to Lake Tahoe. The earliest one was in the morning. "I might do that."

"Cool. Do you have time to watch a movie?"

"Always," I said. I put my phone on silent to spend uninterrupted time with my favorite person.

Sophia grabbed the remote and pressed the voice control. "Play *Hunger Games*," she said. She always picked that movie; it was her favorite.

"May the odds be ever in your favor," we said in unison.

* * *

This could blow up in my face, but it was too late to turn back. Besides, I was never one to turn down a challenge. I was fearless.

Except right now.

I was halfway between Lake Tahoe Airport and my home. After crossing the state border from Nevada to California, I turned on some music to keep my mind from imagining how Isaac would react to my impromptu visit. I drummed the steering wheel of my rental in time to the beat, trying to fight the urge to take the next exit and turn around. Since when had I become wishy-washy? "Fuck," I groaned and pulled over, grabbing my cell from the middle console.

What's up, Mac? Enjoying your stay? I reread the text, making sure it sounded casual, before pressing send. Seconds later, my phone pinged.

Big Mac: *Hey! I was about to text you. Yes, your place is incredible. Just finished training and we're heading back.*

Me: *Great! There's a hot tub on the second level overlooking the mountains. You should check it out.*

Big Mac: *I have a date with that hot tub tonight.*

Me: *Want company?*

Big Mac: *I asked Alex, but she's meeting her friends later.*

That was enough for me. He didn't say he wanted to be alone, so that was as good as an invitation. OK, yes, it was a stretch, but my confidence was returning. I checked traffic before pulling back onto the road, blasting Bruce Springsteen's version of 'Fire'. Rivals could be friends, right?

Seventeen: Isaac

Surprise Visitor

"Is your hand OK?" Alex asked, looking at my right hand as I stretched it.

The practice was going well until I pushed myself too far and crashed mid-track during a sharp turn. The fall could have been worse, but it was bad enough to aggravate my old injury. "Yeah, I'll ice it when we get back." I wasn't sure she believed me, but the concern in her eyes faded and she entered lecture mode.

"Next time, listen to me. And I'm not gonna repeat my-self—don't jeopardize your future by being reckless."

It was a risky move, but I wanted to shave more time from my second training run, even after she'd told me she had a plan for tomorrow. "Yeah, that was my bad. I'm sorry. I'll rest tonight."

"Give me the keys. I'll drive." She held her hand out until I relinquished the car key.

"Alright, boss," I mumbled.

"Damn right." Alex closed her hand around the key and walked around to the driver's side.

I buckled my seatbelt and faced Alex, who was adjusting the

automatic seat to her height. "Um, what's the plan tomorrow," I asked hesitantly.

She didn't say anything, just shook her head with a dry laugh. "So?"

"Mac! We literally just finished, and we're not even sure if your hand is well enough for tomorrow."

"It'll be alright, I promise. See?" I held out my wrist and rotated it. I managed to keep a straight face as a sharp pain and tingling sensation shot through it.

"We'll talk about it tomorrow." She directed her attention to the road and started driving.

"But—"

Alex gave me a quick death glare.

"OK, you're the boss," I conceded.

"Who's that?" Alex asked as we pulled through the security gate at Foster's place and saw a black SUV.

"No clue," I said. Weird, Foster had told me no one was going to be there.

"Whoever it is, they had the code to the gate."

"Let me check it out." I hopped out of the car and headed toward the parked SUV. The back-seat windows were tinted, so I walked to the front of the car and peered through the windshield. "Foster?"

He waved, a huge smile on his face.

"Hey, Alex, it's just Foster," I called out, and waved her toward the SUV. I opened the door and was welcomed by his scent, that fancy cologne that was already tattooed in my memory after one evening with him. "What are you doing here?" The slight look of uncertainty on his face gave him an air of vulnerability. "I mean, it is your place, but still?" He hadn't moved a muscle, so I stepped back and waved him out.

He hopped out of the car and reached out to give me a hug just as I was reaching to shake his hand. "Oh," he said, jumping when my hand brushed his crotch.

"I'm sorry!" I reversed actions to return his hug, only to have his hand brush my bulge as he did the same.

His eyes widened, then he threw his head back and laughed. The veins across his neck protruded; oh, how I wanted to run my tongue along them. It was clear that Foster and I were both alphas when it came to relationships. How would that even work between us? Wait, what was I doing thinking about a relationship? The R word brought me back to reality. What happened that night couldn't and wouldn't happen again. We were peers. Nothing more, nothing less.

Alex stopped when she saw what happened and gave me a hand signal telling me she'd be inside, and then winked.

"What...um...why are you here?" I asked again.

"I'm sorry to come unannounced, but I wanted to watch the race this weekend. I hope that's OK?"

"Of course it's OK. This is your place. Why wouldn't it be?" Was he here to watch the event, or to watch me in particular? Was he here to scout the competition?

"Are you sure?" Foster asked.

"Of course. Why don't we get inside? It's cold out here." I almost wrapped my arm around his shoulder when I caught myself and put my hands in my pockets instead.

Alex was waiting in the kitchen, leaning on the island counter. "I'm Alex, Mac's coach," she said, offering Foster her hand.

"Foster. It's nice to meet you, Alex." He accepted her hand before he continued. "I hope I'm not imposing. I just wanna see the event this weekend."

"I told you it's fine," I answered for both of us. "Let me get your coat."

"I got it," he said, but I was already taking it off him. "Oh, OK." He chuckled.

My hand brushed the back of his neck and I didn't miss the way he shivered, goosebumps appearing on his exposed skin. *Calm down, Isaac. He's probably just cold.*

Alex's cell buzzed. "I need to take this," she said. "See you around?" Foster gave her two thumbs-up.

"How was your training?" Foster asked after Alex's voice had faded up the stairs.

"Well," I replied quickly. He didn't need to know about the little tweak of an old injury. He was my competition and I couldn't show him my weaknesses.

"Good. Have you done your workout?" he asked.

I hadn't, and I was planning on taking it easy to rest my hand, but I couldn't tell him that either. "Yeah. I'm all done for today."

"Oh. Wanna spot me? I've skipped three days in a row."

"Sure."

* * *

In the gym, we stretched side by side on a rubber mat. "How long have you been working with Alex?" Foster asked.

"Almost a week. The World Cup was our first race together."

"What? Really? That's impressive."

My pride swelled at the compliment, especially coming from him. Would he still think it was impressive if I had beaten him? "Thanks. Alex and I just clicked."

"It's amazing. How haven't I heard about you until last week?"

What was up with these questions? I thought we were here to work out, not for an interrogation. The funny thing was, I didn't mind answering his questions. That was new for me. "I mostly raced locally."

"Why?" he asked, leaning forward over his straight legs to touch his toes. "Afraid of competition, are you?" He wore a cocky grin.

I couldn't tell him why, but I could match his arrogance. "You should be thankful, you know."

"Oh yeah, why is that?" He bent his knee and leaned back, propping his body up with his elbows.

"You wouldn't have won all those medals if I had been competing against you." I stood and grabbed my left foot behind me to stretch my hamstring. I delivered the statement as a joke, but it was half true. I knew I could go toe-to-toe with Foster, the World Cup result was proof of that.

"Oh really, you think you have the skill?"

"Absolutely." I enunciated every syllable.

"The stamina?" Foster raised an eyebrow.

He should know the answer to that just from the other night. "Jump by jump." I crossed my arms, looking down at him.

"Please, you can't even do two workout sessions in one day."

Damn him using my competitiveness against me. No way would I give him the satisfaction of having the last laugh. Against my better judgment, I asked, "How much can you lift?"

Eighteen: Foster

Who's Your Daddy Now?

I'd seen Isaac naked and memorized his every muscle, but seeing him in just sweatpants exposing the waistband of his black underwear made me lose my fucking mind. The plan to start a friendship with him was getting more difficult the more time I spent with him. His body glistened with sweat and his face was flush from exertion. I'd asked him to spot me for my workout, even though I didn't need help, but my teasing made him reconsider and he'd met my challenge and decided to train his legs.

"One. Two. Three," he counted in between grunts. The carnal sound he made at the end of each rep did all sorts of things to me.

I repositioned my semi-chub at the same time Isaac decided to peer my way. "What?" I asked, feigning innocence." I'd been caught.

He shook his head. "How do you get any exercise done? You're so slow."

"You're distracting me, man." The admission was out of my mouth before I could stop it.

"You're the one who asked me to join you, remember?"

"I didn't think this through." I gestured between us.

Isaac walked over to the machine where his shirt was hanging and began to pull it back on.

"What are you doing?" I asked.

"Putting my shirt on so you can focus."

"Isaac, it's hot as fuck in here. Don't be ridiculous." It *was* hot in here, but I would be lying if I said that was the only reason I wanted him to remain shirtless.

"Is that right," he smirked, tossing his shirt on the bench. "Take yours off then."

"You can't handle all this." I motioned to my body from head to toe.

"Please. I handled you just fine, if I remember it right."

"Is that what you did? Not how I remember it."

"Drop the shirt, pretty boy!" he barked, a delivery that was too playful to be serious.

"Oh, you think I'm pretty." I waggled my eyebrows.

"Drop the shirt or I'll take it off you," Isaac warned, his eyes dancing with mischief.

"I'd like to see you try."

Isaac strode toward me and I braced myself. He was breathing hard, but it couldn't have been from the five-meter walk to reach me. "Take. It. Off."

We stood face-to-face. I puffed my chest. "Make me," I said, looking at Isaac's mouth.

He grinned, and before I knew it, I was lying on the floor, Isaac straddling me and pinning my arms over my head. "Don't say I didn't warn you, baby."

"Cocky motherfucker," I said. I rolled over and used my hands and legs to push Isaac off me. He landed hard on his back, but didn't wince. I grabbed both his hands and brought them to his sides, using my knees to lock them in place. "I'm not your baby." I moved my face closer to his. "I'm your daddy." Leaning down had been the wrong move—Isaac peeled himself from my hold. "Shit."

He freed his hands and put my right arm behind my back as I lay face down. "Who's the daddy now, Foster?" he whispered in my ear, bending my other arm behind me. With my hands immobilized, he used his free arm to try and lift my shirt off.

I wiggled as hard as I could, but the fucker was too strong.

"Damn it," he said, stopping halfway. He couldn't progress any higher with my hands in the way.

I looked over my shoulder to watch him. "Out of moves?" I taunted.

He leaned forward and lifted the hem of my tank top to his face. He bit the edge with his teeth and ripped my shirt in half.

Respect. He'd won. I laughed hard, my body heaving in convulsions.

"Yeah!" Isaac waved my torn shirt, proud of his victory.

"Well played." I offered my fist and he met me halfway. He joined me on the floor, and we laid our sweaty bodies on the mat until our heartrates calmed.

"What a workout," Isaac said and stood, extending his hand to help me up.

"I'm spent. Wanna shower?" We were standing face-to-face, breathing in each other's breath.

Isaac looked at me suspiciously. "I don't think that's a good idea."

"It's just a shower. That room is big enough for ten people." And that was the truth. One of the reasons why I'd bought this place, aside from the view, was the state-of-the-art gym with adjacent shower.

Isaac led the way, stopping by the towel cabinet and grabbing two. He tossed one to me. He was very attentive. I noticed him doing that a lot. He took his sweatpants off, bending over to pull them from his ankles. He folded them and put them on the counter before pulling off his briefs, exposing his muscular ass.

I swallowed hard and took my gym shorts off, followed by my boxer trunks, and tossed them in the hamper. "Just shower," I mumbled when he was out of sight. I could do that.

* * *

"Are we all set?" I asked the private chef and waiter I had hired to prepare and serve us a six-course meal tonight. Pulling this off was harder than I expected, and I practically had to beg Isaac to stay away from the kitchen. I told him I was *having some work done* when he asked why. He seemed to buy it, and spent the next two hours in his room.

"Just one last thing," the waiter said before lighting the two long candles in the middle of the table. The white linen and table setting was similar to the gala setup in Aspen. "This is so romantic."

"Oh, this is nothing like that." I said, watching the chef and waiter exchange glances. "No, really. We're...buddies." I hoped they didn't see me cringe after saying that last word. *Buddies? What the fuck was wrong with me?* "You know what, it doesn't matter what we are, let's just make this evening special. Can we do that?"

"Copy that," the chef said. The waiter nodded.

"Thank you." Time to go get Isaac.

I took a long drag of air to calm the tension growing in my body. This wasn't a date. *You're doing him a favor,* I told myself to rid my stomach of the butterflies taking up residence. I knocked softly. "Isaac? You awake?"

I heard the bed shift, and Isaac answered the door wearing a tight gray polo shirt and jeans. "Hi!" he greeted. His face broke into a smile when he saw me. His short wavy hair wasn't styled, making him appear more relaxed than the usual wound-up look he sported.

My face felt warm, my throat became dry.

"Can I come out now? I'm starving," he asked. He took one step closer and leaned on the door frame, his smile turning into a smirk. "Foster?"

I cleared my throat and swallowed hard. "Sorry about that. They're done working downstairs. I've got something to show you."

"You do?" Isaac raised an eyebrow.

"Yeah. Let's go to the dining room," I said, turning around before I embarrassed myself.

"What is it?" he asked, grabbing my arm.

"Can you just come down or whatever. It doesn't matter." *Way to be smooth, Foster.*

"Let's go then," he said, closing the door behind him.

The closer we got to the dining room, the more nervous I became. Was this a good idea? *You're just trying to do something nice for a friend.*

Isaac stopped walking when we reached the dimly lit room, shadows dancing with the flickering candles. "Foster, what is this?" His eyes widened. "Did you do all this?"

"Well, I had some help. They're in there." I pointed to the

kitchen, and the waiter emerged and filled our wine glasses with the merlot I'd picked from the cellar downstairs. "I remembered how distraught you looked during the Winners' Gala."

Isaac was planted in place, staring at me.

"I don't want you to ever feel inadequate, so I thought we'd have a private dinner so we could practice."

His eyes softened, his Adam's apple bobbing.

"I hope this is OK?" I was beginning to think this was stepping over the line. He didn't ask for my help, and I hoped this dinner wouldn't make him feel worse.

"Thank you," he said in almost a whisper. "This is one of the nicest things someone has ever done for me."

"You're welcome," I said. "Class is in session." I motioned for Isaac to sit down.

The first course arrived, and once our waiter was gone, I gave Isaac the rules of thumb when it came to formal multi-course dining. "Regardless of how many courses the meal is, the basic rules are—" I pointed to the silverware in front of me "—forks are always on the left, and spoons and knives are always on the right."

Isaac nodded, bouncing his attention from my face to my hands.

"And you always start from the outside."

"Always?" he asked.

"Always."

One by one, the waiter served us dish after dish of delicious food, and I showed Isaac which utensils to use, until the last plates were cleared from the table.

"Is this the work you were having done?" Isaac asked, finally connecting the dots.

"Yup. Smooth, huh?"

"Very smooth." He grinned while nodding.

"Sorry you had to stay cooped up in your room for a couple of hours."

Isaac's grin faded momentarily before he answered my question. "Oh, um, that's OK. I was on the phone with my parents, so no big deal."

"That's good. Are you close with them?" I asked.

"Yes." He took another sip of his wine. "My dad was my first coach." He appeared nervous, rubbing his palms on his thighs.

"That's cool. Was he a pro?"

"Um, no. He learned how to ski by reading books and watching videos."

"Oh wow. It must be nice to have a dad like that." A small part of me was jealous; my own father barely bothered to congratulate me after winning a race. I couldn't remember the last time my dad and I had a conversation that didn't include an argument or some form of criticism.

"Thanks for this, Foster." Isaac put his hands over mine. His thumb rubbed small circles on the back of my hand, igniting warmth in my chest. "That was a hundred times better than the gala." He smiled, his piercing brown eyes focused on mine.

"You're welcome, Isaac. Did you notice the portions were bigger?" I winked. Joking was easier than analyzing how his touch made me feel cherished and his gaze made me feel seen.

Isaac leaned his head in and laughed. He squeezed my hand. "I did notice. Thank you for that, since I don't think Lake Tahoe has a hot dog stand." He lifted my hand and intertwined our fingers. He didn't say anything else, and neither did I. We were just satisfied to be in the moment.

* * *

The following evening, Isaac hopped in the jacuzzi after our less formal dinner and I joined him. He propped his arms up on the side of the jacuzzi, extending his legs to where I sat opposite him. We were both wearing underwear; might as well, since my balls were still strained after he wrestled my shirt off. He took a sip of his coffee, as he had a rule of not drinking alcohol when he had a race coming up. Since I wasn't racing this weekend—not that it had ever stopped me before—I opted for a much stiffer drink: Irish coffee, heavy on the Irish.

I pressed a button next to me and the tub lit up, jets spraying water against our backs.

"Ahhh," Isaac groaned and tilted his head back, eyes closed.

"Is that enough pressure?" I asked, ignoring how my body came to life once again.

"It's perfect." He brought his attention to me, and then out to the dark skies. "It's really nice up here."

"It is. I wish I could spend more time out here."

"How long have you had this place?"

"Three years. I stayed here during the World Cup."

"Oh, yeah. That was your first World Cup, right?"

"Yup. Fun times." I winked, proud that he knew that about me.

"You shut the doubters up. They were so wrong about you" he said, chuckling.

I had some critics after winning the gold medal at the Olympics almost four years ago. They questioned my motivation and compared me to my father, doubting that I would be able to follow in his footsteps. They quieted after that World Cup, and were ultimately silenced after my three-peat. "Anyway, we stayed here and I fell in love. It wasn't for sale, but I called the owner and asked what they wanted for the place, and the rest is history."

Isaac nodded before submerging his body up to his neck in the warm, bubbling water.

"It's a treat coming down here. I love living in high-rises, but I like a change in scenery once in a while." I copied Isaac and slid my body into the water, the jets' pressure massaging my shoulders. I realized that, once again, I was talking about myself too much. Isaac was right. It was a bad habit I needed to stop. I cringed when I thought about the number of times I'd spent hours talking about myself, from first dates to casual occasions. "What got you into skiing?"

"I didn't know anything about skiing till I was nine. I was watching the finals of the 2006 downhill skiing and I just fell in love. I've been skiing ever since." Isaac's face lit up as he spoke.

I understood why. I'd been skiing since I could remember. Thankful that I was finally getting more than single-sentence answers from him, I continued. "What's next on your schedule?"

"A break before the World Championships in Whistler."

It was my next race too. And just like the World Cup, I was the defending gold medalist.

"I'll be at a camp before Whistler," Isaac said. "One of my good friends, Sawyer, is a pediatrician who specializes in developmental medicine and he holds an annual camp for skiers. I try to volunteer every year."

"That's amazing that you chose to do that during the busiest weeks in the ski season."

"It's something that brings me joy. Are you familiar with developmental medicine?" he asked.

I knew what it was; Sophia had been seeing a doctor specializing in that field. "I'm very familiar with it," I admitted. I didn't usually tell people about my sister. My dates never seemed to care after I told them about her, so I just stopped doing it. But it was different with Isaac. "My sister has been seeing one since she was little. She's almost eighteen now." Thinking about her always brought a smile to my face.

"Is she OK?" Isaac's eyes softened when he asked.

"Yeah, she's awesome. She has Down syndrome."

"Some of the kids at the camp have Down. They're awesome. Some people think that it's too difficult for them to learn how to ski, but they're so wrong. They just learn differently. What's her name?"

"Sophia. I call her Red or Dot sometimes because she's obsessed with ladybugs and her favorite color is red."

"That's so cool. She's probably a good skier since you and your dad are pros."

This was the first time someone other than my family and friends spoke about Sophia like an actual person. Isaac didn't say, *Oh, I'm so sorry*, like being born with a different ability was something to pity. I didn't expect this side of him. "No, she doesn't ski."

"How come?"

"Actually, I don't know why," I admitted, feeling a little guilty. My parents always took me to clubs when I was younger, and I just assumed Sophia didn't like to ski since she never asked.

"Do you think she'll enjoy spending time and learning how with other teenagers?"

It didn't escape me that Isaac said *other teenagers* and not *others like her* and honestly, I could have kissed him for it. Sophia might actually love it. "I can ask her later. Do you think your friend Sawyer would mind?"

"He won't," Isaac assured me.

"If Sophia wants to join, and it's OK with your friend Sawyer, do you think you'll need another volunteer?"

"You mean, you?" he asked in surprise. "It's the week before the World Championships."

"Yes, me. And you're doing it, and I am way better than you," I joked.

He rolled his eyes and ignored me.

"Are Sawyer and you…"

"A couple?" Isaac finished my question. "No, we're best friends. We met during a ski camp when I was twelve and he was fifteen. He's like a big brother to me."

I sighed in relief.

"Plus, I never would've spent that evening with you if I was in a relationship. I'd never do that."

"Same. Is the ski camp near Portland?" I asked.

"Yes, Mount Hood."

"Were you born and raised in Portland?" I remembered he lived there from our past conversation.

Isaac sat up abruptly and water splashed over the side of the hot tub onto the wooden deck. He swallowed hard. "Um, yeah." He took another sip of his coffee and glanced back at the door, as though he wanted to escape. Hmmm. What is this man hiding?

Nineteen: Isaac

All the White Lies

Everything was going well until Foster's last question. It was a simple question, but my answer was two thousand miles east of Oregon. I didn't want to lie to Foster, and it was just my luck that the one person I'd like to be honest with was the last person I wanted to know the truth. What started as a white lie when I was younger had turned into something I now wore whenever I left the four corners of my sad and empty apartment.

* * *

Twelve Years Earlier

I peeked outside when the bus loaded with kids pulled into the ski resort. This was my second year in a row attending the camp, and I was excited to see my best friend, Sawyer. Even though he was three years older than me, at sixteen, he didn't want to stop hanging out with me. He never made fun of my clothes or the way I spoke. He was like an older brother and had protected me against the bullies who made fun of me at camps because I was different. I didn't have a lot of friends, since our house was far from my school and my mom had to homeschool me when blizzards snowed us in, which happened often in the mountains.

I didn't have a cell phone like most of my classmates, but Sawyer always called our house. Sometimes we spent hours talking about skiing and what we wanted to do when we were older. Unlike me, he didn't want to be a skier. He wanted to be a doctor. And I didn't doubt that he would be, because he was really smart.

From my seat in the lobby, I watched as, one by one, kids exited the bus, hauling carry-ons and zipping up jackets. Then, finally, there he was. I leaped to my feet.

"Sawyer!" I hollered out the sliding glass doors, waving and grinning.

He looked up and hurried toward me, and we hugged like long-lost brothers.

"You're taller now," I said, looking up at him.

"You are too," he replied, ruffling my hair. He wrapped his arm around my shoulder, and we walked together to join the rest of the group to receive our room assignments.

"Sawyer Montgomery," the camp coordinator called. "You and Isaac McAllister are roommates."

"Yes!" I put my fist in the air, exhilarated that I would get to spend every minute of the entire weekend with my best friend.

"Let's go," Sawyer said, and we set off to find our room.

* * *

As we did last year, we started our days warming up on the bunny slopes before transitioning to bigger hills. Since I hadn't graduated from my age group, there were some familiar kids from last year.

"Isaac," *our camp leader called.* "Can you show everyone what you did earlier?" *It had been easier for me to follow his instruction this time around as my dad had been training me in the correct techniques he learned from reading ski books. For once, I was ahead of the game.* "Alright everyone, I'd like you to watch Isaac and try to do it too, OK?"

"But it's hard," *one of the kids whined.*

"Yeah, and Isaac is way better than us," *another kid echoed.*

"It's not hard, I'll go slow so ya can follow," *I assured them. We positioned ourselves and waited for our leader's directions.*

"Ready. Set. Go!" *he shouted, and everyone slid on the packed snow.*

Some of the kids wiped out halfway, and some of the kids who followed my guidance made it to the bottom of the hill.

"Good job," *I said to the two kids who had thought it was hard, and gave them each a high-five.*

After a minute, the kids who wiped out joined us. "Good job, guys," *I said, encouraging them for the next round.*

"Shut up," *one kid snarled.*

"Why do you talk funny?" *another kid asked.*

What was he talking about? I'd always spoken the same. "What do ya mean?" *I asked.* "I talk just like anyone else."

"No, you don't. Your accent sounds weird and dumb." *He laughed, and the two boys hanging out with him laughed too.* "Where are you from?"

I was about to answer when the camp leader joined us at the bottom of the hill. "Great job, Isaac," *he said.* "Great job everyone."

"Thank ya," *I said.*

"Thaaaank yaaaa," *the boys trilled, mocking my words and*

making goofy faces. I turned away.

* * *

"Sawyer?" I asked that evening, as we relaxed in our room after the first day.

"Yeah?" His head appeared over the edge of the top bunk, his brown hair hanging around the sides of his face.

"What's an accent?"

"It's the way we talk, the sound we make when we say things."

I frowned. "I don't wanna have no accent."

"Why? Everyone has an accent."

"But I don't want mine."

"Why?"

"The other kids think I'm stupid." I placed my hands behind my head, resting them on the pillow. "Can ya teach me how to talk like ya?"

"Don't listen to those losers. They're just jealous because you're better than all of us." He jumped down, and I sat up to make room next to me on my bed. "You're fine. There's nothing wrong with the way you talk."

"I jus' wanna be like e'eryone else." I swiped at the tears sliding down my cheeks and looked at Sawyer. "I'm tired of bein' different."

He took a deep breath. "OK," he said.

"Will ya teach me how to talk like ya?"

Sawyer nodded. "We'll start tomorrow."

"Thanks."

* * *

"Hey, you cool?" Foster tapped my leg to get my attention.

I realized I'd been staring at the door. "Yeah." I looked at Foster and nodded. "I'm just a little tired, I guess."

"What happened to the guy with all the stamina?" he teased, splashing me gently. His smile faded when I didn't respond to his taunt. "Isaac, you sure you're OK?"

"Yeah, I'm alright, ya ain't got nothin' to worry 'bout."

"There's that accent again. Where's that from?"

I shook my head and stood up, grabbing a towel and stepping out of the tub. "I'm gonna call it a night. Alex and I have a big day tomorrow." I needed to get out of there before I revealed more than I already had.

"I'll call my sister tomorrow and ask her about the ski camp," Foster said.

"Yeah, just let me know so I can tell Sawyer."

"Thanks."

"You bet." I wrapped the towel around my waist and headed toward the house.

"Good night, Isaac," Foster called as I closed the sliding door behind me.

Once in my room, I grabbed the pillow from the bed, covered my face, and screamed. The cushion barely muffled the sound of my frustration.

I heard someone on the stairs, too heavy to be Alex. They stopped in front of my bedroom, their shadow visible in the space under the door, and stayed there for a couple of minutes. I walked to the door and opened it.

Foster jumped, a look of shock quickly replaced by one of

concern. "I just want to make sure you're fine, man," he said. "Sorry if I said something that upset you."

"You didn't. I just have a lot on my mind."

"Wanna talk about it?" His voice was low, dripping with hesitation. "Do you want me to leave?"

I didn't move, afraid to say anything.

Foster came inside the room and closed the door behind him. "Hey, it's OK."

He leaned against the door and I moved closer to him, bringing our foreheads together. I closed my eyes, inhaling his scent, cologne mixed with chlorine. His breath fanned my lips; I detected a hint of alcohol and coffee. I opened my eyes and found his blue eyes boring into mine. "Please stay?" I begged, because the last thing I wanted was to be alone.

Twenty: Isaac

Game of Inches

"Something's bothering you, Isaac. Would you like to share? I'm a pretty good listener."

"No. What I need is something different," I said, pushing him hard, pressing his back against the door. "Can we just do this?" I reached into his wet briefs. Both of us were still wearing what we had on in the hot tub, and I wondered why we hadn't gone in the buff to begin with.

"Mmmm. That feels good," Foster moaned.

"You like that?" I asked, gripping his growing cock. I cupped his balls and slowly moved my palm up the side of his cock, stopping at the head and giving it a gentle squeeze. "Impressive. Probably a good thing I'm a top, wouldn't you say?"

"Still on that, are we?" Foster said. "What would you do if I actually said go for it?" He pushed his cock hard against my hand, moving his hips forward.

I grabbed his hand and moved it to my erection. "I'd say this." He let out a soft chuckle at the feel of my throbbing dick. "See the effect you have on me? Just the idea of topping the king of the slopes makes me hard as fuck."

"So you want to put this," he squeezed my cock again, "into

my virgin ass? Is that what you're thinking about, rookie?"

"Hey, it's not my fault your ass looks so enticing. Don't tell me you weren't showing it off in the locker room earlier. Come on, dude, I can take an obvious hint." I nuzzled my face into the crook of his neck. "You'll like it," I whispered, twisting my fingers over his slick pre-cum, enjoying when he tensed.

"OK then, show me how much you want it."

I moved my lips to his and darted my tongue across the soft skin, slowly parting them so I could taste his sweet velvet. He opened willingly and we explored one another, savoring each other's flavor. The kiss became more intimate; the manhandling stopped and our connection deepened. It was sensual, tender. The feeling was overwhelming and unexpected. *Foster Donovan is a romantic?* "That was incredible," I whispered, after pulling back and staring directly into his cool blue eyes.

"Then why did you stop?" His thumb traced my lips. "Kissing might make me more pliable, if you get my drift." He dropped his hand and returned my gaze. He was extraordinary, even in the dimly lit room. Seeing him naked again stirred feelings deep within my soul. It wasn't a feeling I was accustomed to either. I felt weak. My heart thumped harder.

"There's...there is just..." My words were getting jumbled and stuck in my throat. "I can't explain what you do to me, Foster." I knew I wanted him. My body ached with a desire that told me to take him, control him, and make him mine. I desperately wanted my cock buried in his ass, but there was another gnawing desire as well, and that was what made my heart pulse as hard as my dick.

He pushed down on my shoulders and lowered his eyes to his erect cock. "Don't overthink it, Isaac. Show me what your words can't explain." He pulled his briefs down to his knees and leaned back against the door.

I found myself sinking to my knees with no hesitation. I placed my hands under his sack and squeezed gently as I brought my mouth to his cock, slowly taking him in.

"Yes, that's it. I'm hearing you now." He held the sides of my face and guided his cock in and out of my hungry mouth. "You *do* like me, Mac, don't you?" I had to laugh at that sweet joke, but all I accomplished was a stifled gurgle due to the nine inches of meat in my throat. "Swallow every inch, rookie, and if you're really good, I might consider sitting on yours."

I lost my shit at that comment. I had mad cock-sucking skills, in my opinion, but I would have to perform like I did on the slopes if I hoped to win the ultimate award: his sexy ass.

I pulled my mouth off the joystick and slid his briefs to his ankles, tapping on them so he would step out. "You might wanna sit down for this then, big talker," I said. I stood and led him to the edge of the bed. I spied my duffel bag a couple of feet away. Good. It would come in handy should I get the ultimate prize tonight. I pointed at the bed. "Sit."

"Yes, sir." He half laughed. "I like that tone, Mac. You have my permission to keep that the fuck up as long as you want. How do you want me? Ass up already, or maybe some more head first?" He stood there naked, full mast and ready to sail. His strong legs were ripped, the moonlight filtering through the window reflected their muscled edges. My eyes moved to his obliques, sharp as knives sticking out of his sides and supporting an impossibly perfect six-pack. "You like what you see?" he asked, staring at me as if he actually needed me to confirm that he was flawless in every physical way.

"You're beautiful, Foster." It came out before I had road-tested it in my mind. "I mean, like, really fucking hot." My cheeks flushed. I wasn't sure why I was embarrassed by calling him beautiful, maybe it was too soppy or sentimental. But he *was* beautiful.

"That's the sweetest thing anyone's ever said to me." His words cracked with sincerity. "Now, how do you want me?"

I motioned for him to be seated. He sank onto the edge of the bed. I stood motionless save for my eyes, which moved slowly across his nakedness, stopping at my favorite locations. He brought his hands to rest on his knees, slightly obscuring himself from my gaze. "Are you being shy?" I asked. "You shouldn't be, Foster."

"I bet you say that to all the boys, Mac." In a wondrous show of teasing, he leaned back on the bed and brought his hands over his head. The muscles on his body were taut and stretched. His flat stomach showed the years of grueling training a world-class athlete suffers through. Slowly, he spread his legs, and his balls hung heavy between them. When he flexed his erection, I was reminded that I had a duty to fulfill.

"Very subtle, Donovan." I smirked.

"Well, what does it take for a guy to get attention around here?"

"Trust me, you have my attention," I growled. "Question is, do you want *all* of my attention?"

"Get back to sucking and then I'll let you know, Mac. Pretty please?"

I yanked my briefs off and spat in my hand before slowly bringing it to my cock, rubbing and pulling back and forth. I stared at him as he watched the show.

His face was blank. My feelings were momentarily hurt, but

then he licked his lips. "Come here," he said, using his head to motion to me. "Let me see what I'm up against?"

My cock was still firmly in my grip. I squeezed its length and grinned at him as I took a few steps. "You should probably take an oral measurement. You of all people understand the game of inches. One or two more or less can end up being disastrous. But lucky for you, Foster, I am very patient when awarded with something as hot as your sweet ass."

He sat up and slid to the edge of the bed and pulled my hips forward, bringing my cock into his mouth. He gently rolled his tongue over it and bobbed up and down, taking his sweet time absorbing its length. Pushing me back, he let my dick fall out of his mouth, and looked up at me. "Darn!"

"What? What's darn?" I asked, worried he was changing his mind.

"I think you're a quarter-inch longer than me. You know how I hate coming in second." He massaged my balls, still looking into my eyes.

"Then make an exception."

He moved my cock into his mouth again and worked me over aggressively. He slobbered and stroked. He let it rest fully in his throat before coming back up for air.

"Fuuuck! That is so good. What other tricks you got?"

He moved his feet off the floor and twisted around so he was lying on his back, his head now at the foot of the bed and his feet pointed at the headboard. "Let me show you." He scooted down toward me and dangled his head off the edge of the bed. "Fuck my mouth first and we'll see how you like that."

"You're a little nastier than I imagined," I said.

"Good! How about you join me there then? What do you think, big guy?" He reached up and pulled me closer to the bed, his nose now under my balls. "Now follow my lead and fuck my throat."

I was hot as fuck by then. He was enjoying this game of cat and mouse, and so the fuck was I. I leaned forward and placed my hands on his chest and drove my dick into his throat. It was like a standing sixty-nine. I had never done this before, and Foster was clearly enjoying exposing me to a few of his tricks. As I fucked his throat, he had one hand on his own cock, stroking it slowly, working it to the point that his head was swollen. He was turned on by what we were doing, and it motivated me to get into the spirit of giving. If he was so willing to be this exposed, I could certainly return the favor. I slid my hands down his chest to his tight stomach and brushed his hand away, taking full control of his cock. Every pump of my hips got him a nice long tug.

After a minute or two, I brought one knee up on the bed, then the other, and placed my mouth on him. We worked on each other's cocks while moaning and writhing. He brought his hands to my ass and pulled me harder into him as he moved up and down, fucking me with his mouth. I had never experienced such raw and animalistic sex in my life.

"Jesus! You are amazing," I said. "This is too fucking hot."

"I'm worked up too. Might be a good time to try to...you know," he said. I stood and came around to the side of the bed while he slid back on it. I straddled him and leaned forward, kissing him passionately. He had his hands on my hips and was pumping his cock against me. We rubbed and ground into each other. I could feel his swollen cock under my ass crack. My usual reaction at the first sign of someone knocking on my do-not-enter door would be to get away immediately, but somehow, I felt safe with Foster. That didn't mean I wanted to bottom, but I wasn't completely weirded out by it.

"Roll over." I tapped his hip and moved off him. His eyes widened. "I'm going to introduce you to something. Remember, I've been cooperative so far too." Silently, he rolled over and positioned himself in the center of the bed. His head was still while his eyes followed my movements. I stood and leaned over for my duffel bag, unzipping an inside pocket where I kept my travel lube for jerking off. It could get lonely on the road, and a guy's gotta do what a guy's gotta do. I also retrieved a condom...just in case. Fingers crossed.

"Uh-oh," Foster said, lifting his head up and watching me. "This shit is getting real."

I got serious for a moment. "I'd really like to be the one," I whispered.

"Well, if there *is* going to be a first, you're a great choice, I'd say." His eyes softened; his cockiness gone. He trusted me. "I'm serious, Mac. I have always been curious about it, but never found that certain guy I felt had the ability to top me. I think I may have found that now."

"I'll take it easy."

"Not too easy, OK? I actually want to be properly fucked if you're gonna do it."

I knelt on the bed and moved a knee over the top of him. My weight relaxed into him as I lowered myself onto his back. I put my mouth beside his neck and nibbled on him as I pressed my hips into him more aggressively. His hands were lying palms-down above his head, so I intertwined mine with his as I continued to grind.

"I always think this position is a good starting point."

"Like I said, I'm trusting you. It's not like I haven't been in this position before, just never underneath," Foster said, spreading his legs ever so slightly. He had been in my position before, and now it would be up to me to make this experience a good one.

"I'm going to lube up and fuck you without penetrating, is that OK?"

"Always been one of my fave moves," he said, a little shakily but pushing his muscular bubble butt against my cock. I reached for the lube and lathered my cock generously, then placed it between his butt cheeks and moved my cock between his legs. His back was strong and tapered to an impossibly lean waist, before rising up to two perfectly round mounds of pleasure. I liked how athletic Foster felt under me. I preferred masculine bottoms, and he was the finest example I'd ever been with. The thought of being in him had me near orgasm already. I'd have to take my time if I wanted to actually get to the point of penetration—I could blow my load now if I wasn't careful.

Once I was pumping up and down on him, he began to relax, and he pushed his ass up trying to get the tip of my dick to hit the underside of his balls. "Fucking hot, Mac. So far, so good. You feel amazing. Let's try some tip."

I wanted to laugh and say, *Just the tip?,* but it didn't suit the moment. The scene was hot, and he was moaning and grinding, but still I felt like we were embarking on a more personal journey. My desire to be inside him came from a different place. I was hot as fuck for him, yet I wanted to protect him and proceed carefully so as not to hurt him. I wasn't used to these dueling feelings. "You sure you're up to this?" I asked.

"It just feels right. *Right* time, *right* guy, so how about *right* now? You're not going soft on me, are you?" he asked.

I jammed into his butt cheeks. "What do you think?" I sat up, straddling the back of his thighs, and eyed the impressive ass underneath me. This was going to be heaven; for my cock *and* my heart. I reached down and placed a hand on each of his ass cheeks, massaging and kneading them. I slid my hand between his cheeks and rubbed on his balls, stroking the sensitive skin between them and his hole. I could sense his body tense, so I took my time, making sure to bring pleasure to this new experience.

"That's hot. Keep that up and I'm going to sit on your cock."

I lubed two fingers and circled around his hole, teasing it and applying a bit of pressure between circles. I let a finger push in a bit and left a bit more lube after every exploration. "Feel OK?" I asked, squeezing his ass cheeks with one hand while probing his hole with the other.

"Feels amazing. Reach under my nuts and rub my cock too."

I liked his eager participation and willingness to try this. I slid my hand under his balls and searched until I grasped his cock that was pressed against the bedspread. I began to stroke him and apply pressure at the same time. He lifted his butt up and rubbed against my hand that held his cock while I circled his hole, still probing. I took my time as I tried to get him worked up and receptive to more.

"Deeper," he moaned. "That feels fucking great, Mac. Keep rubbing my cock. It makes me want you in me even more. I am learning some killer shit by doing this, man." He writhed and began to buck his hips as the first finger went through the tight passage. "Fuuuck. Unreal. Keep going further, stay on my dick too though."

"You like that, huh? Good, because I have a thick dick coming next. Work with me and open that asshole up." I brought a second finger to the party and began to swirl it around the other. I moved them in, up to the second knuckle and held my breath. I knew we were near the make-or-break moment. This wasn't my first virgin. Was it my last? *Stop that, Isaac. This is purely about his ass. That's all it is.*

"How many?" he asked, still pumping his ass up and welcoming the invasion.

"Two."

"Grab a condom and lube up your dick, Mac. It's showtime. Now or it's not happening."

He didn't have to ask me twice. I had the condom in my mouth and tore open the packet before he took another breath. I slid it over my swollen cock and applied more lube. I remained straddled on the backs of his thighs and leaned forward slightly, using one hand next to his hip to support my weight, before pointing my cock's head toward his slathered-up hole. I dropped my hips and pressed my head against his opening.

"Nice and easy, baby," he whispered. This was happening. I pushed and he lifted up, equal pressures trying to reach the same goal. We both knew that getting past the first tightness was the main battle. After that, it was all about relaxing and getting used to it. "Ohhh...slow," he whispered breathlessly.

"Relax. I'm in, and it's time to see how much you can take. I'll be patient." I placed my other hand to the other side of his head. I was now in a push-up stance as I looked down and watched my cock sliding slowly into his ass. I pushed an inch and then pulled out an inch, careful to slowly dip deeper into him when I pushed in again. "You're fucking tight. I love it too. You should see my cock going in and out your hot fucking ass. It looks amazing, and it feels even better."

"Give me more. Deeper. You feel amazing inside of me. I can't fucking believe I am doing this."

"You OK?" I asked.

"Oh, trust me, I am better than just OK. Stay focused on the ass you're drilling." He spread his legs wider and curved his ass up, opening as wide as he could. "Come on, all of it!" he growled. "This feels so good, and your dick is so huge, but I love it. Give it all to me."

I pushed deeper and then retreated. Over and over, an inch at a time, until I was completely inside him. I relaxed onto him and let my entire weight rest while my cock stayed motionless, expanding and pulsing inside his hungry ass. "I'm all the way in, stud. How's it feeling?"

"Surprisingly, it's amazing, unreal. I cannot believe this is happening. How does it feel for you?" he asked. I turned my head sideways to where his face was visible. He attempted to catch my eye and I moved my mouth to his. Tenderly kissing him was the best way to answer his question. We kissed as I remained buried in him, not moving, just allowing him to get comfortable. Slowly, I began to move in and out.

He reached back and used his hands to pull his cheeks apart. "I want all of you."

I pushed as deep as I could, and we began to move in synchronicity. I plunged deeper, and he received and pushed back harder.

He reached his hand underneath himself and started rubbing his cock. "I could fucking come, this feels so goddamn good. Who fucking knew?"

"Don't come yet. I want to watch your face as we climax," I said, pulling out of him.

"Aww, I was just starting to enjoy that."

"You'll like this too. Roll over," I said, standing up and moving to the end of the bed. He rolled over and I grabbed his ankles and yanked him to where I stood. His ass was right on the edge as I held his legs against my chest.

His eyes widened and he looked frightened, shocked, surprised, maybe all three. "Holy shit, Mac. You're strong. Am I in trouble?" he asked, smirking like a Cheshire cat. "Because I sure hope so."

I held his ankles to spread his legs apart. "Maybe. Let's see how you like it from this angle." I pushed my dick down and brought it to his sexy hole and entered him slowly, not stopping until I was completely sheathed.

He grimaced at first but relaxed and smiled. "Still fits," he smirked, pulling the backs of his knees to his chest and exposing his asshole fully to me. "Let's go, handsome. Show me how to top."

That was all I needed to hear. I leaned forward and pressed myself against him. He released his legs, and I placed his ankles on my shoulders and started pumping my hips. He opened his eyes and watched as I concentrated on his ass, watching my expressions when his body tightened around me. Our mouths were slack with ecstasy as we locked eyes. His six-pack flexed, and he pulled my hips. He bit his lip while turning his head to the side, breaking our gaze, and closed his eyes as I thrust into him. My pace was gentle and slow at first, and when he spread his legs wider and scooted toward me in between pumps, I took his cue and gave him every single inch of my cock.

"Fuck, man! Do not stop!" he moaned, eyes still closed as I pushed forward, pressing his knees deeper against his chest.

"You like that, don't you?" I asked. "I'm impressed with your skill sets, Foster. Who would have thought?"

"Yeah, whatever. Keep pounding on me. You're rubbing against something in my ass. I've heard a bottom or three mention this before. Holy shit! There! Yes, keep it right there. Fuuuuuuuuck!" His eyes popped open, and I watched sheer pleasure pass over them. He grabbed the back of his knees and yanked them tight against his chest. His teeth gritted. "Yes! Keep going. Harder. Faster. Deeper. Oh fuck, Mac. This is incredible."

His eyes rolled back, and he grabbed his cock and started jacking on it aggressively. "You like that cock in your ass, Donovan? You like being topped now?" I wasn't sure where my words were coming from, but I was hot watching him lose his mind over being fucked.

"Yeah! I fucking love your dick in me. I was right." He looked directly into my eyes. "I knew you'd be great, Mac. I wanted to feel you inside me. I fucking knew it."

"I'm getting close," I said, pulling my length out and watching his eyes beg me to keep going. "You ready to be fucked harder?"

He shook his head and closed his eyes. "Yes," he whimpered.

I picked up the pace and got off watching his face morph with pleasure, sending me closer to the edge. He started moving his head in time to my thrusts. He was moaning and whimpering unintelligible words, and I could only make out a few of them.

"Holy shit. Fuck me. That spot, that spot." His eyes opened again and they rolled into the back of his head. He was jacking his dick with all he had.

"I am gonna come," I growled between gritted teeth. I was torn between watching my cock going in and out of his ass, and watching him squirm with pleasure under me.

"Keep going. I can come at any second. Jesus, keep hitting

that spot in my ass. I love it. Fuck!"

He returned his eyes to mine, and we watched each other as we soared through the hot, crazy, wonderful sex. "I...am...
" I held my breath and felt the load churning up my shaft, "gonna shoot my load!" My body tensed and I dove as deep as I could into Foster's ass while he jerked his cock. My heart pounded and I was hit with dizziness as I gasped to catch my breath. Bright, dark spots danced in front of my vision when I exploded.

Now it was his turn. I refocused on him as a look of pure pleasure spread across his face. "Yes, that's it! Yes! Holy shit, yes!" He stiffened and his ass gripped my cock. I watched his load spill across his stomach as he let out guttural sounds of bliss.

He looked up at me and smiled. "That's some shit there, Mac," he gasped. "Thank you. Tru–truly, the single hottest sex I have ever had." He reached up and wiped the sweat off my brow.

I smirked and collapsed onto him, kissing him until our lips were numb.

Twenty-One: Foster

Your Guy

I t was clear that something was still bothering Isaac.

He was quiet as we lay in the aftermath of another first—well, for me at least. I had never imagined myself submitting to anyone, but I felt safe with him. I trusted my instinct and went for it, and was rewarded with an experience I would never forget. I'd never been fucked, but the ecstasy of it was worth the soreness in my ass. I was surprised I lasted as long as I did.

I was lying on his chest, his arm wrapped around my neck. "I should head back to my room," I said, and attempted to sit up, but Isaac's hold on me tightened. Whatever he was going through lingered even after we'd pleasured each other. God, I hoped he was trying to find the courage to open up about what had upset him. But an explanation never came. Instead, we held each other in silence.

Isaac's breathing slowed and deepened, and I gently peeled his arm off me. I waited before swinging my legs over the side of the bed. I watched him, mesmerized by this beautiful, peculiar and intense man. I was torn between kissing him one more time and risking waking him up, or just letting him be.

In the end, I put on my underwear and headed out. I glanced at him one last time before turning the light off. "Goodnight, Big Mac."

* * *

Isaac and Alex were gone when I made my way to the kitchen the following morning. I'd purposely woken up earlier than usual to see Isaac before he headed up to the slopes, but I was still too late. At least the coffee was done.

"Hey, Red," I said when my sister picked up her phone. I wanted to gauge her interest in the ski camp before I asked Mom about it.

"Hi, Oz. Did you tell your friend you like him?" she asked.

"Not yet, but I'm calling to ask you something."

"OK, what is it?"

"Do you like to ski?" My question sounded odd considering my dad and I lived and breathed skiing, but I felt awful that I had never once asked her if she liked it.

"Like watching you?" she asked.

Her response was like someone stabbing a dull knife into my chest. Did I really make everything about me? "No, not watching me, but do *you* like to ski?" I took a deep breath, hoping she couldn't hear the shakiness in my voice.

"Um…I don't know how."

I placed my phone on my chest and pinched the bridge of my nose. This was fucking insane. Dad and I were world-class skiers and we never taught Sophia how.

"Oz, are you mad at me?" she asked, her voice breaking.

150

"No, not at all. I'm disappointed that I didn't teach you."

"It's OK, you're busy. I understand."

I didn't deserve her kindness. "No, it's not OK. Would you like to learn how?"

"Yes!"

"Do you want to go to a ski camp with other teenagers?" I hoped she'd say yes.

"Do you think Mom and Dad will let me?" Sophia sounded worried. They were overprotective of her, but I would try everything I could to convince them.

"I'm sure they will. I'll be there too."

"You will? That's gonna be so much fun!" she squealed.

"OK, I'll text Mom. I'm sorry I didn't ask you sooner."

"It's OK, Oz, you're still my favorite person."

"And you're mine. I'll talk to you later."

I texted Mom straight away. *Is it OK if I take Sophia to Oregon next week for two nights?* I pressed send and followed it up with *Please.* I needed to make things right with my sister.

My phone pinged. I said a silent prayer before I opened the message.

Mom: *Of course, she'd love that.*

"Yes!" I grabbed one of my insulated portable coffee cups and filled it with black coffee with a little sugar. I wanted to tell Isaac the good news straight away.

* * *

I was prepared to sweet-talk the club manager of the Palisade Ski Resort to let me hit up the slopes, but instead he gave me full access. "Just let me know if you need anything, Mr. Donovan," he said, handing me a pass for the entire week. There were some upsides to fame.

"I will. Thank you. Do you know if McAllister is still up there?"

He looked at his computer monitor and clicked a few keys. "Yes. They have it reserved until ten o'clock."

I glanced at my watch and found he had forty minutes left. Maybe they'd like to go out for lunch. "Thanks," I said, before heading out to take the next chair lift to the summit.

Palisade in Lake Tahoe was one of my favorite slopes, not only for the quality of the snow but its location. When the gondola lifted me higher, I was awed by the lake that sparkled like a sapphire in a blanket of white snow that covered the town.

"Hey guys, it's Foster Donovan," someone yelled.

So much for my beanie-and-tinted-snow-glasses disguise. I waved to the group of skiers, thankful the club wasn't open to the public as it was reserved for competitors. The news of my presence traveled like wildfire. Phones and cameras were aimed in my direction as I made my way to the ski launch.

"Congrats on your World Cup win," someone else shouted.

I nodded to acknowledge him.

"Go Canada," a female voice screamed. That got Alex and Isaac's attention, as they glanced in my direction.

Isaac took his goggles off and rested them on his head. His light-brown eyes were questioning as I approached. "What's up?" he asked.

"Hey," I said, unsure if I should shake his hand or hug him. Instead, I turned my attention to Alex. "How's our guy?" I asked her.

"I'm sorry, *your* guy?" Isaac smirked and crossed his arms, his biceps flexing in his speed suit.

"I didn't say *my* guy, I said *our* guy. Geez, is *our guy* a little slow this morning?" I winked at Alex and returned my gaze to Isaac. "Do you need more coffee?" I offered my cup to him. "Thanks for this, by the way."

"Trust me, *our guy* isn't slow this morning." Alex hooked a thumb at Isaac. "He just did this." She showed me her phone displaying Isaac's training time.

I blinked to make sure I was seeing correctly. Fuck! That was identical to my time when I raced these slopes years ago: *1:28.38*. "Is this today?" I asked.

"Yup," she said, her grin widening.

Whatever. Practice is different from a race. And it was. It was much tougher when the stakes were bigger and the pressure was higher.

Isaac was studying me.

"Good," I said, because I didn't know what else to say.

"What are you doing up here?" he asked.

"I was here to let you know that Sophia is all in if Sawyer doesn't mind."

"Great, I'll let him know. Are you coming too?" he asked.

"Do you want me to?" I teased and took a sip of my coffee. That earned me a chuckle from Alex.

"Oh, I just need to know so Sawyer can plan and reserve extra rooms," he said. "You can go if you want, or just Sophia. I just figured, you know…you said." His face turned red and he stopped rambling. He put his goggles back on.

"If it means that much to you, I'll go," I said, holding a laugh.

"Whatever," he whispered.

Alex snickered. "Are you ready?" she asked Isaac.

He nodded and placed his ski poles in front of him, gliding his skis back and forth. He leaned forward before gripping his poles tightly.

"Remember what I said?" Alex asked him, and I was amazed how quickly she turned serious. "If you can nail that turn, you can shave a thirtieth of a second, a twentieth at minimum."

Isaac nodded and fist-bumped Alex.

"We're about to launch," she said to the guy above us controlling the cameras.

"Ready." Isaac stretched his neck left then right.

"Go!" Alex yelled and tapped Isaac's butt, and off he went.

Alex and I looked up at the screen above. She was biting her thumb as she twisted and turned her body in time with Isaac.

Isaac spent a good amount of time in the air on his first jump. He nailed his landing just in time for the next turn.

"Yes!" Alex yelled, unable to contain her excitement.

Isaac slithered through the slopes turn after turn, jump after jump. He crossed the finish line and the clock stopped. He threw his goggles in the air. "Let's go! Let's go!" he screamed.

Alex nudged me with her elbow and pointed to the screen with Isaac's time. "I think you finally have some competition." She winked before snapping her skis to her boots. "Wanna go for an early lunch?

"That'd be great," I said.

"See you down there?"

I nodded, and she took off. I stared at the monitor with Isaac's face on the screen and the time *1:28.21* below him. He just skied almost a twentieth of a second faster than me.

Are you going to wait until you win silver? Dad's voice echoed in my head.

Twenty-Two: Isaac

Isaac for the Gold

I was so thankful my little injury from two days ago didn't prevent me from training this morning, or worse, cause me to pull out of the race. These were some of the best times I'd ever recorded, even after Foster's impromptu visit. He'd been invading my mind since I woke; I was still reeling from the mind-blowing connection we shared last night. The ecstasy on his face as my cock went in and out of his tight hole made me come harder than I ever had.

I looked up at the scoreboard one more time to stay in the present and shake those memories from last night while I was in the middle of the slopes with a speed suit on. I didn't want to be on TMZ, the subject of some perverted meme.

"Woohoo! That was phenomenal, Mac!" Alex yelled as she skied down the hill. She hugged me and whispered in my ear, "See what happens when you listen to me."

"Maybe," I teased.

"One more day before the race. Let's keep trying our best. We got this, Mac!" She lifted her head up and raised her ski poles in the air, mouthing *thank you* repeatedly.

It was then I realized how much this meant to her too. *A*

female coaching a male skier is almost as elusive as a glitter-winged unicorn, and if you happen to see one, they get blamed for lost races. She told me once. I loved working with Alex. I never thought I would, not because she was a woman but because I'd never worked with anyone other than my pop. Working with a new coach was always going to be a learning curve.

"One more day," I said, echoing her sentiment.

"I asked Foster to lunch. I hope that's OK," she said when we reached the edge of the slope and unbuckled our skis.

"Oh, cool. Should we go to a buffet?" I teased, knowing she wouldn't recommend feasting until after the race

"Um, no," she said. "But could you imagine how stuffy Foster would be? I bet you he's never set foot in a buffet in his life." She laughed good-naturedly.

"He's not that bad." I felt the need to defend him. "He's actually a cool guy."

Alex put her hand on my shoulder and squeezed it. "Mac, I'm kidding. Are you two...you know?"

"Nope," I said, shaking my head. "We're not...you know." Another shake of my head. "Nope. Nuh-uh."

"OK, I get it. He's not *your guy*." She winked.

"We need to change if we're going to lunch," I said, changing the subject and pulling open the door to the club.

"I got us a reservation at The Summit. It's the steakhouse by the lake. Hope that's OK," Foster said when we met him inside.

"Told you no buffet," Alex whispered and chuckled. "Let me go change."

"What was that about?" Foster asked once she was gone.

"She's just being silly, happy with our training today. You know, breaking your record from three years ago and all."

156

"Well," Foster started. "You know they don't actually record training times, only race times. Still good though." He clapped my shoulder before wrapping his arm around it.

"Luckily for you they don't."

"Oh, sick burn!" he exclaimed. Then he lowered his voice. "You need to change, don't you?"

I looked around to make sure no one was listening. "You're not going to take advantage of me while we're in there, are you?"

"Do you want me to?" he purred.

"It depends. What time is our reservation?"

Foster glanced at his watch. "We have thirty minutes."

We hurried toward the locker room and split up to check that no one else was around. Foster opened some of the stalls, and I did the same. The club was reserved for racers and the next group wouldn't be here for another hour or so.

"Clear," Foster said, running to meet me on the other side of the room.

"Here too," I confirmed, and started unzipping my suit from behind.

Foster pushed me to the wall and kissed me without finesse. "Why are you still dressed?" he asked, the unbuckling of his belt echoing through the empty locker room.

"Ahhhh," I groaned when he grasped my hard-on. I cupped his face to kiss his lips, his jaw, and back to his lips before I slipped my hand in his pants and ran my hand down the length of his cock. I looked down and was greeted by the head of his dick glistening with pre-cum. I used my thumb to rub circles on the tip.

"Fuck, that feels good." He closed his eyes and tilted his head back, murmuring incoherent words. He was a goner, and I

157

loved that I had that effect on him.

I licked his neck between nips. My desire for Foster was off the chain. "Look at me," I ordered, and when his glassy eyes met mine, I lifted my thumb covered with his pre-cum and stuck it in my mouth.

"Jesus," he murmured. "Why do you still have clothes on, damn it. Take them off."

"You're so impatient." I pulled his hair gently, exposing more of his neck, and bit the skin behind his ear. He let out a whimper. "What's the rush, baby?"

"I'm not your baby, I'm your daddy, remember?" he asked, pinning my body harder against the wall. He pulled back a little so he could pull his cock out of his pants.

"Hey guys, are you in here?" Alex's voice served as a cold shower.

"Fucking cock-blocker," he cursed, and zipped up his pants. "You need to fire her immediately."

I shushed him with a kiss. "Yes, we're here," I called.

"Great timing too," Foster added, and I shook my head.

"Alright, well hurry up," she replied.

Foster peeled himself off me and headed toward the door. "See you out there."

"Wait, you're not gonna stay with me?"

"Nope. No more incentive for me," he joked and exited the locker room.

* * *

"OK, I have to bounce," Alex said after the waiter cleared our table of plates.

"We haven't even had dessert yet," Foster protested, flashing Alex his dashing smile in hopes of making her stay. It didn't work on Alex, but it definitely worked on me.

"You guys enjoy. I have a video conference with the association to give them a progress report. Sorry to dine and dash." She winked at me before tapping Foster's shoulder on her way out.

There was something I had been meaning to ask Foster that had gnawed on me since our night together in Aspen. "Is any of that true?" I asked him when Alex was gone.

"Any of what?" He placed the dessert menu on the table before looking at me.

"You know…what they say about you in the media. That you only date famous people."

"Was that the interview in *Ski Monthly* magazine?"

I nodded and waited for his response.

"I hate that interview. They took some of the things I said completely out of context."

"So, is it true?"

The coffee we ordered arrived and Foster took a sip before answering. "Yes," he admitted, and my stomach dropped. "But not for the reason you think." A small part of me sparked with hope. "I said I prefer going out with celebrities because they know the pressure of being in the public eye all the time. The scrutiny, the hassles, all of it. They know how to deal with the barrage of misinformation. It's exhausting sometimes, you know. People taking pictures of you all the time, and sometimes they heckle you to evoke a reaction. Same reason I don't go out with family and friends unless I know it's somewhat private. I won't subject them to that. So I said

I prefer dating celebrities because they understand." Foster sighed and leaned back in his chair. His eyes narrowed and his jaw tensed. "But it's a small price to pay, and the reward is you stay relevant. Some people love to build you up so they can tear you apart."

"That's good to know. Thank you for sharing that."

"All that just to say, don't believe everything you hear or read about me in the media. If you want to know anything, just ask me. I'll help you navigate this fun and crazy world. What's important is that you be yourself and live your truth. I won't lie to you."

I admired Foster's honesty, and I felt a sense of shame hiding my past from him. What would he think about me if he knew? Would he still find me interesting? He said to be myself and live my truth. *Tell him now*, my heart said. *Don't do it*, my head argued.

*   *   *

Race day came without any hitches; the weather was perfect, with no delays this time. We'd skipped training yesterday to prevent fatigue, but Alex still made me do a complete body workout with less weight to avoid injuries.

"Ready?" Foster asked after helping Alex and I load my gear in the back of his SUV.

"Ready as I'll ever be," I said, ignoring the pre-competition jitters that coursed through me. You'd think I'd be used to it by now, but the older I got and the longer I stayed in the circuit, the stronger the nerves became. *It means ya care about yer race.* Ma's words played in my head. I made a mental note to call them after the event because it had been a few days since the last time I spoke with them. I didn't even call my pop for a pre-race pep talk. I had a lot on my mind, especially one six-foot-tall man who was currently staring at me.

"You got this, Mac," Alex said, putting her hands on my shoulders. "It's the same course, and if you can do what you did in practice, you're going to be fine."

"We got this," I agreed, hugging her.

I glanced at Foster, who was watching my interaction with Alex intently, but he turned away when he saw me looking. He cleared his throat. "Show 'em what you got," he said.

I opened the back-seat door to let Alex in and I hopped in the passenger seat.

"Let's do this!" Foster climbed in the driver's seat and we took off.

"Our fans are treated with great weather here in Lake Tahoe and the presence of a superstar," the announcer said as the camera swept across the stunning view of Lake Tahoe below to find Foster among the crowd of cheering fans. "You're not seeing things, people. That man right there on your screen is the one and only Foster Donovan Jr."

Alex inspected my skis for the final time, and when she was satisfied, I latched them onto my boots. She handed me my poles and looked up at the screen to check if the last skier had cleared the finish line so I could launch.

"Hey," I called to get her attention. "I got this."

"I know you do. Whatever happens today, I want you to know I'm proud of what you've accomplished this week."

"Thank you."

"We have one final skier left, and all eyes are on the

161

American, Isaac McAllister. Let me tell you, folks, this guy is on everyone's radar right now. And you'll know what I'm talking about in a minute." The television announcer launched into a spiel about my practice times this week, but I stopped paying attention. This was about today, nothing else.

I waited for the bell to ring and the signal to light. The cold winter wind pierced my face like tiny ice picks, but I was made for this. Putting my mental blinders on, I tuned out everyone and focused on three things.

The slopes.

The track.

My victory.

My surroundings quieted; my vision focused. *Just like practice.*

Beep. Beep. Beep. I took off after the third beep, and all I could see was white. I let gravity and the weight of my past pull me as I maneuvered a series of turns while keeping my balance and pace.

I made a small mistake after coming out of the first corner, but I didn't panic. One of my strengths was about to be tested. I might not be the best glider in the business, but I made up for it with my jumps. I tucked my poles under my arms and leaped, suspending myself in the air for a hundred feet at almost sixty miles per hour. I didn't have to look at a screen to know my speed, my instinct just knew. Racers could tell their distance and speed just by *feeling*. I couldn't explain it, but I was feeling pretty spectacular right now.

At the halfway point, bells rang and the crowd cheered when I leaned to my side, bringing my body inches from the ground to exit the hairpin turn coming up ahead. And just like practice, I nailed it. One final jump; I gave it all I had and I propelled forward, flying. I landed and skied the last few yards to the finish line as the crowd erupted.

American flags waved while chants reverberated at the bottom of the hill. I crossed the orange line and knew I'd won before I even looked up to check my time.

"He did it! Isaac for the gold!" the announcer's voice echoed in the speakers below. "He was the favorite this week, and man, did he deliver. Isaac McAllister is the 2022 American Cup Champion."

"Yes!" I yelled.

Alex skied over to me, her face wet, and kissed my cheek. "You did it!"

"*We* did it," I corrected, wiping the tears from her cheeks.

I grabbed her hand and lifted it up in the air with mine. I leaned and whispered in her ear, "This is our victory."

"Our victory," she repeated.

I combed the crowd for Foster. I found him on my right, staring at the scoreboard. He glanced in my direction and nodded, before clapping with the raucous fans. He grinned and gave me two thumbs-up, and pointed me back to the screen.

I looked up. Below my name was my time and the words *new record.* I had broken Foster's record from three years ago. Elated as I was, I couldn't help but wonder how that made him feel.

Twenty-Three: Foster

It's a Small World

"Is there something on my face?" I asked Sophia. We were in her bedroom, grabbing her bags and the new pair of skis my parents had bought her when I gave them the specifics of the two-night camp in Portland. I planned on treating it like a getaway with my favorite people. She was contemplating me.

"I didn't know you could whistle," she said, pulling her red backpack onto her shoulders.

Was I? I didn't know I could whistle either. I meant, I did, but that was a different kind of blowing.

"And you look different," she continued, passing me the handle of her rolling luggage, which was also red.

"Like, I look bad or something?" I checked the mirror on her dresser, but aside from my stupid grin, I looked fine. Really fine.

"It's not bad. I actually love it." She chuckled before grabbing my hand and leading me out of her room.

"As long as you love it, then I love it."

Our parents were waiting when we made our way downstairs. They were standing in the middle of the room, arms folded, and I gulped. *They're not changing their minds about Sophia, are they?* My dad's pursed lips and Mom's forced smile didn't scream *bon voyage* either. "Sophia, I want to show you something." Mom took Sophia's hand and led her outside.

"What's up?" I asked Dad when we were alone, the tension between us so thick you could cut it with a butter knife.

"To the study," he said, and walked away before I had a chance to protest. I hated to admit it, but my twenty-six-year-old ass reverted straight back to being a kid once again, afraid of my dad and disappointing him. I used to think he was tough on me because he wanted me to be the best, that he was ultra-strict because he never wanted my focus to wander, and that maybe he'd change when I achieved the goals I'd set for myself. It had been a decade and I was still waiting.

He was looking out the window at the falling snow when I closed the door. I cracked my knuckles, anxiety building inside me. A huge oak desk sat between us, to the left a small bar cart containing his prized vintage scotch collection. He reached for one of the crystal bottles and poured the liquid gold into a matching glass. This drink was offered to his friends and his friends' adult children, but he'd never shared it with me. He plonked two pieces of ice in and swirled the liquid around, before taking a small sip. He returned his gaze to the window, the peaceful scenery juxtaposed by the tension in this room. A heavy sigh escaped him. "What are you doing?"

"Right now, I am just standing here," I said, a smart-ass remark to quell my inner trembling.

He turned to face me, expressionless. That was one of his unique abilities. "You're always full of jokes, aren't you?" he asked, motioning his fingers in the air.

"What do you want, Dad?"

"Why are you wasting precious time before the World Championships?" He sat on the oak chair that matched his desk. "Going to Oregon for a camp?"

"Wasting time? I'm going to spend time with my sister. Do you think that's wasting time?" I fumed, imagining smoke streaming out of my ears.

"That is not what I meant, Foster!" He slammed his glass, hard, on the desk, its content spilling on the smooth, shiny surface.

"Then what do you mean, Dad? You seem to know everything, so educate me. What am I missing now? What did I do that disappointed you this time?"

"Do you have to do that now? Less than a week before the World Championships here in Canada? The world will be watching, the nation will be cheering. The Austrians have been here since last week practicing and what will you be doing? Playing camp like you live on the old prairie?"

"I don't need that kind of preparation, you know that. We've tried it before; it didn't help me then and it won't help me now."

"All I'm saying is it wouldn't kill you to pay more attention to your training. Your inconsistencies—"

"Dad, stop!" I put a hand up. "If you don't have anything good to say, I don't wanna hear it." I looked up to the ceiling, trying to hold back the tears from cascading down my cheeks. "You know what wouldn't kill you?" I asked, pointing my shaking finger at him.

He sat back and placed his elbows on the armrest, his fingertips touching to form a triangle, his stoic face staring at me. The same emotionless gaze I knew all too well.

"It wouldn't kill you to congratulate me when I win. It wouldn't kill you to invite me here for an actual conversation, drinking with you as you do with your friends." The tears fell, but I didn't care now. I didn't care if he thought I was weak. "It wouldn't kill you to finally admit that you despise having your son break all your records."

Bullseye. He took his glasses off and revealed actual emotion on his face. Anger, resentment, sadness. "Is that what you think?"

"Yes, Dad. That's exactly what I think. Now, if you'll excuse me, I have a sister who wants to learn how to ski, and a World Championships to win." I turned on my heel, yanked the door open, and slammed it so hard behind me the walls rattled.

Mom was standing in the hallway when I looked up. One of her hands was on her chest while the other covered her mouth.

"It's OK, Mom." I kissed her forehead and wiped away the smear of streaked mascara.

"You two will have to find a way to be around each other without hurting one another." She held my face. "He loves you. You know that, right?"

I didn't have the energy to deal with that. All I wanted to do was go away with my sister and spend more time with Isaac. "Where's Sophia?"

"In the living room, waiting for you."

"We'll talk later, Mom. We have to go. I love you."

"I love you too, honey. Be safe. Take care of your sister."

I nodded and hugged her one more time, then found Sophia on her phone. I took a deep breath and combed my hair with my hand, hoping she wouldn't notice the pain on my face, because the truth was, I didn't know whether our dad loved me.

*** * * *

My sadness vaporized at the end of our five-hundred-kilometer flight to Oregon. Isaac waved to catch our attention after we grabbed our bags from the luggage carousel.

"Oh my god, that's Isaac McAllister," Sophia said. "He's going to camp with us?"

"He is. How do you know him?" I asked, stacking our luggage. *How did people travel with all this stuff?* I was struggling to carry our bags and Sophia's skis. I needed to pay the team more, this shit was a lot of work.

"I follow him on Instagram and my friends love him. Act cool, he's coming," she whispered.

"You look like you need a hand," Isaac said, and reached for Sophia's skis. "These are yours?" he asked her.

Sophia nodded, giving him the sweetest smile—the one she usually reserved for me. "Red is my favorite color," she said, pointing at her red-trimmed skis.

"I love red too. My name's Isaac." He offered her a hand. "You must be Sophia?"

"Yes, nice to meet you, Isaac McAllister," she said, shaking his hand enthusiastically. The scene made my heart swell.

"You can call me Mac." He winked. "Let's get this party started!"

* * *

Isaac and I loaded all the ski equipment onto the bus that

would take us to Mount Hood, while the kids, around the ages thirteen to nineteen, played inside. Isaac was right, Sophia was in heaven hanging out with other teenagers she had a lot in common with. She wasn't a shy girl, but I'd never seen her this excited before. The guilt of my negligence pinched at me, but there was nothing I could do about *yesterday*, I could only be better *tomorrow*.

Isaac stood close to me, our hands and hips brushed as we packed in our own gear. "You OK?" he asked. "You seem quiet. Where's the loud, obnoxious, suffocatingly cocky Foster? Don't get me wrong, I like this quiet version too, but I want to make sure you're OK."

The urge to kiss him was all-consuming, it took my breath away. "Was that your way of saying you missed me?" Humor was the best defense.

"There you go. Welcome back," he said, slapping my ass and walking to the Jeep that just pulled up.

My gaze followed him and his ass, and I grinned. After closing the bus storage compartment, I looked up and found Sophia peering out the window at me, a huge smile plastered on her angelic face. I blew her an air kiss, and followed Isaac in case he needed help.

A good-looking man with wavy brown hair past his ears hopped out of the Jeep and his eyes widened when he saw me.

Isaac turned and waved me in. He wrapped an arm around my shoulder and introduced me to the man. "Sawyer, this is the guy I was telling you about. Foster, this is my best friend, Sawyer." *So, Isaac had been telling his best friend about me? Interesting.*

"I know *who* Foster Donovan is," Sawyer said, tapping Isaac's arm. "You didn't tell me the guy you were bringing *was* Foster

Donovan! Nice to meet you." He shook my hand.

"Likewise." I smiled at him, trying to make a good impression. "Thank you for accommodating our last-minute self-invitation. Do you ski too, Sawyer?"

"We're happy to have you, and no, I don't ski. I mean, I did when I was younger, that's how I met Isaac, but I don't anymore."

"Oh," I said. Then how did he know my name?

"Travis just told me you won a big tournament," Sawyer said.

"Wait, Travis?" I asked.

"Montgomery. I'm Sawyer Montgomery."

"Holy shit, you're Travis Montgomery's cousin? We go way back! What a small world." I rushed to give Sawyer a hug, forgetting I had Isaac's arm around me.

"Let's get inside the bus. It's cold out here. Another reason I don't like to ski. Too cold."

Isaac and I followed Sawyer. "What are the odds that *your* friend is related to *my* friend?" Isaac said.

"It's crazy, right?" This thing between Isaac and I just kept getting more interesting. *Small world indeed.*

Twenty-Four: Isaac

The Man Behind the Mask

I knew the next two days with Foster would be different from Lake Tahoe. We would be spending almost the entire time together, and the thought made me nervous and excited at the same time. I enjoyed being with him, we always had fun. Even though Foster was cocky, liking him was easy. I just hoped he wouldn't start asking me questions about my past.

"Where are we staying?" Sophia asked once we made our way to the Mount Hood campground. She looked around the rows of log cabins, their roofs covered in snow. The paths to each chalet were plowed with a mixture of sand and salt for traction, and in the middle was a giant campfire made of stones surrounded by Adirondack chairs.

"The campers are staying in that big cabin over there." I pointed to the building in the middle, where most of the teens would sleep accompanied by camp volunteers. "But if you don't want to sleep with the group, you're welcome to sleep with your brother and me."

Foster snapped his head in my direction, flashing me his Hollywood teeth. I hadn't told him that Sawyer booked us a separate cabin so we wouldn't have to sleep with a group of teenagers.

"I want to hang out with the rest of the campers," Sophia said, and looked to Foster. "Is that OK, Oz?"

"Of course you can. Why don't you head over and we'll bring these to you?" He relieved her of her backpack and she took off running. "Please be careful," he called, and Sophia slowed to a walk.

"Oz?" I asked him.

"Yup, that's me. She used to call me that when she was a kid because it took her a while to learn how to say *Foster.*"

"I like it." It was clear that Foster loved his sister; his face brightened when he talked about her. It was another side of him that tugged at my heart. "She's lucky to have a loving brother like you. That's really sweet."

"No one would accuse me of being sweet. Jackass, yes, but sweet, never." He tried to hide his sigh with a chuckle.

"You are sweet, and it's other people's loss if they haven't tried to get to know you better."

"Thanks, but don't go soft on me now." He laughed, but it sounded hollow. "You didn't tell me we were staying together."

I knew he was trying to change the trajectory of our conversation; I was an expert at that. "Oh yeah, I forgot to tell you when you texted me." Warmth spread across my face when Foster raised an eyebrow and smirked. "There are two rooms though, so we are totally separated."

"Oh good, I was *so* worried about that," he joked. "I don't know what we would've done with just one room." His smile didn't reach his eyes.

"Let's check out our home for the next couple of days." I led him to our cabin, the last one near a ravine. The stand of pine trees was blanketed with snow. The door squeaked open and a delicious heat greeted us from the fireplace.

Foster walked around, examining the cabin. "This is quaint," he said as he took in the small room, dropping one of his bags on the leather sofa facing the fire. "With real logs even." He strolled to the fireplace and ran his hand over the mantel made of river rocks. He came full circle to where I stood by the closed door. His questioning blue eyes stared into mine with an expression I couldn't read. His gaze turned fiery, burning hotter the closer he came. He put his hand on my stomach and gently pushed me backward until my back was against the door. "Did you plan this?" he whispered breathily.

I struggled to find words, his touch and presence rendering me useless. I cleared my throat. "Uh, no. I think it came like this."

"Wrong answer." He brushed his lips on mine.

I opened my mouth to invite him in, but he pulled away and I tried to chase his lips.

"We better join everyone and make sure Sophia is OK."

"Uh, yeah," I said, snapping out of my Foster-induced trance.

"Hey." Foster tapped my shoulder on our way to the main cabin. "We can share a room, or I can sleep in the other room. Whatever you're comfortable with."

"OK," I said, disappointed by his lack of enthusiasm. He was off, and I wanted to figure out how to make him feel better.

"OK...so which is it?" he asked.

"Let's share a room," I answered, holding my breath for his response. That must have been the answer he was hoping to hear, because finally he smiled.

* * *

"Welcome everyone!" I addressed the campers gathered around the makeshift classroom that was provided for us. "My name is Mac, and my buddy and I will teach you some safety tips before we start skiing. Because why?"

"Safety first," some of the kids from last year said.

"Exactly. Safety always comes first." I waved at Foster, who was standing by the window and cracking his knuckles, to join me at the front. "This is my good friend, Foster."

"Hi, Foster!" the group said in chorus, including Sophia, who seemed to be having a great time.

"Foster is here to help, so be nice to him so he'll come back next year." I wanted Sophia and Foster to have a great time, and I wanted them to come back. I stepped aside to let him address the campers.

"Hello, everyone," he said, waving to the group, looking unsure about what to do next. He was like a fish out of water. He glanced at me, and I nodded and gave him a thumbs-up. "Like what Mac said, safety first." I motioned for him to keep going. "We'll start with how to properly attach your skis to your boots."

Foster's stiff posture relaxed the moment he started talking about skiing, and kids began asking him questions about the slopes.

Sophia volunteered to be the model for her brother's demonstration, and his smile and laughter brightened up the room. He even answered some of the questions from volunteers about competing and was gracious with his answers; different from the well-rehearsed ones he gave to reporters during interviews.

My heart beat faster, my pulse became louder with my attention zoomed in on him. I gripped the window frame for support, my legs suddenly weak, when he glanced at me and winked, saying, "Thank you."

* * *

"Thank you both for being here. The kids love it," Sawyer said on our way to the giant campfire the volunteers had started.

"I'm so happy to be here. You have an amazing program for these kids and I want to be part of it," Foster said. "We'd like to come back next year, if that's OK?"

"Are you kidding me, of course! It'll give Isaac the help he needs. I haven't been able to be as involved with the ski activities lately. I get tired more easily these past couple of years."

"Because you work too much, man," I said, squeezing his shoulder. "You need to stop working seven days a week."

"Seven days a week? Yikes," Foster said.

"It's not that bad. I love my patients, and I want to be available when they need me. Man, it's cold. I'm keen to sit down." Sawyer joined the group, and I noticed that even his walking was slow.

"Man, I've heard of doctors working hard, but Sawyer makes them look lazy. He looks really tired too. Is he OK?"

"I think so. He lost some weight, but other than that I think he's fine. He used to be my size."

"Really? He must have lost at least twenty pounds. I mean,

he still looks great."

I nodded. Sawyer *did* look great. He had that All-American look, and was once scouted to be a model, but that wasn't his thing. I made a mental note to check in with him later.

"So you usually do all this by yourself? That's a lot of responsibility and hard work." Foster whistled and shook his head. "Why do all this?"

I glanced at the group of kids, chattering and laughing while drinking hot chocolate. "Some of these kids don't have the luxury of going to ski camps. Their family spends a lot of money on their medical bills, so buying skis is frivolous. Many of them don't even own skis. This is the only chance some of them get to ski and I just want to make it special for them." I knew how it felt to have next to nothing, and I always said if I ever had the chance to lift a kid up, I'd do it in a heartbeat. "Did you know there aren't a lot of charities dedicated to developmental medicine? It was hard to not be cynical about it, but Sawyer used to tell me it's because the cause isn't glamorous." I shook my head and sighed. I still couldn't believe that was true. "I'm sorry, that was a long-ass answer for such a simple question."

"Isaac, that is truly amazing. That breaks my heart." Foster put his hand on his chest and his eyes softened. "I want to be here. I sometimes forget not everyone is like us."

Not us. Just you. "Have you ever had hot cocoa by a campground fire?" I asked him.

"Never been camping."

"Another first that I can show you," I teased.

"I'm in great hands then," he said. "Isaac?"

"Yeah?"

"Thank you for inviting Sophia and me. I've never seen her

this happy." He pointed at her taking selfies with one of the girls. "This means a lot to me. And if you and Sawyer need anything, just ask. Whatever it is. I needed this break."

"Break from skiing?" I asked.

"Not just skiing." Foster placed his hands in his pockets and brought his attention to me, his blue eyes blazing. "Skiing is actually the best part of all this." He shook his head. He seemed to be having a tough time articulating what he wanted to say. "You know what, forget all that. I wasn't making any sense." He took a step forward, but I grabbed his arm to stop him.

"Foster, tell me."

He looked at my hand, then to my eyes once again. "It's the other things that go hand-in-hand with skiing. The constant request for interviews, the photoshoots, the well-curated social media posts, and the lack of privacy." He took a deep breath. "All of that. I just wanna do what I want."

"What is it that you wanna do?"

Foster was thoughtful for a while. "Honestly, I don't even know," he admitted. "I've been doing what I was told was good for my game and I forgot what I wanted to do."

My heart broke for him. "Do you like this?" I asked, motioning around the campground.

"I love this," he said quietly.

"Then that's what we'll do. And maybe after the World Championships, we'll figure out what other stuff you like too."

"You don't have to do that. I don't want you to spend your break doing that." Foster began kicking a small branch.

I stood in front of him and lifted his chin with my finger. "Hey, I'd really love to show you things that you might like. So far, I'm two for two. Remember the hot dog stand?" I winked.

"And now glamping. Pretty good, huh?"

"It's more than just good. It's perfect," Foster said.

I nodded, my throat too thick with emotion for words.

"Now, about that hot cocoa." Foster took my hand and we walked to join the others.

* * *

"I didn't know you wore glasses," I said when Foster was out of the shower. I wanted to join him, but it was new territory for us. It was silly, considering what we'd already done, but taking a shower together was intimate and I was afraid to cross that line.

"Yes. My goggles are prescription. Fancy, huh?" Foster asked.

"Very fancy. Did you have enough hot water?" I asked. I didn't know how big the water heater was in this place, so I had showered quickly.

"Plenty." He sat next to me on the leather couch and placed his phone on the ottoman next to him. "Sophia is all tucked in," he said. Foster was thoughtful for a moment, his attention trained on the crackling fire. I'd asked him several times if he was alright, but his answer was always a short *yes*. I didn't want to push him, but something was definitely amiss. He hadn't laughed at any of my jokes; granted, they were awful, but still. "Are you close to your parents?" he asked.

This question was dangerous territory, it could very easily go to a place I didn't want it to. But he looked so troubled, the best thing I could do was be his friend. *So here goes.* "Very," I admitted. "They're all I've got. I was an only child, and I was very fortunate to have them as my parents."

He glanced at me momentarily before returning to the fire. "That must be nice." The solemnity of his statement spoke volumes.

"Are you and Sophia not close with your parents?" I asked. I only knew of his father from his legacy.

"Sophia is close with both, but I'm only close with my mom," he said.

That stumped me. How was that possible? He and his dad had skiing in common—they even shared the same name. I couldn't fathom it. I'm not sure what I would do if I wasn't close to my folks.

"I wasn't good enough for him. I will never be good enough for him."

"What? That's crazy. You're one of the best skiers of any generation."

"Maybe," he shrugged.

"You're kidding, right?" I turned my whole body toward him. "I'm only going to say this once, so listen carefully: you are the best skier I know."

He didn't say anything, he didn't even react. I moved closer to him, I wanted to put my hand on his lap, but I held back.

He looked down at his open palms before looking at me; the reflection of the fire danced in his watery eyes. He wasn't crying, but the sadness in them conveyed what his words wouldn't.

"Talk to me," I urged.

He started to peel his gaze away, but I touched his chin, his stubble rubbing against my callused hand. His eyes intensified, but he still didn't utter a word. How could someone who had it all look this sad?

"Tell me what to do," I said. I was out of my element; the helplessness was overpowering. I was lost in a whiteout and wasn't equipped to guide him to safety.

"Just be here," Foster whispered. The mask of arrogance and bravado he usually wore was gone, and the man behind it was the most beautiful person I'd ever seen.

Just be here. I could do that.

Twenty-Five: Foster

Keep Your Friends Close, Your Enemies Closer

They say, keep your friends close and your enemies closer. What *they* failed to tell you was what to do with someone like Isaac. Someone who knew me better than any of my friends, but had the power to hurt me more than any enemy.

"Tell me what to do," Isaac had said.

"Just be here," I'd replied. I wanted to be close to this selfless man who gave his spare time to help bring joy to others.

I wasn't sure why it meant so much to me that Isaac was a great listener, but it did. We barely knew each other, but these past few weeks I had found myself thinking about him in different terms than I had expected. I knew better than to allow myself to get wrapped up in someone new during ski season, especially considering he was fast becoming my biggest competition. I knew better, and yet it didn't seem to matter as much to me anymore. I was feeling things for him that I had never felt for another guy.

"I can be here for you," he said, sliding even closer to my end of the old leather couch. "I'm here. Whatever you need." Isaac placed his hand on my knee. "Believe it or not, Foster, I'm not dazzled by your brilliant career. I admire it, but it's you I'm beginning to be dazzled by."

"Are you hitting on me again, Mac?"

"Maybe. Well, yeah."

"Where's your duffel bag?" I asked, raising my eyebrows suggestively.

He looked surprised by the hint. "Seriously? I mean, you would again?"

I shrugged. "Unless you don't want—"

"I want to," blurted. He leaned in and held my face tenderly before planting his lips on mine. He began to unbutton my flannel shirt. Both of us had thick wool socks on and a pair of jeans. He was already in a simple white tank.

"Good. I was hoping that was the case." I moved to the edge of the couch and remained seated. "Come here, let me help you with that." I unzipped his pants and pulled them lower toward his knees. I looked up. "Can I ask you a favor?" He nodded, his cock now peeking through the top of his black briefs. "Can we just get right to the fun part? I just want to feel you in me, like, right now."

Isaac's eyes widened. "You want me to suck you for a bit? Maybe tease your dick some?"

"Nope. I want you in me."

"Stand up then." He got up to retrieve his duffel bag and its magical supplies. "You're sure?" he asked. He dropped his pants and underwear near the bag and padded back toward me. His huge cock was ready to answer the call of duty.

I'd ripped my clothes off and was standing near the couch. "Where would you like me?" I asked, grinning like the horny fucker I was. He came up and pulled me tight, kissing me tenderly. I pulled away. "Where. Do. You. Want. Me?"

Isaac spun me around and pushed me head down, ass up onto the couch. "Grip the back of the couch and keep your knees on the edge," he ordered.

My nuts got the signal from his command and woke my dick up instantly. I knelt on the couch doggy-style and did as he said. He walked up behind me and slid his finger over my ass crack. He stopped at my hole and pressed.

"This where you want me?"

I nodded and arched my back, placing my ass directly in range. I heard the lube cap pop and his hand running over his cock, and then the pressure of his fingers pushing into my hole.

"Get me nice and ready, and then let's fuck, Mac." I was oddly not embarrassed talking to him like this. I enjoyed someone else in control for once. *Wait a fucking second.* Was that what this new pleasure party was about? Was the fact I could let go and be controlled what made the experience so fucking hot? Maybe. Plus the fact it felt so good. But what if it wasn't Isaac?

"Hold on," he said, grabbing a hip and guiding his cock with his other hand. I felt the pressure build and relaxed the best I could. The resistance from my ass didn't last long, partially due to his forceful approach, and also because I *really* wanted him inside me. "Here it comes," he said, pulling his cock out, adding more lube, then pushing deeper. I gritted my teeth; it wasn't easy, but truthfully, part of the thrilling sensation was the *getting used to it* part.

"I am so fucking ready!" he said, grabbing my hips and starting to move in and out, his pace increasing with my moans and grunts.

"Your cock is amazing, Mac. Don't stop. This feels so

fucking hot." I reached for my dick and started stroking it, using my horny-as-fuck pre-cum for lube. His pace was hard and fast now, each thrust buried as deep as he could get. I felt the limit every time he reached it, the thrill sending me over the edge. I buried my head in the corner of the couch and kept my ass high in his target zone. I could hear Isaac moaning, rolling his hips into me over and over.

"Foster! This is so hot, man. I wish you could see my dick burying into your sexy-as-fuck ass! Shit, dude, it's too fucking much."

"Fuuuck." All I could think about was Isaac inside me.

"You're amazing, baby. I'm telling you, I could blow right now."

"Wait!" I said. "Let me flip over, I want to watch you shoot again. That shit was hot." He pulled his cock out, and I missed it already. I laid back while he grabbed my ankles and pushed my knees toward my ears. "Shit, man. Good thing I'm flexible, huh?"

"You said you wanted it. I'm here to deliver it to you." He positioned his cock and pumped it to the maximum depth for our mutual pleasure. "This is fucking hot," he moaned, looking down and watching his cock slide in and out of me. I had my head tilted to the side and was folded into the couch like the letter V, loving every plunge. He hit that spot I had only just discovered—or was it Isaac that found it? Who knew? I had come alive from this angle; he was rubbing that electrifying spot with every thrust. I was losing control; my cock was throbbing. I stared at the intensity on Isaac's face and grabbed my own cock.

He held my ankles and spread me as wide as I could go. "That's it, Mac. That's it," I half moaned, half demanded. "Fuck yeah!"

"You like that?" he asked, grinning and grunting.

"I fucking *love* it." I closed my eyes, lost in the rawness of our physical connection.

"I want to try," he suddenly blurted out in a breathy voice.

My eyes popped open, and I found him grinning from ear to ear. "What?" I asked, stopping mid-jerk.

"You heard me," he said. "I want to experience whatever the fuck it is you're going on about. I'm serious." He pulled his cock out of my hole and backed up, motioning for me to stand. "Get up, let's do this." He grabbed a hand and pulled me up. "I'm serious, so you can wipe that look off your face. You've topped, right, or has all this just been a ruse?"

"Fuck yeah!" I grabbed his ass and ran my hand over the amazing curves. "This ass feels tight," I whispered, pushing him on the couch. His eyes widened with my manhandling. "You sure?"

"Uh…yeah. I think so." He stared at my fully erect cock.

I grabbed it and flopped it around in my hand, letting him get a nice, long look at what I was sporting. I rubbed the lube up and down my shaft, smiling as I teased my cock, letting him make his final decision. "Let's start with you on your knees like I was. You'll fucking love it," I suggested. "I'll be gentle."

He stood and turned to face the wall, quickly looking back over his shoulder. "On my knees, right?" he asked with a nervous chuckle.

I nodded and tapped his shoulder. "Hey, look at me." He turned around. "You don't have to do this. Seriously, I don't need to top you."

"I want you to, Foster. I want to experience this with you. I trust you."

I kissed him, our tongues dancing. I pushed him toward the couch. "Bend over then, Mac. It's daddy's turn."

"Less talk, more action," he ordered.

I slapped his ass cheek with my dick. "What a fucking pleasure this is going to be."

I reached for the lube and held it over his ass crack and let some drip on his hole. He jerked and pushed his ass back toward me. I ran my fingers around his hole, circling the spot I had been fixating on since I first saw him. I'd hoped he was a bottom then, but now, well, who knew what I wanted? Maybe this would be fun, to fuck around with someone willing to share the fun equally. If he liked it the way I'd found out I did, this was going to be fantastic. I pushed a well-lubed finger against his ass, and he slammed shut like a clam during clamming season.

"Wow, that felt strange," Isaac said with a muffled voice. "Do it again."

I moved my finger over his hole and pressed gently at first until I finally had to apply more pressure. My finger moved past the resistance, and I stopped.

"Get used to that for a second, OK?" I said. "Then I'll move in further." I pushed a little deeper, and felt him give in to the invasion. I moved my finger around, exploring and stretching him. "All the way in now," I announced, inserting it in fully and stopping again, before I extracted it and repeated the action. "How's that feeling?"

"Weird, but so good. Give me more." He moved his ass back toward me, an invitation. I removed the finger before adding a second one to the entrance. A little more lube and a bit more patience and both slid in nicely. I stopped and let him get acquainted with his new friends. A nice introduction to the considerably larger friend waiting his turn. "Hey, not so bad. Finger-fuck me a bit while I stroke my dick."

I was happy to fill the request. I moved both fingers in and out more aggressively as he relaxed, his body becoming more willing. Isaac continued rubbing his cock, becoming more receptive by the second.

I slapped my cock against his butt cheek a few times. "You think you're up for the real thing?" I asked, hoping like hell he was, because my cock was purple and swollen, hornier than it had ever been.

"I am so ready. Let's go, Foster."

I sheathed my cock in a condom and re-lubed it. After applying a heavy squirt of lube to his hole, I pressed the tip against his puckered entrance. My swollen head was twice the size of two fingers, but I was a patient man, and this prize was worth the patience of a saint. "It might hurt a little, but it'll get better. I promise."

"Got it," he said, stroking his erection. "Put it in." I pushed against his hole slowly, knowing it would resist. It took a bit more force than I anticipated, but finally, he accepted me. "Ohhh…" he groaned, taking a deep breath to relax. "Keep going." He began to rub his cock aggressively again. "Stick it in, Donovan."

I pressed against him and sunk another two inches in. I held his hips tightly in my hands, reassuring him that he could trust me. "At your pace, Mac." I held the position and let him get used to me. The tension released my cock and I slid further in. Slowly in, slowly out. "How's it feeling, Mac? I'm about halfway in."

"Only half? Feels like your leg's in there," he whispered.

"Not yet, but it's coming soon." He laughed at my poor joke, and I felt him relax. I pushed even deeper. "There you go, Mac. Almost in, big guy. Keep pumping on your cock and open wide." I wanted to pound on his asshole and talk some real smack, but this was an intro lesson. I was delighted to have been invited to instruct.

"It's feeling good. I feel you in me, and it's fucking turning me on. I feel like I could come, it feels so hot," he moaned, beginning to move back against my cock, inviting more of me in. I knew he was feeling the thrill of jacking his dick and getting fucked at the same time. Now that I had experienced the other side, I understood what previous sexual partners had described. It was simply unlike any pleasure a man had ever experienced. If straight men could ever get over the *there's a dick in my ass* feeling, they'd all be doing this, trust me. I picked up my pace as Isaac became more receptive. He rocked back and forth against me while stroking himself, his sounds full of pure desire. He was finding out what every bottom he'd been with had experienced with him, and he seemed to be enjoying the sensation.

"How are we doing there, Mac? Still with me?"

"Keep it up. Give it to me a bit harder and faster," he growled.

"I guess that's a yes then. Hold on." Faster now, I started really giving it to him. He was furiously stroking his cock, moaning and groaning. "You keep that sound up, Mac, and I am going to lose my load."

"Jesus! Holy fuck, Foster. You weren't lying, man."

"Can you flip over? I want to watch you as I fuck you," I asked, tapping on his butt cheek.

"Sure, but hurry. I am so fucking close, and I want to ride this…this…whatever the fuck you're hitting in there." I backed away and pulled his hips back, helping him flip over fast. He rolled over quickly and lifted his legs for me to grab while he kept stroking his dick. "Hurry, put it in. This shit feels so damn good." I lifted his legs apart and let my cock drop close to his hole; without guiding it, it found its way to his opening, and I pushed back in until I bottomed out. "Fuuuuuck," he muttered deeply. "Fuck yes!"

It was amazing to watch the pure enjoyment of his experience. He was moving his head back and forth, mumbling and moaning, all the while jacking on his cock. If he had been self-conscious earlier or embarrassed at the idea of being topped, that shit had passed. He was in a zone of need now. I was sweating and just kept my eyes focused on him. He was sexier than any man I had ever fucked. Not only was my dick aroused, but my brain was thoroughly down for the show. I couldn't believe the array of emotions; excitement and protectiveness over this man who was allowing me to be in him, joined together as one. It was new. I hadn't felt like this before, even with men I had dated more seriously. "I could come, Mac."

His eyes flew open, and he grinned. "Just say when."

We stared at each other as I held his legs high and met his every thrust. He grinned and stared at me before moving his eyes to his cock, asking me to take all of him in. "Hot, Mac. Fucking hot!" I said, my arousal growing at the sight of him jacking his meat while mine was going in and out of his ass. "I'm close, Mac!"

"Good! Keep pumping. Keep pumping. Do not stop pumping." His eyes glazed over; the passion of the moment had taken him completely. "YES! FUCK YES! That's it. That's it…here we go…here we go." He had his dick in his hand, furiously stroking. His legs were tensing and getting harder to hold as I tried to time my orgasm with his.

"I'm...going to..." I moaned.

"Yes...keep it up. Oh fuck! Oh fuck!" he growled. He looked directly into my eyes and grinned like a possessed man. I watched him look at his dick as it exploded over his abs. His ass tightened and I released my load a mere moment after, and we slowly came down from the high once every ounce of enthusiasm was drained. He let go of his cock and held his hands up to me. I let his legs drop beside me and knelt in front of the couch, leaning forward as he wrapped his arms around me. We let our breathing subside and held each other in silence. "You were right, Foster. Jesus! How could we have not known about this?" he said, a soft chuckle in my ear.

"I know, right. Maybe it's just us?" I wasn't sure what exactly I meant by that, but it didn't matter because of his response.

"It has to be," he said, pulling me closer and kissing the top of my head.

Twenty-Six: Isaac

There's Always Tomorrow

Alex and I had opted out of flying to Vancouver and decided to meet up in Seattle and drive the five-hour trip to Whistler. We had been on the road for three hours, crossing one of the most beautiful parts of the drive. Buildings and houses were replaced by boulders that had lost the battle with gravity from the surrounding mountains along the winding stretch of freeway. Aside from the black asphalt, all around was a winter wonderland.

I glanced at Alex, who was taking notes with her leather-bound tickler file, and realized she'd been quiet for a while. "What's on your mind?" I asked.

Alex took a deep breath before closing her notepad. "Are you sure this is a good idea?"

The *this* she was referring to was staying with Foster and his team this week. They were staying at Foster's folks' log cabin in Whistler, which was big enough for both of our teams. "Yeah, why wouldn't it be?"

She put her tickler in her bag and stared at me. "Really?"

I'd told her about Foster and me, minus the flip-flop that was hot as hell. It had been the single most arousing thing I'd

191

ever done. I'd heard about it, and had seen it on countless porn videos, but watching didn't compare to the real-life ecstasy. Not even close.

"Mac, are you listening?"

"It will be fine. We've done it before and we won." I reminded her about the American Cup in Lake Tahoe two weekends ago.

"I don't know, Mac. This is different. You and him, you know." Alex switched her attention to the road, and I thought she was done worrying. "Can you take that exit, please." She pointed to the *Rest Stop 1 Mile Ahead* sign.

Our SUV skidded a little as we entered the rest stop, which hadn't been plowed and had accumulated several inches of snow. "Good thing we rented a car with snow tires," I said after parking. "What are you worried about?"

"This is the final competition before the Olympics in Beijing, and that means a bigger pool and tougher competition. Your last chance to make a splash and be selected by the committee to represent the USA. I'm worried that having Foster around twenty-four seven will complicate things. Not just for you, but for him too."

"Listen, I get it. But we got this. He won't be a distraction. I promise." I placed my hand on her shoulder to assure her that everything would be alright.

Alex sighed and shook her head, but said, "OK."

"Are we good?"

"We're good," she said, and pulled her tickler back out.

"What do you have in there?"

"Notes from Aspen and Lake Tahoe. I started a file with things that you did well and things that you sucked at." She smirked, and I felt better that she was somewhat herself again.

"See...you have your tickler and everything. We got this."

Alex and I laughed and made our way back to the road. But I felt momentarily rattled. The World Championships was huge—should we rethink this arrangement? I shook my head. If we were able to win in Lake Tahoe, this shouldn't be different.

* * *

"I thought you said a cabin—this house is bigger than the Lake Tahoe home. Is this his?" Alex asked as we pulled up next to the massive log mansion. It was three stories, with a center A-frame full of windows that separated two wings.

"No, it's his parents'," I said. We were about to hop out of the car when one of the four garage doors opened, revealing Foster wearing an unbuttoned blue flannel shirt exposing a gray T-shirt underneath, and a pair of faded denim jeans. He waved us in with a big smile on his handsome face.

Alex watched Foster and I hug after hopping out of the car. "Nice to see you again." She smiled at him and shook his hand.

"I'm glad you're here. Let me show you around." Foster led us in and gave us a tour of the place. Framed black-and-white pictures of Foster Donovan Sr. hung on the walls. Each picture had a gold plate at the bottom with the place and date of the competition, reminding me how prolific his career was.

We made it to the main living space; the A-frame structure we saw outside was designed to frame a breathtaking view of the mountains. "Are those—"

"Whistler and Blackcomb," Foster answered.

Whistler and Blackcomb were two peaks considered to be ski heaven, separated by a huge valley in the middle.

"You can see the slopes from here!" Alex exclaimed, her mouth dropping open.

"Pretty cool, huh? Your room has the same view," Foster told Alex. We walked down the hallway of the left wing. "This is you," he said, opening one of the rooms. "The guys will bring your stuff here."

"Alex and I can get our own stuff," I said, not wanting his team to cater to us. "Where's my room?"

"The next one," he said. "You and Alex will be in this wing, and my team is staying in the opposite side."

"That's great." Alex nodded. "Why don't you show Isaac his room, and come get me when you're ready to get our stuff." Foster and I got the hint.

Foster was all over me when I closed the door to my room. "Did you tell her?" he asked in between kisses.

I put my lips on his before answering, cherishing how his body felt. God, I had missed him in the few days since camping. It was odd, I'd never missed anyone the way I missed Foster. It wasn't just the sex, but his laugh, his cockiness, his presence. "Yes, I told her. But I promised her I'd stay focused and work harder for the upcoming competition."

"Harder, huh?" Foster grinned and cupped my face, then kissed my neck and whispered in my ears, "How hard?"

I moaned, intoxicated by his touch. I used the last ounce of self-control to peel myself off him. "Seriously, Foster."

"OK," he said, giving me one last kiss. "You know where to find me if you change your mind."

"I won't, but I'll keep that in mind."

"Oh, by the way, Sophia asked me to give you this." Foster

pulled a folded piece of paper from his back pocket and handed it to me.

I brought the letter to my nose to get a whiff of the scented paper. "Strawberry," I said, and opened the handwritten note.

Dear Mac,

I wanted to thank you for inviting Oz and me to camp with your friends. I made new friends and had the best time of my life. Thank you for making Oz very happy. I haven't seen him this happy in a very long time. He couldn't stop talking about you on our flight back home. I think he really likes you, but he is scared to tell you.

He asked me one time what I wanted for my birthday, but I only told him one of my wishes because I was afraid that it wouldn't come true if I said both. I was so glad I didn't tell him, because it finally came true. I wished for him to meet someone who would make him the happiest, and I think it is you. Good luck this weekend. I wish that both of you could win gold, but I used up all my wishes this year.

XOXO,

Sophia

I swallowed the lump forming in my throat. "What a sweetheart," I croaked.

"What did it say?" Foster asked.

"Just thanking me for inviting you and her to camp." I decided to keep her other revelations between her and I—no one wanted to jinx a wish.

"We're thankful. Let me show you the rest of the house."

* * *

"Goddamn it," I said when I botched my turn yet again during training. I continued pushing to make up lost time, even though I knew it wouldn't make a difference.

Alex was waiting for me at the bottom of the hill. This was our last run for the day, and it had been one of my worst training sessions. She looked up to check my time and shook her head watching me cross the finish line. "Well, there's always tomorrow," she said. She wrote something on her tickler before bringing her attention back to me. "What's happening?"

"I'm getting used to the conditions. I'll get there." I took my goggles off and skied toward the edge of the slope before disengaging my boots from my skis. "The snow on the slopes is packed and hard. I just have to get used to it."

"It's been really cold and the forecast looks the same all week, so you need to get used to it fast. I'll come up with a plan and we'll try again tomorrow," she said, eyeing me warily.

"OK, we'll try harder tomorrow."

"You're not gonna bug me about what the plan is?" She raised an eyebrow

"I trust you," I answered, wondering how Foster's training was going.

"You usually can't wait to hear what the plan is, so I was just...curious."

"I know you got it. I believe in you." I didn't know what she was implying, but I needed to get back to the house because Foster and I had plans. I was going to tell him about my past so we could move forward with our future. I needed to show him the truth behind all the white lies I'd told.

Alex and I made our way to the club to change out of our gear. "I reserved a massage therapist after you cool off from the gym," she said midway to the lobby.

"Oh, I don't think I can do that."

"Why not?" She stopped walking and looked at me, her forehead wrinkled.

"Foster and I are snowshoeing around the property later." I held my breath for her response.

She rubbed her palms on her face.

"What's the big deal?" I asked. I didn't need a massage, and I could cool off after snowshoeing.

"Mac, you just finished a two-hour physical training and you're telling me that you're going to add more stress to your legs by snowshoeing? That's not conditioning," she argued. "You can't do that, Mac."

"You can't tell me what to do." The irritation in my voice earned us a couple of glances from nearby skiers.

"As your coach, I can."

"Do you have a problem with him?" I asked. She hadn't been excited about staying at Foster's, and now she was preventing me from spending time with him. *I don't think so.*

"This is not about Foster. This is about you." She tapped my chest with her finger. "I don't have a problem with you being together. I only care about your success."

"I told you, I'm fine," I said, my frustration growing. This wasn't how I wanted the day to go. First the terrible training, now this.

"No, you're not. You are ten times better than what you did today. You're distracted, and you know it. Where's the Isaac I met three weeks ago?" She motioned to the corner of the lobby with two cushioned chairs so we could talk without making a scene. Once we were seated, she continued. "Isaac, I've seen this before. I was coaching this amazing skier. Full of talent. She reminded me of Lindsey Vonn." She closed her eyes and took a deep breath. "Everything was going well for her until she got involved with a male skier. He wasn't very good, but decent enough to join the circuit. At first it was casual, and I didn't make a big deal because it didn't affect her performance initially." Alex looked out at the falling snow. "But the longer they were together, her game suffered. She started missing training to spend time with him, then lost her timing, and it went downhill from there."

She leaned back in the chair and rubbed her hands on her thighs. "The association called me in for a meeting and they asked if I knew what was going on with her. You should have seen their faces after I told them." She looked at me; she wasn't crying but her eyes were watery, it was clear how much she cared about her former skier. "I thought they were going to fire me. They asked why I didn't say anything. I thought it wasn't my place. But then I thought about it some more, and I asked myself, why *didn't* I say anything? I could've prevented her demise. I was her coach, I should've been guiding her so she could make the best decision. Years later she asked me why I didn't intervene." Alex looked at the ground. "I don't want that to happen to you. I don't want you to wake up one day and wonder why I didn't say anything. So, Isaac, I don't have a problem with Foster, and I'm truly happy for you both. I know you like him, I can see it in your eyes. But I also know what you're capable of, and you're way better than what you showed today."

Alex's story made sense. This was her redemption too. "OK, no snowshoeing then," I said. I was overwhelmed with the realization of how much Alex cared about me. I finally had a team, and I would do anything to make her proud.

198

"OK," Alex said, nodding. "Thank you."

"So what's the plan tomorrow?"

Alex responded with a snort.

Twenty-Seven: Foster

West Virginia

It started to snow, and Isaac and I looked up to the sky. Isaac decided against snowshoeing, and chose to enjoy the hot tub instead. Isaac was behind me, his arms spread along the edge of the tub as I leaned back against his chest. We were wearing swim trunks since there were other guests in the house, but that didn't stop us from touching and caressing each other.

"How did your training go?" I asked, cutting through the silence. I'd seen his time earlier; he could do better than that.

"Um." He stiffened under me. "I'm getting used to the conditions."

"Huh. Don't get lazy on me, Big Mac. I don't want an easy win."

"You wish," he countered. I could hear the smirk on his lips. "Alex and I are working on it. I'll do better tomorrow."

"You better," I urged. The old me wouldn't have cared, but there was a shift happening between us that I was terrified to acknowledge. I was fearless and never backed down from a challenge, but I was out of my element when it came to Isaac.

I scooted forward, shifting my position so I could look at

Isaac. His eyes met mine. I didn't know who could see us, but I didn't care either. I leaned forward and pressed my lips to his. Isaac's lips parted in invitation. There it was, the feeling I'd been trying to deny came rushing in with more force than an avalanche. *How do you deal with someone who has the power to destroy you?*

I opened my mouth to speak, when Stan's voice caught our attention. "Foster, your father is here."

"Oh shit," I mumbled. "I'll be right back."

Isaac went to stand but I put my hand up. "Stay, I'll just say hi real quick."

"Are you sure?" he asked, and looked toward the main room for my father.

"Yup," I called, closing the sliding door behind me. This didn't look good, judging by my father's face. Not the emotionless expression I'd come to know, but his eyes were narrowed, lips tightly closed. *Fuck.*

"Bonjour," I greeted him, hoping that a little French would butter him up a bit. Nope.

He gave me a stern look, and turned toward the library without saying a word.

I glanced back at the hot tub. Isaac was watching, worry in his face. I gave him a thumbs-up and smiled, hoping it would ease his mind. This was the last thing he needed after the day he'd had. I scurried after Dad. "What are you doing here? The race isn't until Saturday," I said when I entered the library.

"Close the door," he ordered. This wasn't going to be a fun visit. He pointed at the blanket draped over the chair when he saw me shivering.

"Where's Mom and Sophia?" I didn't know if my shaking voice could be attributed to being cold, or the irrational fear of

201

knowing I had somehow disappointed my father once again.

"What are you doing bringing strangers into my home?" he asked, ignoring my question.

"Isaac and Alex aren't strangers. Alex is my friend, and Isaac is my…" I struggled to find the words. I was getting ready to tell Isaac I loved him when my father showed up. "Isaac is very special to me."

My dad laughed—actually laughed. "You're so pathetic," he said, looking at me with disgust. "You're calling your biggest competition a *special friend*. Just how desperate are you?"

"What?" I asked, my voice quivering. "Isaac is not my competition. We care about each other."

"Are you out of your mind? You can have any guy out there and you choose him?" His distaste for Isaac was obvious, and I didn't understand why. Isaac was an amazing man, noble and talented.

"What's wrong with him?" I asked.

"Oh, come on, Foster. If you want to have a fling with him, go ahead, but you're not serious about him, are you?"

I wasn't following my father's train of thought. "I thought you agreed that he's an amazing skier. You said so yourself." *What am I missing?* Did Isaac say something he didn't approve of in the press? That couldn't be it, Isaac didn't like talking to the press. "What do you have against him?" I asked. The thumping of my pulse and gushing in my ears made it difficult to hear him. I stepped closer so he could really listen to what I was about to say. If he knew the truth, he might chill. "I love Isaac, Dad."

My father's eyes flared, and he balled his hand into a fist. "I will not let my son be with trailer trash from West Virginia."

I shook my head. Did I mishear him? "What're you talking

about, Dad?"

He looked at me with pity. "You didn't know?"

"Didn't know what? Isaac isn't from West Virginia. He was born and raised in Portland."

"Oh, Foster," he said, but not in a loving, kind way. It was condescending, and I fucking hated it.

"I had a friend look into his background. I was curious about him when he almost beat you at the World Cup, and then when he won the American Cup. I was *curious* how someone that good flew under my radar." He leaned on the frame of the window, partially sitting, his face smug. "Imagine my surprise when I found out that your little friend grew up in the Appalachian Mountains in the middle of nowhere. His carpenter dad trained him until he was eighteen, then he moved west." He laughed as if the mention of Isaac's father left a bitter taste in his mouth. "The association backing him is probably the best thing that ever happened to that kid. What does a carpenter know about coaching? His mom worked two different jobs and they still live in squalor."

It was like someone had dumped a bucket of ice on my head. The way he dodged my questions whenever I asked him about his home, and his occasional slips in his accent. Why would he hide that from me? I didn't want to believe my dad. "You're lying," I said.

Dad walked toward me. He placed his hand on my shoulder and paused. "He's just using you, Foster. I wouldn't be surprised if all this was his ploy to distract you. People like him will do anything to get out of that godforsaken place."

"Stop, Dad," I whispered.

"I want them out of here tomorrow."

He strode to the door and closed it behind him, his words

final. Tears flowed down my face. Why didn't he tell me? Would I even have cared? My knees weakened and I made my way to the chair.

A small knock on the door. It opened, and I knew it was Isaac before he spoke. "I saw your dad leave. Are you OK?"

I didn't move, didn't have the energy to speak. Footsteps approached, and when I glanced up, a concerned Isaac was gazing down at me. He handed me a towel, but I remained motionless. I let my head fall.

"What's wrong, Foster? Are you hurt?" He kneeled down and tilted my chin, urging me to look at him. "Talk to me, please?" His soft brown eyes begged for an answer.

"Why didn't you tell me?" I asked.

"Tell you what?"

"Who you really are."

His hands fell to his side and he sat on the floor. He swallowed hard. "Is that why your dad was here?" he asked.

"Is there any truth to anything you said? Are you even gay?" I hated that I even asked that question, but what if Dad was right? What if Isaac was just using me?

"Of course I'm gay. You know that."

"No, Isaac. I don't fucking know anything. If you could lie to me about something as simple as where you came from, how can I believe in the amazing things we shared?"

"What I felt about—"

"Stop!" I yelled. "Don't say it."

"Please listen to me, Foster." Isaac put his hands together.

"Why didn't you tell me?" I asked him again. "I would never lie to you."

He pulled his knees to his chest and hung his head between his legs. For a couple of minutes, he didn't speak. When he looked up, my heart broke for him. His eyes were red, tear tracks on his face.

You don't know him, Foster.

Twenty-Eight: Isaac

This is Me

We sat in silence. I could barely speak around the lump of shame in my throat, and the fear of losing the best thing in my life. The tears streamed down my face, relentless, unstoppable.

I forced myself to look up and found Foster watching me, pain contorting his handsome face. Then the pain melted into a cold mask of indifference.

"Actually, I don't care. I don't need to know," he spat. He pushed off the chair and stormed past me.

I got up from the floor so quickly the world spun, but I didn't care. I had intended to come clean tonight and now it was too late. I still needed to tell Foster the truth. "Foster, please wait. Let me explain." I grabbed his elbow to prevent him from leaving.

He looked at my hand and returned his hollow gaze to mine. "Tell me this, Isaac. Did you lie to me because you thought I'd care?"

I didn't want to lie to him anymore, so I nodded.

Foster blew out a breath and yanked my hand off his elbow. "You think so little of me that you assumed it would matter?

I'm so fucking stupid." He banged his head with the heel of his palm.

"Foster, you're not stupid."

"I feel pretty stupid right now. When were you going to tell me? Were you ever planning on telling me?"

"I was."

"When?" His face looked like he'd aged ten years since we were outside. "I asked you on multiple occasions. You could have told me then, instead you dodged and dodged and walked away."

"I dodged because I didn't want to tell you another lie."

"Not telling a lie isn't honesty—I doubt you know the difference."

His last words stung, but I persevered. This couldn't end this way. This couldn't end, period. "Please, I'll tell you everything you want to know."

Foster shook his head. "I don't need to know. I think it's best if you and Alex find a different place to stay this week."

I felt numb. My mind flashed back to all the amazing things Foster and I had shared together. This couldn't be the end. If I knew it would be, I would have told him the truth. I would have kissed him harder. I would have hugged him tighter.

I didn't realize Foster was gone until the slamming of a door snapped me from my musings.

I ran to his room, my bare feet slapping on the wooden floor. "Foster, open up, please," I yelled. I knocked, louder each time, but he didn't answer.

Stan emerged from his room, and Alex was coming down the hall giving me a *what the fuck* look.

I ignored them and banged on Foster's door again. "Foster, please? Let me explain."

"Mac, what's going on?" Alex asked, looking between Stan and me.

"I need to talk to Foster." My voice was breaking, panic overtaking me.

"He's not coming out, man." Stan grabbed my arm to stop me banging on the door.

We can't end like this. We haven't even started. I snatched my hand from him. "Don't touch me."

He backed off and looked to Alex for help.

"Can it wait until tomorrow?" Alex asked, concern drawn on her face.

"No. I need to tell him now."

"OK," she said. "Is Foster in there? Can you have him come out?" Alex asked Stan.

The sound of a roaring car grabbed our attention. We all bolted to the living room.

"I guess that answers that," Stan said, pointing out the window at Foster's SUV speeding off. "He must have used the patio door in his bedroom."

My heart sank. "Where's he going?"

"I don't know, maybe his place," Stan answered.

"Give me his address," I demanded.

"I can't do that, Isaac."

"Mac, let's go back to your room, OK?" Alex said, attempting to pull me to our wing.

"No, I need to talk to Foster."

Stan's cell phone pinged and we looked back at him. "Is that Foster?" I asked. I knew I sounded desperate but I'd go down on my knees if I had to.

Stan nodded. "He said you and Alex should stay." He placed his phone back in his pocket. "That's all he said, man. I'm sorry."

"Thanks, Stan," Alex said, placing her hand on my back.

"He's gone," I mumbled to no one.

Alex rubbed circles on my back as we headed to my room.

I grabbed my phone from the nightstand and dialed Foster's number. It rang once before transferring to voicemail. I tried again, same result. I pulled up our last text exchange and typed, *Please Foster. I need to talk to you.* I stared at the screen, willing him to respond, but it went unanswered.

I sat on the edge of the bed with my head hung low, staring at my cell phone. "I need to tell him the truth," I mumbled. I shivered, and Alex replaced the damp towel hanging on my shoulder with the blanket lying on the bed. I grabbed both of its ends and wrapped it around my body.

"What's going on, Mac? Why did Foster leave?" Alex was pacing at the foot of the bed and biting her fingernails. "Did you have a fight?"

"No." I cradled my face with my palms. "I should have told him."

"Told him what?" She squatted on the floor and peeled my hands from my face. When our eyes met, she asked, "What did you need to tell him?"

"Everything."

* * *

Seven Years Ago

My stomach was in knots competing for my first tournament away from home. Pop and Ma couldn't help me move to my new apartment in Portland because of the cost of traveling cross country. I hated being away from them, but they knew that if I wanted to pursue skiing as a career, I would eventually have to move out of West Virginia for more opportunities.

Beep. Beep. Beep

The third beep sounded and I was out of the gate with lightning speed. My true talent would be tested competing against skiers from all over the country. At eighteen, I was one of the younger guys here. The track was easier to navigate than the one I used to practice on back home, and with the two training runs I had at the beginning of the week, I was sliding through the slope with relative ease. I cleared every turn and hurdle and victory was waiting for me when I crossed the finish line.

"I did it," I screamed along with the small crowd gathered at the bottom of the slope. I skied toward the top finisher that I had just replaced to congratulate him and his team on a job well done. "Great job, y'all."

He glared at me. Him and his friends hadn't been the friendliest competitors all week and had been looking at me with nasty expressions. "I didn't know rednecks skied," the runner-up taunted while his minions laughed.

"What did you call me?" I asked. "Do you have a problem with me, man?" I continued, trying my very best to hide any trace of where I came from.

"I said, congratulations, Bubba," he lied before turning his back and flipping me off.

I skied toward him and when I reached him, I slammed into him forcefully, causing him to fall. I towered over him ready to knock some sense into him, when a friend of his grabbed my hand before I had a chance to deck him.

"Get off of him you fucking redneck!" his friend yelled. "This *isn't the swamp."*

Our little commotion caught the attention of other skiers and they separated me from him. What did I do to these guys to deserve this hostility?

After my crazy and insult-filled day, I went home and recorded every single television show I could find and mimicked the way they spoke. So much so, I even convinced myself that I wasn't from West Virginia. This was the new me and no one would ever take me seriously if I couldn't lose my southern twang. I was on my own now.

* * *

Alex sat next to me, and I told her what I should have told Foster. Everything from where I grew up and why I hid my accent.

"Wow. That's crazy, Mac."

"I know, Alex. I'm a fraud."

"You're not a fraud," she said. "I get it, and sadly, you aren't the first or last person to hide something to fit in." She made air quotes around *fit in.* "I'm not saying it's right or wrong, but I understand. Remember Don't Ask, Don't Tell?" I nodded. "How about the actors and athletes staying in the closet because of the millions of dollars at stake from endorsements and movie projects?"

I nodded again, at this point just hoping she'd keep coaching me after my revelation.

"What are we gonna do?" she asked.

"We?"

"Yes, you and I are a team. But no more lies, OK? Not even white lies."

"OK."

* * *

Alex and I were getting ready to start training when every single screen on the launch pad showed Foster's picture.

"Defending World Champion Foster Donovan has withdrawn from this Saturday's race," the voiceover said. "We've reached out to Foster Donovan, and his agent told us he'll release a statement soon. Donovan was the heavy favorite to win and defend his title, so the field now is wide open."

Oh my god, Foster. What have you done? "Give me my phone, please," I asked Alex, who kept it for me during practice.

My hands were shaking as she handed it to me. I dialed Foster's number, and just like last night, it went to voicemail. "Foster, what are you doing? Please call me back. I really need to talk to you." I looked at Alex, and she shook her head.

"This is his decision, Mac."

"It's all my fault." I disengaged my skis from my boots and sat on the bench nearby. "I can't believe he withdrew."

Alex grabbed her phone from her backpack on the floor and made a call. "Hey! Are you guys ready? Do you want to switch training times with Mac and me? We're not quite ready." She paused. "Great, thank you. I owe you one."

"What was that?" I asked after she hung up.

"I switched training times with the guys scheduled after us. I won't let you hit the slopes like this." She moved her hand up and down. "I'm not going to risk you getting hurt."

"Thank you."

"Let's grab our stuff and go to the lounge to clear our heads, OK?"

I let Alex guide me to the lounge. I couldn't believe Foster withdrew from one of the biggest races of the year, and the last race before the Olympics in Beijing. Was it because of me?

Alex pulled me to her side so I could avoid bumping into a group walking toward us. "Sorry about that," she said to the passerby, who smiled and waved to her. Her phone buzzed and she looked at me. "Foster's statement is posted on his IG account."

We grabbed the first available chairs and checked Instagram.

Dear fans,

After consulting with my team, it is with a heavy heart that I withdraw from this year's World Championships. It is one of my favorite events of the year, made even more special as it's hosted by my beloved Canada. I love skiing, and I give my all whenever I do, but I am unable to give the race my undivided attention this year. To my Canadian fans, I know you are disappointed, but I promise I will make it up to you and try my very best to win gold at the Olympics in two weeks. Thank you for understanding, and please know that I am OK.

Thank you all for your love and support,

Foster

Twenty-Nine: Foster

You're the Insecure

Not even Sophia could bring me out of my gloom. It had been a few days since I'd seen Isaac and withdrew from the World Championships, but I was nowhere near the end of this long, dark tunnel. The truth was, I loved Isaac. I thought he was different, but he was just like the other guys. I didn't know what hurt the most. His lies about who he was, or the fact he thought I'd care. I wanted to believe that what we had shared was real, but how could I possibly believe anything when the foundation of what we had was based on pretense and lies?

"Two more skiers are left before the new World Champion is revealed," Andrew Sorensen said when the broadcast came back from a commercial break. I shouldn't be watching this. But, like always, I was a glutton for punishment. "Two skiers from Norway currently occupy the top two spots, but World Cup silver medalist and American Cup winner Isaac McAllister is yet to hit the slopes."

The mention of Isaac's name roused all kinds of emotions. The anger, sadness, disappointment and longing came in droves. I grabbed the remote control and my thumb hovered above the power button, but I couldn't turn it off. Mad as I was, I wanted him to win, and I wanted to witness it. What started out as a rivalry turned to friendship that blossomed into something so much more. But I was so fucking wrong.

"Fuck!" I rested my head on the back of the couch and stared at the ceiling. *I need to get him out of my head.*

The call box hanging on the condo's kitchen wall rang and I ignored it. It stopped after several rings. *Good.*

My cell phone rang, but I didn't even bother checking who it was, since it wasn't the ring tone I had assigned for Sophia or Isaac. I couldn't believe I gave that fucker an assigned ring tone. Calling him *fucker* didn't sit well with me, and I realized just how messed up I was over him.

"Leave me the fuck alone!" I yelled after the call box buzzed again. It was more persistent this time. *Goddamn it.* Walking like a zombie, I bumped into chairs, a coffee table and almost tripped on a rug on my way to answer the call. "What!" I barked when I pressed the button.

"I'm so sorry, Mr. Donovan," our building's bellman said. "But your father is here and is demanding to see you."

Great. Just what I fucking needed, a visit from daddy of the decade. "Fine. Send him up." I looked down and studied my appearance. "This'll do," I said. Once upon a time I would have changed out of my green plaid pajama bottoms and the old UCLA T-shirt I'd had on for days, but not anymore.

"Why aren't you answering my calls?" he asked after he stormed in.

"I was busy," I said with a dry tone.

"Doing what?" he asked between gritted teeth. He studied me with disgust. "Why did you forfeit?"

"I didn't forfeit, I withdrew. Forfeit means ceding mid-race."

215

"I know what the difference is. They're the same to me. *Losing*," he snarled. "So why did you choose to *lose*, Foster?"

"Just not feeling it, Daddy."

"You're throwing opportunities away because of that man. I raised you better than that." He pointed his finger at me, fuming.

"Incorrect. You didn't raise me. Mom raised us. You, on the other hand, just criticized."

"You embarrass us," he said, his chin up. For a moment he looked like he was about to hit me, but of course he wouldn't. He didn't need to. He knew his words would hurt me more than any physical blow. He'd been playing with my mind since I could remember.

"Embarrass us or you?" I retorted. I wasn't in the mood to deal with his bullshit.

He was about to speak when Andrew Sorensen introduced the final skier. "Alright, ladies and gentlemen. The man on your screen is American Isaac McAllister, the final skier of the day. The weight of USA's expectations is on his shoulders after three of his compatriots failed to make it to the top three today. Can McAllister replicate his World Cup and American Cup success? We will find out in less than two minutes."

Isaac's eyes were red, their puffiness exaggerated by the dark circles around them. His facial hair was longer than usual, making him look older than twenty-five. He looked gaunt. He nodded as Alex whispered in his ears then gave her a fist-bump. He put on his goggles and gripped his poles, flexing his forearm muscles. He moved his skis back and forth.

Beep. Beep. Beep.

Isaac staked his poles on the snow with force then propelled himself down the hill with high speed. The television switched

216

to the aerial camera and Isaac glided around the first turn flawlessly. He slithered through the next couple of turns, and when the first jump approached, he tucked his poles to his sides and remained suspended in the air for a distance longer than any of the skiers before him.

"My oh my! Look at that flight from McAllister. Nice high racing line," Andrew Sorensen said. Isaac spent what seemed like four seconds in the air; he landed with a thud, loose snow floating in the air where his skis made impact. A green arrow appeared on screen, showing he was ahead of the current race leader, and if he continued at this speed, he would beat the best time of the day.

My heart pounded; I crossed my arms to hide my heavy breathing from my dad, who was also glued to the television.

The bells rang, signaling the midway point. One of the hardest turns was coming up. Three of the skiers today wiped out navigating the unforgiving curve, taking them out of the competition completely. "This is where it could get complicated, folks. By far the toughest section of this slope. McAllister is taking his time. Is he going to make it?" Pause. "He did!" Isaac slowed down a notch and the strategy paid off; he came out of the turn perfectly and kept his lead.

The end of the slope neared and, barring any catastrophic move, he'd win gold. "Can McAllister keep this up? You're witnessing the birth of a star. This is it. The final turn." Isaac put everything on the line; I held my breath as he sped across the finish line. "Isaac McAllister is the new World Champion with the fastest time by half a second!"

The camera zeroed in on Isaac as he removed his goggles and looked up at the result. He raised his fist in the air, but his smile was subdued—he seemed more relieved than happy about winning the biggest title in his career so far. The sidelines were a sea of red, white, and blue as the roaring crowd cheered for their new champion.

Alex joined him with a hug that almost knocked him over. "You did it!" she yelled, jumping up and down, her excitement practically leaping through the screen. I couldn't help but smile.

Isaac was surrounded by people giving him fist-bumps and high-fives; someone even wrapped an American flag around him. My smile faded. He was the only one yet to show joy for his flawless victory.

My father grabbed the remote and turned off the television. "That could have been you," he said, throwing the remote on the couch with force. It bounced and landed on the floor.

"Nope. That couldn't have been me, because I'm right here."

"Oh, you think this is a joke? That impostor is taking your limelight."

I had the urge to defend Isaac, but I clamped my mouth shut. He didn't deserve it, and my dad would not have cared anyway. "Why are you here?" I asked instead.

"Why am I here? To make you listen to reason. You're going to snap out of your little crush and get back to practice."

"No. No to all of that."

"It's not up to you. This is an order."

"No, Dad. I'm not leaving here, and you can't make my decisions for me."

"You really don't have what it takes," he spat. "You're weak. And they said you're like me." The disgust on his face was palpable.

"Why do you always play mind games with me? What did I ever do to you?"

"What games?"

"Your mental sabotage, Dad. *That* game." My father had used that ploy on me my entire life. "You know my every insecurity, and you know how to play them against me."

"You're losing your mind, Foster." He straightened his suit jacket. "I wanted you to be strong *up here*," he said, pointing to his temple.

"No, that's not it. The real truth is, you actually never wanted me to be better than you. It reminds you of your own shortcomings."

"Don't talk to me like that. I made you who you are." His face flamed red, a side I had never seen. *Is he losing his tightly controlled façade?*

"No, you didn't." I walked to the door, opened it and looked him in the eye. "Now tell me, Father, who's the insecure one? Me or you?"

His blue eyes darkened. He balled his fists, but being the proper man he was, he released them and stood proudly before heading out. "We're not done here," he said, pausing at the doorway.

"I think we are. Oh, and one last thing—I don't want to see you anywhere near Beijing." I slammed the door.

My knees were weak and trembling, but my heart felt light. Family could hurt you more than anyone else because they knew your weaknesses. But finally—*finally*—his criticism didn't cut through. I was enough. I was good enough.

Thirty: Isaac

Winner Takes All

I'd been staring at my gold medal since we left Whistler after the ceremony. I flipped it between my fingers, shifted it from one palm to the other. Its cool weight felt foreign somehow, heavy. I still hadn't found it in me to celebrate. I put the medal back in my pocket and focused on the view of Downtown as we approached Vancouver. *Would I have won had Foster been there?*

"Thinking about him?" Alex asked, glancing between me and the road.

"I still can't believe he withdrew," I said. "Does he really hate me that much?"

"It was his decision, Mac. I'm sure he had his reasons."

"Do you think I'd have won if he had been there?" The question had plagued me since I crossed the finish line.

"Absolutely," she insisted. I knew she'd say that; she was my coach, after all. "This is a big deal, you know? And I'm very proud of you."

I knew it was, but the happiness I thought it would bring was nowhere to be found. I wanted to win for my family, to help my parents out for all the sacrifices they had made to get me here. We didn't have a lot of money when I was growing up, but they made sure I had the right gear for training. "Did you know that my dad was my first coach?" I asked Alex.

"I don't think you told me that," she answered. "He must be very good then." Alex glanced at me, a warm smile on her face.

"He is."

"I'd love to meet him one day. Is he going to the Olympics?"

I nodded. With my prize money from the last three events, I could easily afford the tickets and a hotel room for my parents in Beijing.

"That's great, Mac." Alex took the exit to Downtown.

"I think I'm just going to stay in my room."

"OK, I'll just drop you off."

"You sure?"

"Of course." Alex pulled up in front of the hotel and put the car in park. "Hey, I'm sorry about you and Foster. I know how much you care about him."

"Thank you." Hearing his name out loud made my heart feel like it was being shredded into pieces.

"I'll call you tomorrow to plan our trip to China, OK?"

"You're that sure the committee will send me?"

"What're you talking about? You won the World Championships! Of course they will."

"OK," I said. I hopped out of the car, and Alex popped the trunk.

"Just grab your luggage, I'll take care of our gear."

"Thanks."

"Please get some rest, OK?"

As if operating on autopilot, I nodded and headed inside. Later I wondered how I made it to the room, because I didn't remember checking in and getting my key.

Sitting on the bed, I stared at my phone. I dialed Foster's number and it immediately went to voicemail. I needed to tell him the truth, and knowing that he'd never pick up, I took a deep breath and left him a message.

The phone beeped partway through my spiel, signaling I was out of time, so I called his number again and continued.

I looked out the window and reached into my pocket for my medal. I'd worked my entire life to get here, only to find that it didn't make me happy. I made a decision. After canceling my flight to Portland and booking the next flight to West Virginia, I called my mom.

"Isaac, honey, are ya OK?" she asked.

"Yeah, Ma. Sorry to wake you."

"It's alright, love. Why're ya callin' so late?"

"I'm comin' home."

"Ain't that great, Isaac. It'll be nice to see ma baby before ya go to China. We're so prouda ya."

"Thanks, Ma."

"Ya just won today against the best. That has to be some-thin'."

No, Ma. The best wasn't there. "I just miss ya and Pop." I didn't want to pretend anymore. I didn't want to hide who I was, especially to those who cared about me.

"We miss ya too, honey. I'll make a roast for ya."

"Thank you, please let Pop know."

"You betcha."

"I love you, Ma." *And I'm sorry I did everything I could to wipe out my past with lies.* I found what I was looking for, but somewhere along the way, I lost myself.

"Oh, honey. I love ya too."

* * *

My flight home was the longest trip of my life, although a part of me didn't think it was right to call the Blue Ridge Mountains of West Virginia my home. I'd erased all the evidence that could be traced back here. My heart didn't feel like it belonged anymore. It no longer fit the hole that was created when I walked away from the only home I'd ever known.

The one-way road narrowed, and I took the next turn to the stretch of dirt road that led to my family's cabin. A house that my dad built and my mom made into a home.

My tires crunched through the mix of gravel and snow. The sun had just set when I pulled up in front of our home. I grabbed my cell phone from the glove box and saw twelve missed calls and four voicemails from Alex. She had been blowing up my phone since I texted her this morning that I wasn't flying to Portland.

The door opened, and Ma and Pop came out to greet me.

"Here's our champion," Pop said, hugging me.

"How was ya trip, honey?" Ma asked.

"It was fine," I said in almost a whisper. I caught my parents' worried glance.

"Why don't cha put yer bags in yer room and I'll get dinner ready," my ma said as we entered the house.

I inhaled deeply, that familiar, comforting scent, and asked myself why I tried to hide this part of me. The love that flowed through this home was more than many got in their lifetime. I headed to my room and passed images of me hanging in the hallway. One was taken when my parents gave me my first skis. In another picture, I was helping my dad repair a damaged section of the house after a windstorm when I was thirteen. I was wearing his tool belt, which had been wrapped around my waist twice because it didn't fit. The last picture was from winning my first tournament at twelve years old, a huge smile stretched across my face. I hadn't felt that happy again until I met Foster.

My room hadn't changed in years. I only came home during spring and summer to help my dad with carpentry. It was my way of repaying them for all their sacrifices, for encouraging me to follow a dream that might or might not have happened.

* * *

"Are ya not hungry?" Ma asked.

I blinked at my plate. I was off in my own world and had been playing with my food. "Oh, I just have a lot on my mind," I answered before taking a bite of the roast my mom made especially for me. "This is really good, Ma."

My dad cleared his throat and glanced at Ma. "What's goin' on Isaac, yer not yerself?" he asked.

"Let him eat first," Ma said.

"Oh, it's OK, Ma." I met Pop's eyes. "No, I'm not myself."

Pop's brow creased. "The committee didn't pick ya?"

"It's not that, Alex thinks they will," I said.

"Then what is it, Isaac? This is yer dream. Ya been waitin' for this since ya were a lil' boy."

"I'm not happy anymore," I admitted.

"What makes ya say that? Yer the new World Champion!" Ma exclaimed.

224

Truth time. No more lies. I told them about Foster, and how I lied about where I came from and hid my accent, which ultimately led to Foster ending what we had before it had the chance to begin. "I'm so sorry I disappointed ya when all ya did was put me first." I sobbed, letting go of all the pressure and pain of these past few days. "I miss him."

Ma stood and cradled my face against her chest. "It's gonna be alright, baby. Yer home now. Everythin's gonna be just fine."

"We only want ya to be happy, ya can stay here as long as ya want. Is that what ya want?" Pop asked.

I didn't answer, because honestly, I didn't know what I wanted.

* * *

"Hey, Isaac, ya up?" Pop called.

I'd been home for three days, and all I'd done was sleep, eat, and sit in the living room, staring into space. My folks had been understanding, and never pushed for more information. They'd been disappointed, but they never judged me. That must be what they called *unconditional love*.

"Come in," I said.

He peered around the room, then picked up my gold from the World Championships from my nightstand and hung it with the rest of my medals and trophies.

"I'm sorry, Pop, for letting you and Ma down."

He stood silently, studying me.

"I'm sorry that all the sacrifices you made were for nothing.

I was selfish."

"Get up," he said

"What?"

"I wanna show ya somethin'. Get ready and meet me outside."

I found Pop waiting in his truck. I spotted my old ski gear in the bed when I walked to the passenger side. "Where're we goin'?" I asked.

"I got somethin' to show ya."

"What is it?"

"Hop in, Isaac."

We'd been driving for forty minutes when the surroundings became familiar. My dad was taking me to the slopes where I first learned to ski. He parked without a word, walked around the front of the truck, and opened my door.

"I don't wanna ski right now, Pop," I said.

"I just wanna show ya somethin', and if ya still feel the same way after, then I won't talk 'bout skiin' no more."

"I can't do this, Pop."

"Isaac Connor McAllister!" That got my attention. He only used my full name when I was in trouble—and it had been a while. "Grab your skis and follow me." This was a side of my dad I rarely saw.

I followed his request and waited for the next ski lift to take us to the top. The sun had only been up for an hour, so we and two other groups were the only people on the slope.

"Why are we here?" I asked when we reached the summit.

"I wanna show ya where yer dream began." He looked me in the eyes. "Remember when I asked why ya wanted to learn how to ski?"

I nodded. How could I forget?

"What did ya tell me the reason was?"

"Because I wanted to be an Olympian," I muttered.

"What was that? I didn't hear ya." He definitely did hear me.

"I said, because I wanted to be an Olympian."

"That's right." He closed his eyes and nodded. "I remember that." He opened his eyes and started fastening his boots. "Ya were so excited and yellin', *I wanna be an Olympian,* over and over again." He attached his skis to his boots one by one. "Somethin' changed, and it became more about winnin' and provin' somethin', and payin' me and yer ma back, and ya forgot to have fun."

"I wanted to help you and Ma," I explained.

"And we appreciate that, Isaac, but we don't need help. We're happy here. We don't have a lot, but we ain't strugglin' neither, we have what we need. This is the life we chose and we're happy. And we have an amazin' son. That's the life we dreamed for ourselves."

Speechless, all I could do was stare at my dad.

"What happened to the kid who used to love skiin'? That was all he talked about all day long. What happened to the kid who couldn't wait to wake up on a Saturday mornin' so he could hit the slopes and have fun? What happened to the kid who wanted to be an Olympian? That kid had a spark in his eyes, such passion at a young age. What happened to that kid?"

"He's gone, Pop," I said.

"I don't think he is. I think he's still in there." My dad placed his hand on my chest. "I know ya, kid. Don't ski because ya have somethin' to prove. Don't ski because you wanna make millions of dollars. I want ya to ski like the nine-year-old kid I remember, because that kid can do anything. That kid can

227

go anywhere. That kid is a future Olympian."

I fastened my boots and latched them to my skis.

"Let me ask you again, bud." My dad grabbed his ski poles. "Why did ya learn how to ski?"

"I wanted to be an Olympian," I said.

"What? I didn't hear ya."

"I wanted to be an Olympian!" I yelled.

"Atta boy!" he tapped my cheek and took off down the slope, me following his lead.

* * *

"Isaac!" Alex exclaimed when she answered my call. "Where have you been?"

"Long story. How soon can you get to West Virginia?"

"You're home?"

"Yes, and I was hoping we could train here before we head to China."

"Of course. Let me book a flight."

"Let me know when you land and I'll pick you up at the airport."

"I'm on my way."

* * *

"This is us," I said as we pulled into our gravel driveway. I filled Alex in on my sudden change of plans. After giving me an earful, Alex switched to planning and coaching mode.

"Oh my god, this cabin is beautiful," she said. "Your dad built this himself?"

"Yup." I couldn't believe I had been ashamed of this place. It really was beautiful. "Have you heard from him?" I asked Alex.

Her eyes softened. "No, I haven't. Stan told me they're heading for Beijing tomorrow."

"Oh. Well, that's good that he's going."

Alex snaked her hand around my waist and leaned her head on shoulder. "Sorry, Mac."

"I'm OK." I wasn't OK. "This is my dad, John McAllister, and my mom, Brittany McAllister." My parents were waiting outside for us. "Ma, Pop, this is my coach and friend, Alex."

"It's nice to meet ya, Alex," my dad said, offering his hand to her.

"It's a pleasure to have ya out here," Ma said.

"Thank you for having me. You have a beautiful home. This is exactly what I want to build on my property in Montana." Alex pulled her cell phone from her purse. "Is it OK if I take a picture of the cabin?"

"Absolutely," my mom said.

"I can give ya a copy of my design if ya like," my dad offered.

"Really? I would love that."

"Yes, yer family now. Let's get ya inside."

Thirty-One: Foster

We're Not Friendly

I didn't want to talk because it only made me bluer. I severed two ties in just a couple of weeks. Confronting my father had been a relief. But then there was Isaac. How could something so beautiful end in such disaster?

"Hi, Oz, can I come in?" Sophia asked, peeking through the ajar bedroom door.

Mom and Sophia were spending the night at my place so we could all leave on the same flight to Beijing tomorrow. Thankfully, my father respected my request and didn't plan on going. The little boy in me still wanted him to be there, but I was starting a new chapter in my life, and although he'd always be a character in that story, he didn't have to be a part of my journey. It was a sad thought, but it needed to be done.

"Come in," I said, and cleared my bed of luggage. "Perfect timing. I just finished packing."

She sat on the bed, examining the room. "Can I ask you something?"

"Anything," I said, flopping down beside her.

"Don't you love Dad anymore?"

"Of course I do. What makes you say that?" I held my breath

for her response. I didn't think Dad would say something hurtful about me in front of Sophia, but what did I really know? Two of the most special men in my life ended up hurting me.

"I heard him talking to Mom and he said you didn't want him to see you in China."

"Oh, Red. Look at me." My bed creaked as we shifted to face each other. "I love Dad, and I always will, but sometimes people we love do things we don't like and we don't have to see them for a while, and that's OK. That doesn't mean you stop loving them. You just need time and space. Do you understand that?"

"I think so," she said, nodding. "I love you, Oz, and I don't want to stop seeing you."

"I love you too, and I'm always here for you. You're one of my favorite people."

"One of?"

"Yup." I reached over and kissed the top of her head.

"You used to say I *was* your favorite." She chuckled. "Is Isaac your other favorite?"

Oh god! I didn't want to have this conversation about Isaac too. "Maybe," I said, and forced a laugh. "Why don't you show me your outfit for tomorrow?" She took the subject-change bait and led me to her bedroom.

* * *

"She's out." My mom said, glancing over me at Sophia who was sitting by the airplane window. "Completely passed out."

231

"She's a trooper. Fourteen-hour flights are no joke," I said to my mom, who was sitting on the other side of the aisle.

"She loves you so much, you know. She thinks the world of you."

I pushed loose locks of hair from Sophia's face and nodded. "I know."

"What's with you and Isaac?" she asked. "Sophia has been talking about how great he is and that she's never seen you happier."

"Do I look happy?" The sarcasm came out before I had a chance to filter my words. "Sorry, Mom. I just have a lot of stuff going on."

She reached out to touch my hand. "That's OK. Is it about your dad, or did something happen between you and Isaac?"

"Both," I admitted.

"Oh, sweetheart. I talked to your father and asked him to get some help. He didn't have the best relationship with your grandfather, you know."

"What do you mean?"

"Your grandfather died when you were young, so you may not remember much about him. He was always hard on your father. He treated your dad like he was never good enough. Always comparing him to his older brothers, the successful businessmen."

"He never talks about him," I said. *He never talked about anything.*

"I'm not making excuses for him, but he really loves you. He might not be able to show it, but it is hard for him to express himself. He promised he'd get help."

I nodded slowly. It made sense why he treated me the way he did—but I wasn't him, and he wasn't his dad.

"Now, this Isaac. Do you like him?"

"A lot. But it's over now."

"Why?"

"Because he did something. It doesn't matter. It's over now."

"Was it something unforgivable?"

Was it something unforgivable? I studied her face as I considered the answer. What Isaac did hurt, but it wasn't unforgivable.

My mom saw my response on my face. "I think that answers that."

"I don't know, Mom. It's more complicated than that," I insisted, frowning at the seat in front of me.

"You'll figure it out. You always do." She tapped my hand and leaned back, reclining her seat.

* * *

"Welcome to the Mandarin Oriental Hotel," the concierge greeted us when we entered the five-star hotel. The white marble floor reflected the chandelier suspended from the high ceiling in the open lobby. There was an abstract sculpture of a red dragon hanging on the wall, and traditional Chinese calligraphy adorned the space behind the glass-topped reception desk.

"Hello, my name is Foster Donovan, we're checking in."

"Three suites, is that correct, Mr. Donovan?" the man asked, glancing at his computer. "Your other party arrived yesterday."

"Yes, that's correct," I answered. Stan and the rest of my team flew in yesterday to get everything ready for training.

We'd decided to add training runs as it had been weeks since I'd hit the slopes.

"You have a beautiful hotel," Sophia said.

"Thank you. This is one of the best in Beijing," he said.

The concierge waved someone in, and a gentleman in a black suit with white gloves arrived to load our luggage onto a rolling cart. "Please escort Mr. Donovan's party to their suite," the concierge said, and handed us our keys. "Enjoy your stay, and please let me know if we can assist you further."

"Will do. Thank you."

"Is Isaac staying with us?" Sophia asked.

"Um, I don't think so. I'm sure he's probably staying with his team," I said.

"Oh, OK. When can I see him?"

"Sophia, honey," my mom said, touching her arm to get her attention, "I'm sure Isaac and his team are very busy. They have a big competition coming up. So does your brother."

We entered the elevator, and Sophia continued her line of questioning. "How about after the race?"

My mom glanced at me, unsure how to answer. I didn't want to lie to Sophia. "Hey, Red. Isaac and I aren't..." I tried to find the words to describe the touchy situation.

"Aren't what?"

"We aren't together. We were just friends and right now we're not..."

Sophie studied my face, waiting for me to finish.

What the fuck is wrong with me? Why was it so hard to say that Isaac and I would never be together? Why couldn't I tell Sophia that she might not see him again? Why was it so hard to say that she should forget him altogether? "We're not friendly right now." I cringed.

"Oh." Sophia's smile faded. "I'm sorry to hear that. I like him."

I do too.

* * *

A soft knock woke me from my nap. I rubbed my eyes and stretched before answering the door.

"I have a package for you, Mr. Donovan," the bellman said, handing me a box from Lululemon.

"Thank you," I said. I opened the package, and felt a ripple of excitement—the official Canadian gear for the opening ceremony. My cell phone on top of the nightstand started vibrating. I was surprised to see Travis Montgomery's name across the screen.

"Hey, Travis!" I said.

"Hey, Foster, how are you?"

"I'm fine. What time is it over there?"

"Very late," he said, chuckling. "I just wanted to see how you're doing and wish you luck in Beijing."

Travis had been texting me since my withdrawal from the World Championships, but I hadn't told him the reason why. I felt guilty giving him a generic response, and figured this was the reason he finally called. "I'm doing well," I lied.

"You know I'm here for you, right? I know how much pressure you're under. I've been there myself."

"It isn't the pressure," I admitted.

"Then what is it, man?"

I sighed and told Travis everything. How Isaac and I met,

how I felt about him, and all the lies he'd told.

Travis was silent after I finished. "Wow," he said finally.

"I know, right? Who would do such a thing?"

More silence followed before Travis cleared his throat. "Do you remember when I used to pretend to like women?"

"That's not the same, Travis," I argued.

"Isn't it, though? It sounds like Isaac hid who he was because of his fear of being accepted. I get that he hurt you, Foster. But I also understand Isaac because I hid in the closet for years, lying about who I was."

"I don't know, man. It's more complicated than that," I insisted.

"I guess. I'm just saying that hiding in the closet is not much different than hiding where you came from."

We chatted a little longer about the Olympics and Ashton. After I hung up, his comments lingered. *Had I overreacted?*

Thirty-Two: Isaac

The Opening Ceremony

Excitement buzzed in the air. The corridors that housed the athletes before they entered the Olympic stadium hummed, chatter in all different languages drowned each other out, and everywhere faces were filled with pride and elation. Each nation's representative was donned their country's colors. Giant flags stood next to each country's name, which was written in English and Mandarin, the representatives waiting for their chance to be in the spotlight.

Oversized television screens hung from the ceiling, allowing us to watch the Parade of Nations until our countries joined the festivities. The crowd cheered, and the cameras fanned the stands full of fans from all over the world waving mini flags. The orchestra started playing an upbeat song as the officials representing China and the Olympic Committee occupied their box seats.

The lights dimmed. A low hum vibrated through the stadium before more than a hundred drones flew, forming Chinese characters that became the words *Welcome to Beijing 2022 Winter Olympics.*

The cameras returned to the center of the stadium, where several men stood in front of large traditional drums. The music stopped, and the men beat a rhythmic pattern I could feel outside the stadium. After a short, energetic performance, the beat became a steady drum roll that morphed into loud bangs, just in time for the speaker to announce the first nation to enter the arena. "Albania," the female announcer said in English, then in Mandarin.

One by one, countries were called, and I held my breath when I saw Canada's flag. "Canada," the announcer stated, followed by a group of men and women wearing hooded red winter coats over black tracksuits, the word *CANADA* printed in white on their chests. Foster wasn't Canada's flag-bearer, but he was standing next to the female athlete who was, waving a mini flag.

He looked dashing in everything he wore, and my stomach fluttered seeing him in his official Olympic gear. I missed him, and wished we were still talking because I would have loved to see him after the ceremony. He and everyone on his team had their cell phones out, filming the celebrations.

Being from the United States of America meant we were always one of the last countries to join the Parade of Nations. "Ukraine," the announcer eventually called.

The USA was next, so we lined up to take our turn. We were dressed in Polo Ralph Lauren from head to toe. Literally. I looked down to make sure I was presentable for my first Olympics. My white pants with the Team USA logo near my thigh were crisp, and I had opted for the thick blue knitted sweater with the American flag above the five Olympic rings. All of our winter jackets were the same, a red and blue plaid with solid blue sleeves and hoodie.

"The United States of America," the announcer said.

I fixed my hat—blue with red and white trim—tightened the blue laces of my red boots, and had my cell ready so I could secure the memory of this momentous event; the second most unforgettable evening of my life. The surrealness of being at the Olympics lessened the throb of missing Foster for a brief moment.

We walked out to a stadium full of bright flashing lights from spectators. The beating of the drums and pounding of our boots heightened my excitement, and I moved my phone around to capture as much as I could.

The countries that had already marched observed us, and when we passed by Team Canada, my screen filled with Foster's face, watching me. I lowered my phone and our eyes met.

He didn't seem mad or happy. He kept his unreadable eyes on mine until we passed them.

I chanced a look back and saw him still staring at me, but he quickly shifted his gaze away.

* * *

The following morning was my first training run, and I invited my parents to come with Alex and me. They had never been to a competition on this scale, so I wanted to make this Olympics special for them.

"This is where you can watch us." Alex had found a place for them at the bottom of the slope. "You can see Isaac on that big screen too." She pointed to one of the two giant screens on both sides of the finish line.

"Have a great practice, honey!" Ma called.

"Just have fun," Pop added.

"I will," I said, and hugged them. I checked the screen and saw that Foster was leading the standings after his practice run, by a lot.

"Dang," Alex whistled, looking at Foster's time.

"We have our work cut out for us," I said.

* * *

"Great job today, Isaac," my mom said on our way to lunch after training. I recorded a great first practice time, one-twentieth of a second behind Foster's, putting me in second place.

"Thanks, Ma. Alex has a plan for tomorrow."

"I got this, Brittany," Alex said to my mom. "John and I chatted a little and we're gonna try something tomorrow." My heart swelled with the inclusion of my dad.

The second day of practice came, and again my parents watched from the stands. Red lights along the finish line flashed to let us know that a skier was about to launch.

"It's Foster," Alex said, and I looked up to see him on the screen. He was talking to Stan. After a fist-bump, Foster jumped and hit the slopes, sliding and passing every single turn without hesitation. His airtime had extended, and before we could even process his greatness, he was already crossing the finish line, recording an even faster time than yesterday.

My parents clapped, always appreciative of a top performance. "Good job," my dad even yelled.

Foster took off his goggles and looked up, pumping his fist in the air after seeing his time. He casually glanced around, and his stare intensified when he saw me. His team joined him and they skied away from us.

"Foster!" I hurried to catch up with him and his team, but he didn't stop. He didn't even slow down. I managed to reach him. "Do you have a minute? I just want to talk."

He gave me a quick glance, his eyes narrowed, lips pursed. "I don't have a minute. Not even a second for you."

I deserve that. Stunned by his coldness, I watched his back as he moved further away. *You can't give up.* I jogged to catch up with him again. "I just need to explain," I pleaded.

He stopped and looked at his team. "I'll catch up with you later," he said to them. When they were out of earshot, he looked at me. "We don't have anything to talk about. You had all the time in the world to tell me the truth, but you didn't." He lowered his voice, as we'd started earning several glances from others. "Don't bother me anymore. I have more important things to do than listen to liars." He walked away.

Alex came up behind me, her hand on my back.

"He's never gonna forgive me," I said, feeling exhausted. "I hurt him so bad, he won't even talk to me."

"I'm sorry, Mac. You think you'll be OK to practice?"

"Yes. We have work to do."

* * *

Alex and Pop's plan worked and I finished the day with the best time, placing me ahead of Foster after the final training run heading into tomorrow's race. I balled my right hand into a fist and a sharp pained traveled to my wrist, making me wince.

"Great job, Mac. You did it!" Alex exclaimed.

I nodded, and prayed it wasn't as bad as it was four years ago. The thought of not being able to compete again made my chest tighten, and I wheezed. It didn't escape Alex.

"Hey, are you OK?" she asked.

"Yeah," I answered after taking another deep breath.

"Why don't we cool off, then we can talk about our plan for the final race tomorrow?"

"Actually, is it OK if we go back to the Olympic Village?" I avoided her gaze and continued walking. "I can use the gym over there."

"Then that's what we'll do," she concurred. "I'll bring these." She grabbed my skis. "Why don't you go ahead with your folks and I'll see you there."

"You're not coming?" I asked.

"I need to pick up a couple of things." Alex headed inside the club and, obviously sensing me still there, turned and waved. "You go ahead."

"What's on yer mind?" Ma asked when we were inside the van. "Ya been quiet since we left practice."

I stared at my right hand laying over the left in my lap. Outside was a blur as we sped along the highway to drop my parents off at their hotel.

"That was some good practice, kiddo. Ya should be very proud," Pop added.

I glanced at our driver before I turned to face my parents. "I hurt my hand again," I whispered.

"Oh, sweetie." Ma placed her hand to her chest, her eyes

tearing up.

Pop reached over to touch my knee and gave it a gentle squeeze. "Is it bad?"

I shook my head, and opened and closed my hand slowly, repeatedly. "I don't know, Pop. I...I..." Tears came to my eyes, shutting off my throat. *This can't be happening.* I'd worked so hard; I was so close.

Our driver glanced at us in the rearview mirror, sympathy in his eyes. He nodded once before bringing his attention back to the road.

"It's OK, love. We're here for ya, whatever ya wanna do." My mom pulled me into a hug and kissed my head.

"Ya gotta tell Alex, Isaac," Pop said.

He was right, Alex needed to know. I was just afraid she'd recommend I pull out of the race. "I will, Pop."

* * *

Later, after my modified cool-off and early dinner, I went to the village rooftop to admire the slopes from a distance. Heat lamps and a gas fireplace provided warmth in the brisk winter air. I asked Alex to meet me up there so we could speak privately. *No more lies.* She needed to know the truth.

The metal door opened, and Alex came out carrying a small bag. Her serious eyes traveled quickly down to my hand as she walked toward me.

"I hurt my hand again, during practice," I said when she was a couple of feet from me. "I don't know what to do."

She held my right hand and slowly lifted it to inspect. It was swollen, and the pain was worse than it was earlier. "I kinda suspected that, because you had that same look when you hurt it at Lake Tahoe." She led me to the bench and we sat side by side. She reached into her bag and retrieved a packet. "That's why I went to the Olympic medical team to ask for advice." She unwrapped a wrist sleeve and put it on me. "It's supposed to be tight to help with the swelling."

I cleared my throat and asked the question I had been dreading. "Did they tell you to... pull me out of the race?" I held my breath.

"No. But they gave me a list of meds you can take that are approved by the committee," she answered. I let out a laugh of relief. Alex opened a small container of pills and tipped one into my good hand. "They told me that you should take this every six hours. It's not prescription."

"What are they?" I asked, popping the pill in my mouth and accepting the bottle of water Alex offered. I gulped it down.

"It's an over-the-counter anti-inflammatory. Let's hope the sleeve and the pills help."

"What if they don't? I'm not quitting," I said with conviction. I would race even if it killed me.

"We'll worry about that tomorrow."

Thirty-Three: Foster

I've Already Won

Whoever came up with the idea to send a reminder of pictures taken in the last month needed to get fucking fired. As if seeing Isaac training, not talking to him, not holding him, not kissing him, wasn't torture enough, my iPhone flaunted a selfie of Isaac and I in front of Oh My God It's a Wiener. Who the fuck named a hot dog stand that? Although, if I was being honest, it was kinda genius. Whatever. That wasn't the point. I tapped my phone and the picture filled up my screen, Isaac sporting a too-cool-for-a-selfie-but-I-actually-love-it smile, while I beamed behind him, my free hand wrapped around his shoulder. Our faces were touching, and if I closed my eyes, I could still smell him.

I was a jerk to him earlier, but I had to be. It was that or profess my love for him, and the latter wasn't going to happen. I let myself gaze at the image for a couple more seconds before the dull ache in my chest was too much to bear. After closing the picture, I stared at my phone before going to my voicemail, where two messages from Isaac had sat for days. My curiosity finally won. I got up and headed to the mini fridge, and grabbed the first mini alcohol I could find. After gulping the first bottle, I reached for another and downed that too. Lubricated enough to face the music, I pressed play.

"Did you know that my first ski poles were made out of wood? It was so cool. My dad made them. He's a carpenter, and he's very good at making things from scratch. My mom painted them red, white, and blue so they would look like regular poles. My parents are a great team like that." Deep breath. *"My dad coached me until I was eighteen years old. He took me to every competition within driving distance. We couldn't afford to stay in a hotel, so traveling out of state wasn't an option. It's the same reason I only skied locally until the US Ski and Snowboard Association provided their support.*

"My parents saved up so I could go to ski camp every year. That's where I met Sawyer. Some kids made fun of the way I talked. They called me 'stupid' because I talked slow, so I begged Sawyer to help me hide my accent. He still doesn't approve, but he knew it was important to me, so he helped."

The message cut off, and with a trembling hand, I played the second message.

"It's me again, the last message was too long. Aside from where I grew up, everything I told you was true. What I feel for you is real. I love you, Foster, and I'll keep calling until you talk to me. I'm sorry I lied. I'm sorry I hurt you. I miss you."

"Fuck you," I whispered, and threw my phone on the bed. *You don't get to lie to me and say that. I was fine without you.* My mind was running a million miles per hour, torn between confronting him and forgetting his existence altogether. I hated how I felt when I found out he lied, and I hated myself even more for loving him despite it.

Twenty minutes and two more mini bottles of Johnnie

Walker later, I grabbed my wallet and Olympic credentials and headed out.

Pounding the L button didn't make the elevator move any faster, and I was convinced it slowed down to punish whoever did such an act. "Come on! Can you move any slower?" I almost let out a curse when the elevator stopped on the sixth floor, but I behaved. "Hi," I said to the couple who entered, both dressed to the nines. The man was wearing a charcoal suit with a crisp white shirt and no tie. The woman was wearing a double-breasted red wool pea coat over a pleated skirt. "Hello," the man said, and wrapped his hand protectively around her waist, eyeing me.

Not my type, buddy. The elevator opened in the lobby and I made a beeline to the reception. "Good evening, Mr. Donovan. How can I assist you today? Is the suite to your satisfaction?" the concierge asked.

"Oh yes, it's perfect. Can you please arrange a ride for me?" I usually preferred to drive, but this was my first time visiting Beijing and I didn't want to get lost, not to mentioned the four mini-bottles I polished minutes ago.

"Of course, sir." He picked up the phone and greeted the person on the other end in Mandarin. He placed the receiver to his chest and asked, "Where are you headed, Mr. Donovan?"

"The Olympic Village."

"Do you need the driver to wait for you?"

I didn't know how to answer that since I didn't know myself. This was not a well-thought-out plan. "I'm not sure yet. Can I call the hotel when I'm done?"

"Absolutely, sir." He finished his conversation on the phone. "The driver will be here in two minutes. Take your time and call this number when you're ready to return." He handed me a matte-black calling card with the hotel logo embossed on the top. "That's my direct number," he said, pointing to the bottom of the card.

"Great. Thank you," I said, and headed outside to wait for my ride.

* * *

I started to second-guess my decision the closer we got to the Olympic Village. The Scotch whisky courage was diminishing, and I was two seconds away from asking the driver to turn around.

"We are here, Mr. Donovan," the driver said, and exited the car to open my door.

I looked up. The modern buildings were adorned with flags from different countries displayed in windows. Between each complex was a garden illuminated with hanging red lanterns and portable heaters.

Before I could change my mind, I stepped from the car. "Thank you."

"May I see your credentials, sir?" the security guard asked when I tried to enter the village.

"Oh, here." I showed him my photo identification.

He examined the badge and looked at me, comparing my face to the photo. "You're going to have to wear that inside, Mr. Donovan," he instructed.

I knew safety was their top priority, so I put the lanyard over my head and did what I was told. "Thank you. Can I ask you where Team USA is?"

"They are located in the Peace building." He pointed to the third-to-last building. "Floors eight to sixteen."

"Xie xie," I thanked him.

Well, this was going to be an adventure. There were eight floors where Isaac could be, and each floor had about thirty rooms. Never one to back down from a challenge, I started my search on level eight.

"Hey, Foster, what're you doing here?" An American athlete I didn't know sidled up to me. I quickly glanced at his credentials: his name was Conrad and he was a speed skater.

"Hey, buddy! Just here visiting a friend. Do you happen to know where Isaac McAllister and his coach, Alex, are?" I asked.

"Alex is right there," he said, pointing down the hallway. "Yo, Alex! My man Foster is looking for you!"

I fought the urge to roll my eyes and instead searched in the direction he was pointing.

"If you need anything, just holla," Conrad said, walking away. *What a tool.* "Thanks, man."

"Foster?" Alex hesitated before deciding to give me a hug. "It's nice to see you. Great training today."

"Thank you." I glanced around to see if Isaac was behind her.

"Looking for him?"

"Um, yeah. I just need to speak to him real quick." The longer I stood there, the more I questioned my decision for coming. But I needed to ask him.

"Rooftop."

"Thank you, Alex." I jogged to the elevator.

More red lanterns were strung across the rooftop. Lounge chairs with red cushions were arranged around a giant rectangular gas fire pit, producing enough heat to warm a small section. Isaac was looking toward the slopes lit with LED lights, his hands spread on the rail; his right hand was covered in a sleeve. "Was any of it true?" I asked, coming up behind him.

His body tensed. He turned slowly, shock on his face.

"Were any of the things you said in your messages true?" I asked again, showing him my cell phone.

His eyes softened and he nodded.

That wasn't enough. I needed him to tell me. "Say it," I demanded, and moved one step closer.

He swallowed hard, and the lanterns above us made his teary eyes shine. "I meant everything that I said. I love you and I miss you. And I will do anything to prove it to you. Just give me a chance."

I rushed to him and he met me halfway. All the pent-up emotions came rushing out of me; I reached for him and he dove into my lips. We devoured each other, the best way I knew how to express how much I missed him.

"Tell me what I need to do to make you believe me?" Isaac asked.

"I don't want you to do anything but love me. To love me without ifs and whens. Just an all-consuming love that you can't bear to live without. Because no matter what happens tomorrow, if we have that, we both win. So, what's it going to be?"

"I already do." He cupped my face and placed gentle kisses on my nose, cheeks, lips. "I'm gonna hate being the one that hands you your first Olympic defeat tomorrow."

A rowdy laugh escaped my mouth. "We'll see about that, rookie." I held Isaac's wrapped hand and tenderly ran my fingers over it. "What happened?"

He looked down at our joined hands and lifted them to his lips. "I hurt it during practice."

"Oh shit. Are you gonna be OK?"

"I think so. Alex met with the medical team, and they gave me something to reduce the swelling."

"What about the race tomorrow?"

Isaac's face became serious. He combed my hair and whispered, "Being with you, I've already won." He pulled me into his arms and whispered through my hair. "I really want to take you to my room and show you how much I love you and how much I've missed you, but with tomorrow's race, we need to take it easy. We can't risk one of us being *sore*."

"Making excuses already, are you?" I teased. "This is going to be a problem in the future."

Isaac became rigid under me. "What's gonna be a problem?"

I peeled from his embrace and looked into his eyes. "You know, we race the same events."

"OK?" he asked, clearly not following my train of thought.

"We'll have to share a room, and it'll be a torture to not do it, you know?"

He turned me around and wrapped his arm around my chest as we admired the view of the Olympic venue. "I could just lay there and let you do all the work," he growled and ground his growing erection on my ass.

I elbowed him harder and he squeaked.

"Are you trying to injure me?" Isaac joked.

"I'm sorry, that was harder than I intended."

"Oh, I see. Pulling a Tonya Harding on me. That's low!"

"I didn't know you were this funny," I said.

Isaac tightened his hold on me. "I hope that's OK."

"Are you kidding me? I fucking love it," I assured him.

"It's so beautiful out here," Isaac said, looking up to the sky. "When you look up and see the billions of stars, do you ever think that there could be another you out there?" he asked.

"Sometimes," I whispered. Isaac shifted, turning his gaze from the inky black sky, peppered with incandescent specs of light, to me. "But if there are billions of Fosters out there, I hope they're doing the same thing as I am. Because being with you in this lifetime, doesn't feel like enough, Isaac."

"I love you so much, Foster. I am sorry I hurt you. I will never lie to you again," Isaac said, his voice quivering.

"I know you are, Mac. I'm sorry I iced you. With what happened with you and me and then my father, I was all over the place. I promise to always hear you out whenever we have a problem." Listening to my mom and Travis made me realize how I overreacted, but I was hurt and stubborn so I disregarded Isaac's feelings. I would never do that again.

Isaac kissed my lips and then asked, "What happened between you and your dad?"

I told Isaac all about the fights I had with my dad, up to and including his recent visit to my place where I finally confronted him.

"I'm sorry, Foster." Isaac placed his hand behind my neck, bring our foreheads together.

The metal door on the rooftop opened and out came Alex holding three glasses of a steaming drink. "I brought you drinks."

Isaac raised an eyebrow, and Alex continued. "Well, also to let you know that you two need to get to bed. Big day for both of you tomorrow."

"I need to go anyway." I moved, but Isaac wouldn't let go of me.

"You don't have to go now. Let's enjoy some hot tea first," Alex suggested, and we each took a cup of tea from the tray.

"Can you stay for a little?" Isaac asked, his puppy eyes begging. "Please?"

"You can't use that look on me all the time. That's not fair."

Thirty-Four: Foster

The Battle for Gold

My agent and good friend Aaliyah Price had secured us a private lounge in the club at the ski venue where Isaac and I could stay until our turns for the final race. We helped each other get ready, and it took all our self-control to keep from bending each other over the couch.

"There," Isaac said, zipping the back of my red-and-black speed suit emblazoned with *CANADA* in white font on the front. He turned me so I was facing him and placed his lips on mine.

"I love you," I said.

"I love you too," he responded, or at least I thought that was what he said, since our lips and tongues were tangled in a sword fight. Sword fighting sounded good right now. "You're totally hard, aren't you?" he asked, and cupped my bulge.

"I can't help it. Is it bad that I'm more excited to bone you than to race?"

"Not bad at all, I was thinking the same, only I was the one boning," Isaac said with a low chuckle.

"How's your hand?" I asked when he tried putting his glove

254

over the hand sleeve.

"It's better," he said, opening and closing his injured hand. "It's not one hundred percent, but good enough to ski without risking permanent damage. I'm taking a break after the Olympics to let it heal completely."

I wrapped my arms around him, thankful I got to experience this moment with him. "I'm really glad too." I planted a soft kiss on Isaac's lips, which he met and turned into a passionate one.

"Knock, knock," Alex called, and I groaned.

"Your coach is a cock-blocker. She needs to pay for all the interruptions. When are you firing her?" I joked.

"You like her. Admit it."

I did like Alex. She was a cool gal and took no bull from anyone, Isaac and I included.

"You wouldn't believe the conversation I had with the association," Alex said the moment she entered the room. She was slightly out of breath.

"Did you sprint to get here?" I asked. "Why don't you sit down?"

"Can't, I'm too keyed up." She took another deep breath and removed her jacket. "Anyway, I just got off the phone with Jonathan from the association's office in Utah, did you meet him when you were there?"

Isaac nodded. "What about him?"

"Well, he just told me that an executive from Rossignol, you know, one of the biggest ski and outdoor brands in the world—"

Isaac motioned for her to get to the point. "I know who they are, Alex. What did Jonathan say about them?"

I sat down on the couch and watched their conversation.

"Right," she said, shaking her head. And I couldn't blame her lack of articulation. I had a decent guess why an executive of a ski brand was in town, and it was worth getting excited about. This probably meant good news for Isaac. "Jonathan told me the executive is here to speak to you and wants to sign you to a contract. So I asked Jonathan if I could have that person's name and contact number, and because I'm your coach, he gave it to me. So I called them and told him who I was, and I told him where we're staying." Alex looked like she used up all the oxygen in her lungs delivering those words without pause.

Isaac put his hands on her shoulders with a smile on his face. "Alex, breathe with me, OK?"

She nodded and took a few deep breaths.

"Right. Now, what did they say?"

Alex exhaled. "They would like to offer you ten million dollars to endorse them."

Isaac's jaw dropped; his eyes widened. He looked at me and then back to Alex. "Did you say...?"

"Yes, I said yes!" she declared. "Ten million dollars!"

Isaac put his hands to his head. "Ten million dollars."

I stood and hugged them both, such incredible news. Rossignol couldn't have picked a better person to endorse them. "Congratulations, Mac. I'm so proud of you." I turned to Alex next. "Great job, Alex. You both deserve this."

"Thank you. We're gonna need a lawyer or an agent to facilitate all this," Alex informed Mac.

"I wouldn't even know where to begin looking for one," Isaac said, still looking shellshocked.

"My agent, Aaliyah, is in Beijing to watch the race. I can connect all three of you together. She's amazing. She represents Travis Montgomery too—you know, the tennis star."

"Thank you," Isaac said. "I can't believe this is finally happening."

"Believe it," I said. "This is the first of many more, I have no doubts."

* * *

Isaac and Alex joined our team at the launch gate, where skiers and their entourages waited for their turns. "The Chinese Olympic Committee did an amazing job with this," Alex said as she looked around the room equipped with ellipticals, stationary bikes and treadmills to keep skiers warmed up for the race. Television screens were everywhere we looked, with plenty of stations and languages to choose from. Usually, the area where skiers waited for their turn to race was a small room, but the Yanqing Ski Resort built a spacious lounge complete with bars for complimentary beverages, a restaurant with healthy meal choices, available masseuses, and plenty of seating arrangements.

Isaac turned the channel to NBC Sports and raised the volume. "Is this OK?" he asked as the cameras panned to Andrew Sorensen.

"It's perfect," Stan and I said at the same time.

"The medal race for the men's alpine downhill skiing at the 2022 Winter Olympics is underway in Yanqing District. Welcome everyone, to the steepest downhill track in Olympic history, and one of the most challenging we've ever seen. We are just moments away from crowning this year's Olympic champion. My name is Andrew Sorensen, and I'm so excited for what is bound to be an action-packed day." He turned to his fellow broadcaster. "OK, Larry, let's talk about the competitors. A heavy favorite to win his second consecutive Olympic gold is Foster Donovan, skiing for Team Canada."

Stan slapped my back, and Alex and Isaac clapped at the mention of my name.

Andrew and Larry continued their analysis of each racer. "Isaac McAllister is making his Winter Olympics debut at twenty-five years old. He and Foster Donovan are fighting for the lead after each had amazing training runs. Foster was successful in leading the first day, then Isaac stepped it up and took the lead yesterday. Few outside of skiing were aware of Isaac McAllister's talents, but I think he's about to become a household name."

I whistled, and Alex and Stan gave each other high-fives.

"May the best team win," Stan said to Alex.

"Good luck guys," she responded.

One by one, racers skied and recorded their times. A small section below was dedicated to the top three times, and a revolving door of skiers replaced each other as one knocked the other from the podium. The field of fifty-six skiers from different countries was now narrowed down to six.

"Yoshi is next," Alex said as Yoshi walked toward the platform.

"Yoshi!" Isaac called, and Yoshi headed in our direction. "Good luck, bro."

"Thanks, Mac. By the way, this is my last race with Japan."

"What? Why?"

"I think my work ethic will *gel* more with the US, and I have more in common with my peers from the US, so I'm meeting with the US Association next month."

"That's great, Yoshi. Good luck out there."

Yoshi's coach urged him to move it along, so he gave Isaac a quick fist-bump.

"Good luck, Yoshi," I yelled, and he waved to acknowledge me.

Yoshi hit the slopes and surprised everyone with his time, placing himself as the current leader. An image of him appeared on the screen, tears welling in his eyes.

"Go, Yoshi!" Isaac cheered, clapping loudly. "Yeah!" My respect for Isaac grew. I could learn a thing or two about being supportive myself.

He glanced in my direction and winked. *I love you*, he mouthed.

I love you too, I responded.

Isaac and I started stretching and preparing for our turns when the third-to-last skier stepped up. I was next, and Isaac was the last skier of the event.

Stan grabbed my skis and we headed to the gate.

"Foster!" Isaac called, rushing toward me. "Show 'em why you're the best." He hugged me, and I could feel his heart beating as fast as mine. "You got this."

"Whatever happens, we'll have each other," I said before kissing him on the lips, earning us shocked glances from onlookers.

"You have me and I have you. This is just something we have to do," Isaac said.

I nodded.

As I put my goggles on, I realized this was the first time I had felt inspired. Sure, I was excited every time I raced, but I didn't think I'd ever been *inspired.*

I was gone right after the third beep, soon passing the first turn with perfection. I swooshed and slushed my way to the first hill, and when I jumped, I had more airtime than in my trainings. That meant shaving off time spent on the ground, and ultimately adding to my lead. The next tricky turn approached and, just like Stan and I planned, I rounded it tightly, and my execution was better than our training runs. I was on track to break the Olympic record I had set four years ago.

I slid through the track with ease and precision. Before I knew it, the bells were ringing at the halfway point. The second hill approaching was the biggest of the three. I tucked my body into a ball before pushing off the edge and leaning forward to reduce lag. After a perfect landing, I took advantage of the steeper slope to increase my speed. This was where most racers would slow down to prevent a wipeout. But I was a champion, so I rode it all the way down.

Pandemonium greeted me when I crossed the finish line. Canadian flags waved, and chants of "Fo-ster! Fo-ster! Fo-ster!" echoed through the valley. I looked up to check the standings. Not only had I replaced Yoshi in first place by three seconds, I also beat my old record by two. "Yes!" I yelled. I took my goggles off and threw them into the crowd.

I combed the screaming spectators for my mom and Sophia, as only family and friends made up the front of the crowd. As soon as I found them, I skied over.

My mom kissed my cheeks when I reached the out-of-bounds ropes.

Sophia was jumping up and down. "I'm so proud of you, Oz," she said, kissing me. "You're the best!"

"Thanks, Red."

My finish-line support team joined me and lifted me up on their shoulders. They carried me to the podium, where Yoshi had moved to the silver medal position. I took my place next to him in the slot for gold.

Someone offered me a Canadian flag, and I wrapped it around my neck like a cape.

"Congrats, Foster," Yoshi said. "That run was sick, dude. I don't think anyone can beat that."

"Thanks, man. That was the best I've skied. Ever!" I looked up to the gate, where I knew Isaac was watching.

Come on, Mac, you got this.

Thirty-Five: Isaac

Mac and Oz

"That's my man!" I screamed to Alex, who was watching the replay of Foster's incredible run.

"Holy shit," she said. "He just beat his own record from four years ago." One of the organizers gave us the green light to get ready for my launch. "Are you ready?" Alex asked.

"Let's do this," I said, and we headed to the gate. I fastened my boots and engaged them to my skis, going through my usual ritual. A dull ache traveled down my wrist after stretching my right hand.

Alex checked my ski poles before handing them to me. "Hey, Isaac."

"What's up?"

"You would tell me if your hand was not better, right?"

"Of course," I said, and that was the truth. "It still hurts, but it's better than before. I can do this."

"OK." She exhaled. "I just want to let you know that I'm proud of you. Being here with you is a dream come true." Her eyes welled as she spoke. "When you hit the track, I want you to forget about the million-dollar contract. I want you to just have some fun. You're already an Olympian. Not a lot of people can say that."

Just have some fun. Like Pop always said. "Thanks, Alex. I'm here because of your help. Remember when you told me you only coached winners?"

"Damn right I do," she said.

"I'll make us winners."

"You're already a winner in my eyes." She pulled me in to kiss my cheek.

"Here we go." I put my goggles on just as the first beep sounded.

"Go get 'em," Alex said after the second beep.

Third beep. "Just have some fun," I said, and jumped toward my dream, channeling the nine-year-old kid who could win anything. I set aside the pain and focused on the glory. *I can do this.*

* * *

Sixteen Years Ago

"Hey, Pop, I did it!" I yelled when I made it to the bottom of the bunny hill without falling on my butt. I'd been trying since the morning I unwrapped my Christmas present from my mom and dad. It hadn't been hard to guess what it was because of the size and shape of the gift. My folks had promised me a pair of skis if I stayed out of trouble and did well in school. I thought they'd forgotten, and since we didn't have a lot of money, I didn't ask. But it had been the best Christmas morning when Pop brought the gift from his shop outside.

"Ya did it, buddy!" My dad matched my excitement, giving me

high-fives. "I knew ya could."

"That was a lot of fun, Pop."

"See what happens when ya work hard and have fun at the same time?" My dad sat on the snow, leaning back with his elbows on the ground. "What do ya wanna be when yer older?" he asked thoughtfully.

"I wanna ski all the time. Can I do that?"

"Ya can do whatever ya want, Isaac," Pop said. "But promise me one thing."

"What?" I asked.

"Be happy. Whatever you choose. Be happy. Because if yer happy with what ya do, nothing else matters."

"Skiing makes me happy, Pop."

"Then let's keep skiing." He stood and gave me a piggyback ride to the top of the small hill.

* * *

The finish line approached, and all the hard work, pain, joy, fun, and love of the last sixteen years propelled me to heights I always knew I could reach. My body moved left and right as I slithered through the last turns. "Go! Go! Go!" the crowd yelled. "Keep going, Isaac, you're almost there!" someone screamed.

I had given it my all. I crossed the finish line and spread my arms wide, tilting my head to the dark-blue sky.

Screaming and yelling erupted, spectators pointing to the standings with shocked faces. I looked up and saw my name sitting on top of Foster's—on top of everyone's.

I did it.

I won the Olympic gold medal.

Foster rushed toward me, a huge smile and tears on his face. "You did it! You fucking did it!" he exclaimed, and hugged me tight. "I fucking love you, champ."

My joy momentarily stopped when I realized that my win prevented Foster, the love of my life, from winning back-to-back gold. "I'm sorry I beat you."

"I'm not. I'm fucking proud of you, Big Mac."

"Are we good?" I asked.

"We're more than good. We're perf—"

I didn't let him finish because I cupped his face and kissed him, right there in front of the entire world. The spectators went ballistic. Two champions competing for one glory, in love. Even Hollywood couldn't have made this up.

I searched the group of fans lining the rope for my parents, and when I found them, I took Foster's hand and skied toward them.

"You did it, honey!" Ma said, wiping her face with a tear-soaked handkerchief.

"I'm so proud of ya, kid. I always believed ya could do it," Pop said.

"Thank you, Ma and Pop."

Foster waved to someone from the crowd, then returned his attention to us.

"Ma, Pop, this is Foster. My boyfriend."

Foster spoke first. "Nice to meet you both." He gave them both a hug. "Congratulations," he offered, knowing this was a group effort.

"It's so nice to finally meet you," Ma said.

"Congratulations to you too, Foster. Ya should be very

proud." Pop extended his arms to Foster.

"I am, sir," he replied.

"Please, call me John."

"I will, John."

"Isaac!" Sophia called. That must have been who Foster was waving to. "You did it! I'm so proud of you and Oz."

I skied over and hugged her. "Thank you, Red. Can I call you that?"

"You can," she said, and kissed my cheek.

"Mom, this is Isaac," Foster said. It was a shame his father wasn't here, but I was so proud of Foster for standing up to him. I hoped they would find a way to be in each other's lives eventually. "Isaac, this is Vivienne Donovan, my amazing mom."

"It's nice to meet you, ma'am."

Mrs. Donovan pulled on the hand I had extended to bring me in for a hug, and she kissed both of my cheeks. "Vivienne, darling."

"Nice to meet you, Vivienne. These are my parents, John and Brittany."

Our families exchanged pleasantries before Alex joined us. Both of her hands were covering her mouth as she shook her head.

I whispered to Foster, and he nodded with a grin. We rushed to meet Alex, and lifted her on our shoulders.

The crowd responded with whistles and cheers, and the official race results were posted on the screen above.

We put Alex down, and she joined my parents as we got ready for the medal ceremony.

"Congratulations, Mac! That was insane!" Yoshi exclaimed.

"Thank you. Congratulations to you too," I said.

"You two put on quite a show out there—and not just the race," Yoshi teased.

"Our sport could use a little spicing up," Foster said. "It was getting boring."

The three of us laughed as the announcer called our names.

"Ladies and gentlemen, please welcome back your bronze medalist, Yoshi Shimojo, from Japan."

Yoshi stepped onto the podium, leaned over to receive his medal, then waved to the crowd.

"And now, for your silver medalist, Foster Donovan Jr., from Canada."

Foster waved to the crowd and stepped onto the podium. He bowed his head for the medal to be placed around his neck. "Thank you," he said.

"And your 2022 Olympic Alpine Downhill Skiing gold medalist—Isaac McAllister, from the United States of America."

I waved to the fans before claiming the middle spot on the podium. I leaned forward and felt the longed-for gold find its place around my neck. *Finally.*

"Please stand for the United States of America's national anthem."

I placed my hand on my chest as the music played, and let the tears fall from my eyes.

I'm gonna be just like him someday. I remembered saying that when I watched Hugh Olivier, from France, win his Olympic gold medal sixteen years ago. I hoped that somewhere out there, kids were watching me and dreaming that they, too, could be just like the three of us.

* * *

After the medal ceremony, Foster had arranged for the limo to take us back to his suite. We walked through the lobby of the Mandarin Oriental, international press following our every move. They had a twofer for their headline stories—I had the gold medal around my neck, and Foster and I were an out couple.

"Shit, Foster. This place is nuts. Makes the Olympic Village look like a dump."

"Right?" he said. "OK, champ, hold my hand and let's pause and turn so the press can get their images. Two minutes of smiling could get us hours of privacy. I'll lead." I reached for his hand and we stopped, posing for the cameras but ignoring the shouted questions. Foster leaned closer to my ear. "That's enough, let's get upstairs. I'm horny as fuck."

He didn't have to ask me twice. We let go of each other's hands and jogged for the elevator, security running to keep pace. They helped us duck into the staff elevator to his suite. As soon as the doors closed, I slammed my body against his. "Feel this." I thrust my crotch against his hip as he brought his hand down to my official Olympic sweatpants. Foster was in head-to-toe Canadian red, a large white maple leaf emblazoned across his chest. "See what you do to me, Mr. Donovan? I hope you're up for some action."

"If by action, you mean this slab, I'm all in." He ran his hand along my erection. "You look so fucking hot with your gold medal."

"You better strike while I'm hot then."

"You'll be hot forever, Mac." I fell against him and pressed him hard against the mirrored wall. We kissed, and I ran my hands under his zipped-up jacket and T-shirt, feeling his tight stomach, stopping at one of his nipples. "Keep that up, Mac, and I'll drop a load right here," he said, breathing heavier.

The door slid open to his floor and we bolted to his suite. "Couch or bedroom?" I asked with a smirk. "Hey, wait a second. I don't have the duffel bag." *Damn it!*

"I keep a duffel or two myself." He winked "Let's go to the bedroom this time. The bed's a king, fit for the world's most recent gold medalist. I'd like to worship your scepter." Foster steered my shoulders to the right, toward a pair of double doors. "The love palace awaits," he whispered in my ear. Quickly, he kicked off his shoes and pulled off his sweats, revealing his briefs—the one piece of clothing not covered in a Canadian flag.

I closed the gap between us. "Here, let me do the rest." I unzipped his jacket and threw it on a nearby chair. Tugging on his shirt to get him to lift his arms, I pulled it over his head, leaving his face covered while I teased a nipple with my tongue. A muffled moan escaped him. "You're cute like this," I said, licking his neck and tightening my grip on the T-shirt wrapped around his head.

"You're kinky, Mac. What's next, cuffs?" he asked, the outline of his face smirking beneath the soft fabric.

"Good idea. Let's save that for when we get home." I pulled the tee off him and kissed him hard. I grabbed his wrists and pushed him back toward the oversized bed. At the edge of it, I spun him around and shoved him down on his front. "Let's start here."

"Mmmm, my fave," Foster said.

I pulled his briefs down, exposing his exceptional ass. I

stood gazing, taking in every inch of him.

"You like that?" he asked. He turned his head sideways and rested his face on his folded arms.

"It's perfection, Foster. You're amazing. Kind of takes my breath away," I said. "I love you."

"Show me," he urged. "My *duffel* is in the nightstand."

I walked over to the nightstand and opened the drawer, finding lube and an entire box of condoms. "A twelve pack? That's a lot of rubbers, don't you think?" I said, tearing the box open and removing one for my use.

"We don't leave for a couple of days…and…well, there are two users here." He lifted his ass cheeks off the bed and wiggled them toward me. "But tonight's your turn. Lube the beast up."

I lubed up and laid on top of him, pushing my cock between his muscled cheeks. "How bad do you need this? Do you want it now?" I asked.

He nodded and pushed against me. I put the condom on, and slathered lube in his hole before sliding back on him. I lined up the head as he arched his back, waiting for his prize. He was incredibly tight, but receptive and willing. Things were easier now that we both had some practice. I sank deeper into him as he relaxed and welcomed my cock. I reached underneath his chest and held him tightly as I slowly made love to him. Our motion was synced; we were breathless in our ritual of passion. His broad back was moist with sweat as we built up our rhythm, me moving in and out of him, him pushing back and meeting me halfway.

"Incredible, Mac. Keep doing that," he mumbled, reaching back and placing his hands on my flexing biceps. I held him tight and rolled my hips across his ass, penetrating him as deep as I could go. "Jesus! Fuck! You're so amazing. I love how you make me feel."

"I'm going to roll to my side, and I want you to roll with me. I have an idea I want to try," I said, leaning to my right. He was still wrapped under my chest, so we remained attached, lying on our sides with my cock still buried in his ass. I tapped his left leg. "Bring your knee up." He did as I asked, and I was able to get a better angle to his exposed ass. "How's that feel?" I asked, leaning back so my cock could go as deep as possible.

"Fucking. Amazing!" He moved his left arm back to my ass, gently pulling it toward him. "Your ass is killer, Mac. Keep fucking me hard." He pulled his left knee closer to his chest, his right leg still straight like mine. I could see his asshole stretched around my girth, and it was driving me fucking crazy.

I pumped into him over and over as he squeezed my ass and kept rhythm with my thrusts. I grabbed the lube and slathered my left hand, and brought it around to his cock. "Let me do this. You concentrate on the dick in your ass," I said.

"Give me some lube."

"For what?" I asked, wondering what the fuck he was up to.

"Just do it. You'll see." I squirted lube on his fingers and continued sliding in and out of his spread ass. "Keep it up. Fuuuck, it's so good," he said. He moved his head back against mine, arching his back even more. His bubble ass pushed hard against my dick. Our breathing became heavier as our sweaty bodies melted into each other. "I'm getting there, Mac. This angle is hot." I stroked his dick harder while watching my cock get milked by his amazing hole.

"I'm almost there too," I moaned, my body stiffening. That's when shit took a wilder turn.

"Trust me, Mac," he whispered, moving his lubed fingers back to my ass.

I felt him probing near my asshole. "What's this?" I gasped.

"Relax. Roll with it. Just a new trick you might like. That's all." He slammed his ass back hard on my cock. My balls gave that first hint that matters were about to be taken over by desire. His fingers found the target; he pushed one into my asshole and began to massage.

"Holy fuuuck!" I yelled. I bent my knee and opened my lying stance to make it easier for him. "Jesus! Shit, baby. What the fuck?"

"You like, right?"

"Fuck that! I love!" I whimpered, electricity shooting through me.

He fingered me harder and deeper while I jacked his cock, picking up my pace as my cock dove deeper and faster. We were bucking and writhing on the bed, clinging to each other, filling holes, sweating, panting, and just fucking letting go with our pleasure. I let out some unknown guttural sound as my ass exploded with fire.

"Harder, Mac! I'm fucking close."

We became rigid as I stroked him faster and he fingered harder. Electrical currents pulsed through my eyes as he fondled my prostate and my cock prepared for blast-off. "Fuck, baby, I'm gonna shoot!"

"Keep jacking me. Keep fucking me hard. I'm...going...holy fuuuuuuck," Foster screeched. I slammed into him, his finger pressing harder on my spot, and then it was showtime.

"Oh my fucking god!" My ass clamped down on his finger as my balls released their seed into my man's asshole. I felt his shaft pulsing as his load left the station, and he bucked against me hard, convulsing and moaning wildly. I pushed my cock in as far as it would go and held it there. His hole tightened, milking every last drop of my cum. He shivered as the last of his orgasm escaped his body.

"That's some shit right there," was all I could say. I went limp; our legs straightened. I held him tight, my chest to his back, panting in spent unison. "That is my new fave trick, Foster. Not that I need a lot of tricks. Being inside you is all I'll ever need."

"Trust me, there are other tricks. And I can't wait for you to show me some of yours. Two tops, learning new bottoming tricks? It's all I can think about now."

I buried my face against the back of his neck. "Let the games begin."

* * *

Fifteen Months Later

"We look like a couple of lumberjacks with these outfits on," Foster said as I parked the rented Jeep in Missoula, Montana.

"You look pretty hot in plaid." He did, but he looked so out of place in the wilderness.

"When you said you wanted to show me one of your favorite things to do, I didn't think it was fishing."

"It's not just fishing; this is *fly* fishing, and it's way more fun." We grabbed our backpacks from the trunk and put them on. I initially thought about dry camping, but I didn't think my Oz was ready for that.

I'd been calling Foster *Oz* since the Olympics, when I asked

Sophia if I could use the special nickname, and she said yes without hesitation. *It'll be just for the three of us*, she had said. "You wanna go ahead and grab the poles, and I'll carry the cooler." I knew Oz would have a comeback for that request before I even finished it.

His face lit up with a mischievous grin. "Right here? Right now?" He walked toward me before looking around. He grabbed his crotch, then grabbed mine. "These poles, Mac?" he whispered against my lips.

My whole body tingled with his touch. "Not quite." I bit the lobe of his ear before continuing. "We're fishing for trout, baby, not eel."

He shivered. "Mmmm. I'm not your baby, remember?"

Neither Oz nor I had conceded the daddy role in our relationship, and it didn't look like being resolve anytime soon—or *ever*, as the argument always led to a more fun activity. The phrase *the battle on top* meant a different thing in our books.

Honk, honk.

"Goddamn it, Alex!" Foster cursed, and laughed.

Alex and Stan had started seeing each other at the Olympics, and their relationship had blossomed. Alex owned a ten-acre property outside Missoula and had invited us to her brand-new cabin, designed by my dad. She fell in love with our West Virginian home and decided to turn her own home into something similar.

"You really need to fire your cock-blocker of a friend," Oz said, all empty threat.

"She's the one who invited us here," I replied, chuckling.

"Hi, CB!" Oz greeted Alex, waggling his fingers at her.

"CB?" she asked.

Stan dissolved into fits of laughter. Dudes understood.

"What's funny?" Alex pinched Stan's side, and he leaned down to whisper in her ear. Her eyes grew wide, and she threw her baseball cap at Oz. "I'm not a cock-blocker!"

"A little," I teased. "But we still love you."

"I don't!" Oz said, laughing and picking up Alex's hat off the ground. "I've been asking Mac to fire you." He adjusted the hat to fit his head.

"Whatever. Let's go, babe." She took Stan's hand and led him to the river.

"I guess we'd better follow them then," Oz said.

"Wait a sec." I grabbed Oz and leaned him against the side of the Jeep, and kissed him tenderly. "I love you so much, Foster. My search for gold led me to you, but what I found was so much more, and when we're both ready, I will spend the rest of my life with you."

"I love you too, Isaac." He caressed my cheek and brought our faces together. "You're not proposing, are you?"

"No," I said, subtly touching the small box in my pocket. "Definitely not." It would be the last white lie I would ever tell.

THE END

About the Author

he is a Seattle based author who loves the outdoors, fashion, documentaries and tennis. His imagination will take you to the grounds of the US Open and to the sun kissed beaches of Hawaii. His stories will feature sports, medicine, politics and a whole lot of love.

Follow him on Instragram @author_garry_michael to learn more about his current projects.

Also by Garry Michael

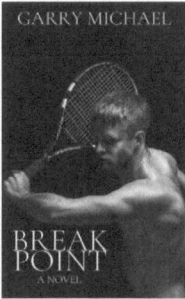

BREAK POINT

Tennis's golden boy Travis Montgomery is at the apex of his life and his young career after winning the US Open yet, his mind and heart is somewhere else. Somewhere deep inside the closet of his past and the secrets he hides even from those who are the closest to him. He is flashing back on another time, another dream, and another love when he is reminded of the only success that eludes him.

Fresh out of medical school, Dr. Ashton Kennedy moves back to Seattle to complete his medical training and start the new beginning he has wanted since Travis walked away six years ago. The task is proving to be harder than he anticipated, especially when Travis returns waving a white flag.What will happen when these two men meet again after six long years? Will Ashton get his questions answered or will Travis' ambition force him even deeper into the closet?Heartfelt and sometimes comical, Break Point is a story about friendship, love, forgiveness and living an authentic life.

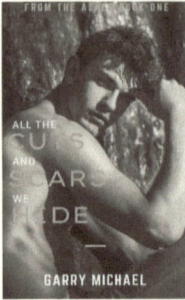

ALL THE CUTS AND SCARS WE HIDE

Ex United States Marine, Wyatt Miller, was living a low-key life keeping those around him at arm's length. Fearing that the shadow that had been haunting him for four years would swallow everything and everyone he touched, he commits to living a solitary life. Until one night when a beautiful stranger came to his rescue during one of the darkest points in his life.

Caught between his guilt and his love for his family, architect Kai Lobo left Hawaii in search of a fresh start and a new place to call home. What he didn't expect was to meet a mysterious stranger that will change the course of his quest for a new beginning.

What will Wyatt do when the only man that can save him is the same person who will drive him over the edge?

What will Kai do when the only man who can free him is the same person that reminds him of a ghost from his past?

Will Wyatt and Kai be able to see past their differences and rely on what they have in common to alter their futures?

All The Cuts and Scars We Hide is a story about healing, redemption and love.

Made in United States
Troutdale, OR
04/28/2025

30951001R00173